"Justice, Miss Lockett."
McClure reached out and slid
his fingers through the hair falling
along her shoulders, slow and easy.
"He'll have it. I swear."

She wanted to believe him. More than anything. So much, she didn't even protest when he took the liberty of touching her hair.

She shouldn't be here with him. Alone, in the middle of the night. In her nightgown, feeling miserable and in sorry need of having his arms around her.

Because it'd been so long since a man had held her.

And she was so afraid.

He stepped closer, a slight shift of his body moving toward hers. Anticipation coiled through her, the knowledge of what he might do.

His fingers curled around her neck, rough skinned but gentle, sure. Carina couldn't have resisted him if she'd tried. And she didn't.

* * *

Untamed Cowboy
Harlequin® Historical #857—July 2007

Praise for Pam Crooks

The Mercenary's Kiss
Romantic Times BOOKreviews nomination,
Best Historical K.I.S.S. Hero

"With its nonstop action and a hold-your-breath climax,
Crooks' story is unforgettable. She speaks to every
woman's heart with a powerful tale that reflects the depth
of a woman's love for her child and her man. The power
that comes from the pages of this book enthralls."
—*Romantic Times BOOKreviews*

Wanted!
"With her signature talent for setting the gritty reality
of the west alongside a sweet, tender romance, Crooks
entertains with a tale that satisfies as it warms the heart."
—*Romantic Times BOOKreviews*

"*Wanted!* was a superior historical western. Fast paced,
realistic characters and a very well put together story
put this at the top of the genre. Pam Crooks has been a
longtime favorite and *Wanted!* was no exception."
—*The Best Reviews*

PAM CROOKS

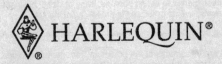

HARLEQUIN®

TORONTO • NEW YORK • LONDON
AMSTERDAM • PARIS • SYDNEY • HAMBURG
STOCKHOLM • ATHENS • TOKYO • MILAN • MADRID
PRAGUE • WARSAW • BUDAPEST • AUCKLAND

ISBN-13: 978-0-373-29457-2
ISBN-10:   0-373-29457-3

UNTAMED COWBOY

www.eHarlequin.com

Printed in U.S.A.

Author Note

For all the appeal of the Old West era, there was nothing more challenging—or more romantic—than the cattle drive. The phenomenon was comparatively short-lived, beginning around the Civil War and ending in the mid-1880s, but it's estimated a whopping 10 million cows walked the trails during that time.

While all those beeves were heading north through hundreds of miles of rangeland, America's cities were growing at an astounding rate. Crime grew, too, with schemes more sophisticated than ever before.

Counterfeiting was one. E. W. Spencer, better known by his alias Bill Brockway, was the most notorious counterfeiter of his time. Nathan Foster was indeed one of his accomplices. Both Brockway and Foster pitted their genius against the government, and soon became two thorns in the side of the Secret Service. In reality, Brockway lived to the ripe old age of seventy-four, and continued his boodling until he died.

Because Denver's Brown Palace Hotel fit so well for this story, I tinkered a bit with history. In reality, the hotel was completed in 1892, and is still a remarkable showcase of architecture today. Fort Supply was indeed a welcome piece of civilization, as I've described it.

And, of course, Dodge City continues to enjoy its place in Old West history. Carina Lockett and Penn McClure experienced the cow town as it was then, a thriving railhead for all those cattle heading to Eastern markets.

I hope the glimpse into their world is a pleasurable one. Look for Callie Mae's story in mid-2008, from Harlequin Historical.

Prologue

Denver, 1885

Penn McClure wasn't a man prone to impulsive decisions, but asking Abigail Whitmore to marry him... well, hell, it just happened.

It didn't matter he knew her barely a month. Nor did it have anything to do with the fact they both worked for the United States Treasury Department and were assigned to the same counterfeit ring case. She was smart and beautiful, loved adventure and danger and had an air of mystery about her which he found fascinating.

That's why he'd asked her to marry him, he decided finally.

Mysterious and fascinating.

It was a matter of timing, too, he thought, settling back into the carriage seat leather on his way to the Brown Palace Hotel where she was staying. It was just the two of them in this part of the country. Neither knew a soul in the entire state of Colorado, let alone the city of Denver. She'd never been this far west before; he'd never been this far north.

Their work on the counterfeit case had thrown them together. Kept them that way. Inevitable the attraction between them would start to sizzle a little.

Make that a lot.

He was ready to get married, besides. Came a time when a beautiful woman got a man to thinking about settling down, and Abigail had done that for him. She'd been surprised at his proposal of marriage, but got over it fast enough. Once she'd agreed, it hadn't taken long to make arrangements.

Penn's plan was to escort her to the judge's chambers for a quick ceremony. From there, they'd go back to the Brown and the honeymoon suite she'd reserved for them.

What would happen after that stirred up a slow fire deep in his groin. They wouldn't have much romantic time to themselves until after they finished up their case, but he intended to give her a wedding night she'd remember forever.

The carriage pulled up in front of the hotel doors. He stepped out into the crisp January air, onto a sidewalk neatly swept clean of the morning's snow. He handed up a bill to the driver. Far as he knew, Abigail had never been late a day in her life. It was one of the things he admired about her. Punctuality. But he was early, and he figured she wouldn't be ready to leave just yet. He wanted to make sure the carriage was still waiting for them when she was.

He entered the Brown Palace's lobby, his mind more on straightening his tie and adjusting the cuffs on each sleeve than the grandeur of the place. She had high tastes and that concerned him some, but they'd work through it. She knew as well as he did what a government agent's salary entailed. They wouldn't be able to afford to live as she was accustomed, and she had to know that, too.

But they had the rest of their lives to iron out the differences between them, minor that they were. Husbands through the ages did what they could to make their wives happy. Penn would try as hard as the best of them.

His heels clicked on the onyx floor as he headed toward the electric elevator. While he waited for the doors to open, he blew out a breath to quell the anticipation of his impending wedding and lifted his gaze. The place was unique in its triangular shape, eight-story-high atrium, and tier after tier of ornate balconies.

Abigail had luxurious taste, for sure.

Her room was located on the fourth floor, and for the time it took the car to return to the ground level, Penn could've taken the stairs and been halfway there by now. He fought down his impatience and slid his gaze up the atrium. There he could see the elevator on the top level, and he tried to discern if there was a cause for the delay.

There was. Three men. And his blood turned cold.

They stepped out the car's door and lingered at the balcony, as if to marvel at the expanse and beauty of the lobby below. Recognition hit Penn hard. Bill Brockway, a notorious counterfeiter recently released from a New

York prison. With him, Nathan Foster and Rogan Webb, his accomplices. All of them members of a slick and very elusive ring of thieves.

Penn swore.

He'd studied the set of photographs sent to him by the Secret Service often enough this past month to have no doubt of their identity. They'd swindled hundreds of thousands of dollars from banks scattered throughout the eastern part of the country with bogus notes they'd expertly forged and distributed.

They had to be stopped. The money they'd stolen returned. The tools of their trade destroyed.

His impending marriage warred with the need to capture them. When another elevator came down and its door whooshed open, the marriage part lost.

He bolted inside. He'd worked too long and hard to lose these criminals now. Penn levered the elevator doors closed himself, before the attendant had a chance.

"The eighth floor," Penn barked. "Hurry."

"But, sir." Clearly taken aback, the bellman glanced at the startled guests prepared to exit before Penn denied them the chance. "There are others who must get off on this level."

"They can do it later. Let's go." He lifted his arm and pulled the cable that would take the car up again. "What's on the eighth floor besides the ballroom?"

The car began to lift, gather speed toward the second floor, then the third.

"The Men's Club Room," the attendant said, eyeing him with uncertainty. "And the Ladies' Club, too."

He hoped the lounging places weren't busy this time

of day. Things could turn ugly in the next few minutes if they were.

The fourth floor passed by, and with it the opportunity to reach Abigail, but there was no time to rush to her room, to inform her of his discovery. She was his partner and entitled, but she'd just have to accept his decision to attempt an arrest without her.

They headed toward the fifth floor, the sixth. Adrenaline simmered in his veins. By the time they finally reached the uppermost level, Penn was all but shaking from it.

The car stopped, the door barely open before he angled his body through and burst into the carpeted hall. His gaze shot along the balcony and found the trio sauntering toward the Club Room, talking quietly amongst themselves, again in no hurry. Penn would've given his right arm to be carrying a weapon.

How he would manage to bring in three men by himself he had no idea, but he had to try. He sprinted toward them. "Excuse me, gentlemen. May I speak with you a moment?"

Their conversation halted. In unison, they turned toward him. Brockway, in his fifties, sporting a moustache and beard, narrowed an eye. In light of his experience and lengthier arrest record, he fit the role as leader of the group.

"That would depend, I suppose, wouldn't it?" he said and smiled.

Penn wasn't fooled by his demeanor. The man was smooth. Wouldn't be long until he got desperate. He'd know an arrest would keep him behind bars the rest of his life.

And if he didn't suspect Penn was a government agent, he would soon enough. Penn kept his features impassive, his manner polite. The last thing he needed was to have the men bolt in three different directions. What would he do then?

He paused in front of them, acutely aware of their uneasy scrutiny. Nathan Foster, small-boned and looking nervous, remained silent. But it was Rogan Webb who studied him with outright boldness, as if the man tried to delve right into Penn's brain to determine his motive.

Handsome and dressed in a smart black suit with crisp white shirt, he looked like a walking bankroll. Wasn't hard to guess it'd been counterfeit money that helped him look that way.

"I don't believe we've met," Rogan said, his tone cool.

"We haven't." Penn indicated the nearest door, the entrance to the Men's Club Room. "Introductions are in order. Let's go inside, shall we?"

The men didn't move, as if they knew that despite the privacy the room offered, it'd have only one means of escape.

Penn knew it, too. He had to get them inside. Fast. He had to find some way to get word to Abigail, and round up a little muscle from the police besides.

"Gentlemen," he said, waiting, his heart pounding, his arm extended toward the closed Club Room door.

Which unexpectedly opened.

But it wasn't a man who stood in the portal. Instead, a woman did, and she wasn't wearing her wedding dress as she should've been. And why was she here on the eighth floor coming out of the Men's Club Room when she should've been in her own room, four levels lower?

Rogan whipped out a pistol from an inside pocket of his jacket and pointed it at her bosom. "I never expected you to double cross us, but it seems I was wrong, my dear Abigail."

Penn's confusion left him stunned...

"Double cross you?" she asked, going very still.

Too stunned to react to the weapon Bill Brockway suddenly produced and leveled right at him.

Seeing it, Abigail's attention jerked toward Penn. For a moment, the *barest* of moments, something that looked like guilt flashed across her features.

His brain began to function, bit by bit. The realization that Rogan knew her, had called her by name, hit him hardest of all.

"Penn!" She stepped toward him, looking beautiful and frantic all at once. "Thank God you're here! We must act quickly—"

"Damn you!" Rogan snarled.

A gunshot ripped through her, and she spun from the force. Her blood splattered onto the wall, the Club Room door, the thick floral carpet that cushioned her fall.

She lay motionless. White-hot rage erupted inside Penn, and he flung himself at Rogan. The tackle knocked the revolver from the man's hand, and Penn scrambled to retrieve it, the need to kill as strong as his need for justice, his fury blinding all reason.

"Let him go!" Brockway yelled. "Or I'll shoot!"

He held his weapon in both hands and aimed it

straight at Penn. With cold, methodical intent, Penn twisted, lifted Rogan's revolver and pulled the trigger.

Brockway clutched his chest and fell dead.

Nathan Foster whirled and broke into a run. Penn shot him, too, and he landed spread-eagled on the rug.

Doors opened, doors slammed. Shouts erupted from the Men's Club Room, screams from the Ladies' Club Room.

Penn ignored them all. He had one man left....

A small sound from behind stopped him. A moan. Abigail's. Stunned that she wasn't dead, gripped by wild hope that she'd survive, that things could be right between them again, he swung toward her.

Rogan Webb took advantage and lunged toward the stairwell. A coward's escape, but Penn didn't care. Not anymore.

He crawled toward Abigail and slid his arm beneath her shoulders. Every breath rattled, her face was chalk-white, and God, there was so much blood. He eased her up, as carefully as he dared, to help her breathe.

"I'll get a doctor," he said.

But he didn't call for one. Her gaze, often seductive, always intelligent, but now fading from life, clung to his.

"You never knew, did you?" she whispered.

A heavy dread filled him at what she implied, the truth he didn't want to hear. "Don't talk, honey. Don't do anything. Save your strength."

Yet, slowly, her hand lifted. Touched his cheek with fingers smeared crimson. "I tried to...love you. You have to know I tried."

The words slashed through him, left him staggered from hurt. From her betrayal.

Then her eyes closed, her head lolled, and he lost her forever.

Chapter One

Texas, Three Months Later

Some days, Carina Lockett despaired of finding decent help.

Today was one of those days.

She eyed the ranch hand sleeping in the shadows of the chuck wagon with disgust. If she hadn't been looking for him, she would've missed him, half-hidden there behind a pile of bedrolls. His intent, no doubt. To let the rest of the C Bar C outfit return to work after the noon meal while he stayed back and took a leisurely snooze.

"Tsk, tsk," Woollie said from his saddle beside her. "He's not used to hard work, is he? Guess he's plumb wore out from having to do some."

Her foreman, Woollie Morgan, was the closest thing she had to a father since her own was killed almost a dozen years ago. He knew as well as she did spring roundup on her ranch required every man to pull his weight. No exceptions.

"I should fire him, the lazy bastard."

Woollie squinted into the sun, and all traces of his mockery faded. "You've already fired two men this week. We're short as it is."

She made a sound of impatience. It hadn't been easy scraping up a few good men to add to the Lockett payroll, the extra hands she needed for this year's roundup. Every rancher in these parts hired additional cowboys, too, to do the same thing she was doing—gathering up the stray cattle from the range for branding before the herds went on the market.

Which made ranch hand pickings scarce. She paid the ones she took on as much as she could. A fair wage, for sure. And she expected each man to earn it.

"Give him another chance, Carina," Woollie said. "Reckon he could've done worse."

As much as it pained her, she didn't have a choice. She'd have to keep the worthless lout, but she refused to tolerate his laziness.

She dismounted. Her boot soles crunched dirt as she strode toward the chuck wagon. She flung one bedroll away from the heap, another and then another, until she exposed Orlin Fahey sprawled full in front of her. His hat covered his face, his hands clasped over his potbelly, and he was so blazes deep in his nap, he didn't even realize she was there.

She toed him hard in the ribs. "Get up, Orlin."

He jerked, whipped his hat from his face and sat bolt upright. "What the—?"

Carina knew she made an imposing figure standing over him with her feet spread and her hands on her hips. Her riding skirt and cotton blouse reminded him she was a woman, but it was the holster strapped to her hips that reminded him she was the boss.

"Now hold on, Miss Lockett." He scrambled to get to his feet, blinking fast to clear the sleep from his focus. He pushed his hat back onto his head and attempted to throw some charm into an uneasy grin. "No need to get yourself in a dither, is there? Might be I shouldn't have fallen asleep, but there ain't been no harm done, has there?"

Dither? Carina Lockett had been called many things in the time since she owned the C Bar C, but a dithering female wasn't one of them.

"I'm not paying you to sleep off your dinner," she said in a cold voice. "But now that you have, you'll feel up to a few hours of cutting wood after you finished the day's work. Sourdough's supply is running low. If you refuse, you're welcome to leave." Hope built in her that he would. "But don't forget you're riding C Bar C horses out here. You're eating C Bar C grub. It's a long walk back to town." She dropped a condescending glance to the flesh his shirt had trouble holding in above his trousers. "And that belly of yours will get to feeling mighty empty along the way."

He muttered something unintelligible, but the distinct sound of an oath came through.

She knew the reason for the curse. Had seen it often enough to know it was coming. "Are you having trouble taking orders from a woman, Orlin?"

His face reddened, and the resentment shimmered from him like heat off hot tar.

"I'll follow your orders all right, *Miss* Lockett," he said finally, pushing the words through his teeth. "That wood'll get cut tonight, like you said."

"I'm glad we agree on the matter." The tension in her eased. "Now, go on. Get to work."

He darted a glance toward Sourdough on his left, Woollie on his right. Two of his own gender, witness to his demoralization by a female younger than himself.

But he said nothing more. Giving Carina a curt nod, he spun on his heel and headed toward the branding fire.

She watched him go. Rebellion didn't flare up often in the Lockett ranks; when it did, she had to fight to keep it from running wild. Like a bronco that needed busting, Orlin Fahey needed to be tamed. For now, at least, she'd succeeded.

"He's about as worthless as a pail of spit, ain't he?" Woollie commented.

"Yes," she said and strode back to her mount.

"He had the scoldin' comin', for sure," Sourdough said.

Flour from the biscuits he'd become known for powdered his apron, but his hands were clean as he handed her a piece of brown paper holding apple slices, sprinkled with cinnamon and sugar. Just the way she liked them.

"Thank you." She took the treat. Every outfit had a troublemaker, it seemed, but loyal and hardworking men like Woollie and Sourdough made up for them. She was grateful for their devotion to the C Bar C. To her. They were her family, and she was their boss, a relationship that had grown to suit them all.

Woollie's gaze slid from Orlin toward the herd milling on the horizon. "Jesse says the morning's gather was good. Almost a hundred head."

Carina's thoughts shifted with his. Taking care of Orlin Fahey's sloth was one detail on a long list she had each day. Now that he'd been dealt with, she dismissed him from her mind.

"Let's take a look." She climbed onto her Appaloosa mare, took the reins in her free hand, and headed out with him.

It was one of her favorite things to do. Watch the size of her herd grow every day. Cows always strayed over the open range when they grazed, and since the roundup was held on C Bar C land, most of the stock the men found was hers. More beef on the hoof meant more money in the bank, and God knew she needed every dime.

They rode past the crude rope corral holding what remained of the remuda. The cutting ponies were gone, chosen by riders already hard at work singling out C Bar C calves and steers for branding. As she drew closer to the milling herd, Carina's gaze skimmed over the men working it, some of them her own, others from neighboring ranches to claim their strays.

She halted on a low rise to watch them, and her attention snagged on a cowboy who rode hard after a steer trying to break loose from the herd. He guided his pony with his knees while he spun his lariat in midair. He drew closer, threw the hemp over the animal's horns and pulled the loop tight. Riding almost parallel, he slapped his rope against the escaping animal's flanks, then expertly angled his horse and flipped the steer into a bone-jarring somersault.

Horse and rider skidded to a stop. The stunned steer

lay still on the ground. The cowboy freed him from the rope; the steer heaved to his feet and headed back to the herd with all signs of defiance gone.

Woollie grunted his approval at the cowboy's skill. "He's good."

"Who is he?" she asked, her gaze still on him while she chewed an apple slice. He relooped his rope into neat coils, getting himself ready for the next steer who tried to best him. His Stetson shadowed his features, but Carina was certain she would've remembered him if they'd met.

"A drifter who rode in this morning. Name's Penn McClure."

"Tell me he's C Bar C."

"He is." A smile appeared through the graying curly beard that had given Woollie his nickname. He looked pleased with himself. "I figured we could use him as short as we were."

She nodded. The drifter's expertise, his strength and speed, made him a valuable asset to her outfit. He could likely do twice the work of someone like Orlin Fahey, and she was lucky to have him on the payroll.

Her gaze lifted from McClure to linger over the day herd again. By the end of the afternoon, calves separated from their mothers would be reunited. Cattle, some doctored, some dehorned, would be sorted into groups according to brand. Riders would be stationed throughout to keep them together before they were trailed back to their home ranges.

Carina took it all in as the bellows of the cattle and bawling calves surrounded her. Dust hung in the air, already hot from the sun and acrid with the scent of burned hide from the branding irons. Men shouted above the ruckus. They worked hard and sweated harder, and Carina reveled in the whole event.

This was Callie Mae's heritage, even more than her own. From the time the C Bar C bore Carina's name on the deed, she'd worked tirelessly to grow the operation into something her daughter would be proud to own someday. The roundup promised to be a success and · brought Carina another year closer to seeing it done.

"She should be here with you," Woollie said.

Carina refused to look at him. It was uncanny how he could read her thoughts as if she'd scrawled them on paper. Most times, she didn't mind he knew her so well. But other times, like now, she did.

"She's only ten, Woollie," Carina said. "Not yet."

"As I recall, you were that age when your pa brought you out here."

His swift reminder stung. The truth in it, too. "Yes."

Being a part of the Lockett roundup had been as natural to her as breathing. An integral part of her child-hood. Her life, her soul.

But Callie Mae was different.

"She's the second C in your brand." Woollie squinted an eye over the herd. "You're the first. It's up to you to make sure she's as much a part of this ranch as you are. Reckon you can't start her too young."

Rebellion stirred within Carina. He felt she coddled Callie Mae too much, she knew. Most times he had enough sense not to say so.

"You telling me how to raise my child, Woollie?" she asked coolly.

A moment passed. "No, ma'am."

"Funny. I thought you were."

"Guess you thought wrong then." He gathered up the reins. The tight set to his mouth revealed he understood who was boss between them and that he'd crossed the line. "I'll go down and check on Jesse. He's looking mighty busy over there by the fire."

Her irritation stayed after he left. The tallyman could handle the job of keeping track of the branded and castrated cattle just fine without Woollie's help, but Woollie needed the excuse. Callie Mae tended to be a sore spot between them. And more often of late than ever.

It didn't matter if he had a different opinion about how she should bring up her daughter. Carina didn't have a husband, so Callie Mae didn't have a father. Not in the usual sense, anyway. Grandpa was the only man Callie Mae could claim in her life, but he was getting on in years, doted on her far too much and didn't really count.

No, Carina was the sole parent in the family, and she made the decisions. She put bread on the table and a whole lot more besides. Callie Mae would grow up to be a fine ranchwoman some day. A cattle queen like herself. By then, the C Bar C would be one of the finest ranches in the state of Texas.

A few more days, when the roundup was over, she'd finally head home. Suddenly, the time she'd have to wait to see her daughter seemed liked forever, and an unexpected yearning budded inside Carina, one that warred with her devotion to her ranch. A wish for a simpler life that would keep her at the homestead more often.

To be a mother, all the time. Not just when she could.

Troubled, she finished the last of her apple, hardly aware of the cinnamon-sugar taste the fruit left on her tongue. Time. There was always precious little of it when she had a ranch to run, men to feed, a payroll to meet.

A daughter to raise.

Carina squared her shoulders. Motherhood was only a small part of her responsibilities. One day, Callie Mae would understand why Carina had to be gone so much. When her daughter carried the weight of the C Bar C on her shoulders, she'd tell her children the same thing. She'd have no choice. It was a sacrifice she'd have to make for their future.

The Lockett legacy.

Callie Mae's.

Her own.

Once again, Carina's gaze swept the vast Texas range. Pride swelled through her.

And this big, noisy herd would make it happen.

Four Days Later

Carina couldn't remember being so dog tired. Maybe she'd never been, considering how hard she pushed herself the past few days, last night's rainstorm being only half of it. A couple good claps of thunder had spooked the herd and sent them into a stampede. She'd worked the whole night through helping her men gather them up again.

But they got the job done and without losing a single head. For her trouble, though, she'd gotten drenched, chilled, splattered with mud, and never had a long, hot bath sounded better than it did right now.

"Good to have you back, Miss Lockett."

TJ Grier ran up to meet her as she cantered closer to the ranch corral, and she smiled tiredly at the lanky wrangler. At fifteen years of age, he worked as hard as any of the men. Was as devoted as the best of them, too. Carina hoped he'd stay on at the C Bar C once he was full-grown.

"I'm glad to be home, TJ." She dismounted, feeling nine days' worth of saddle-riding deep in her bones. "Everything go all right while I was gone?"

"Yes, ma'am. Just fine." He waited respectfully while she dragged her saddlebag off the back of the Appaloosa. "Reckon the roundup went all right, too?"

"It did." She draped the bags over her shoulder. "Next year, you'll be ready to join us."

He gave her a grin as wide as the moon. "I'd like that, Miss Lockett. I sure would."

"Good. Next spring, don't let me forget I said so, you hear?" She was only half teasing. At the moment, she wasn't sure she'd remember her own name, she was so tired.

"No, ma'am. I won't forget." He gripped the mare's bridle, ready to lead her into the barn, and indicated the mud caked to the spotted hide. "Looks like she could use a good brushing down."

Carina nodded and recalled the midnight rains. "We got caught in a storm. Give her some extra oats when you're finished. She's earned it."

"Yes, ma'am."

"The rest of the outfit will be riding in later this af-

ternoon." She'd left the men in Woollie's charge so she
could head home early, compelled by a longing to see
Callie Mae—and to indulge in that hot bath. "Let Woollie know not to disturb me if he can help it."

Not that she expected he would. After their long
hours working the roundup, she'd given the men some
time off in appreciation. They'd head to Mobeetie, the
closest town from the C Bar C, for a little fun and a lot
of hard drinking. They wouldn't be in any shape to get
much work done tomorrow.

Looking forward to some time off of her own, she
turned and began walking toward the house.

"Reckon you'll want to know you got visitors, Miss
Lockett," TJ called from behind her. "Callie Mae's
grandmother, for one."

She halted in midstep.

Damn. *Damn.*

Carina bit back a string of oaths. Everyone on the
ranch knew she despised the woman, but she refused to
let the wrangler see her disdain. Men were worse than
a flock of hens when it came to gossip, and for Callie
Mae's sake, Carina didn't want them squawking up a
henfest on her account.

But for Mavis Webb to see her now, fresh and dirty
off the roundup…

"Thanks, TJ. I appreciate you mentioning it."

Teeth gritted, Carina resumed walking. Unable to
help herself, she swiped her hat from her head and
slapped it against her thigh, loosening a plume of dust
from the wide brim. With the other hand, she attempted to restore her hair to neat order, but sweat and

grime and the need for a good washing robbed her of success.

She pushed her hat back on again. To hell with it. Mavis, with piles of her dead husband's money and her hoity-toity way of thinking, didn't approve of Carina anyway. Especially not as boss of the C Bar C, no matter how she looked or how good a job she did. If it wasn't for Callie Mae being the old witch's only grandchild, Carina would forbid the woman from stepping foot on the ranch. Ever.

Her mood soured. Trouble was, the woman was entitled to come for a visit now and then. Callie Mae enjoyed it when she did.

Carina rounded the corner of the barn, and there sat the Webb carriage in the drive, black and shiny and disgustingly expensive. Mavis probably took Callie Mae for a ride in it this afternoon, which her daughter would've eagerly agreed to, a suspicion confirmed by the sight of the pony stand-hitched in the yard. Forgotten.

Displeasure soured her mood further. Callie Mae knew better than to be careless with her horse, something Carina never tolerated.

She headed toward the back of the house to avoid entering from the front. She needed a few minutes to clean herself up before meeting the woman, and on the way, she noticed the weeds choking young bulbs in the flower beds along the foundation. Her patience strained further.

Carina had been clear in telling Callie Mae she'd wanted the weeds pulled while she was gone. Nine days was plenty of time. No excuses.

She'd never thought her daughter was lazy, but damned if she wasn't showing signs of it. Callie Mae had been doing chores since the time she understood the concept. Why was she disobedient about doing them now?

Because Carina wasn't there to see that she did?

She tamped down the guilt. Grandpa had been home in her place, she told herself firmly. After her parents were killed when she wasn't much older than Callie Mae was now, Wesley Lockett took over Carina's raising, and he helped with Callie Mae, too, whenever Carina needed him to.

Which was just about every day.

Callie Mae had a mind of her own, for sure. Was she getting to be too much for Grandpa to handle?

Carina had often thought Callie Mae's independence was a good thing. She tended to air some sass from her mouth now and again, but then, all children did. And if there were times when she and Callie Mae didn't agree, well, daughters disagreed with their mothers occasionally.

Didn't they?

Carina didn't like feeling uncertain, and she set her hands on her hips in frustration. Where was Grandpa anyway?

Her gaze scoured the yard. Beneath an ash tree's shade, a small table held his checkerboard, but no one sat at the chairs to play. The yard and outbuildings were quiet. Even Callie Mae's pet mutt was nowhere to be seen.

Her irritation simmered. Most likely Grandpa was

inside keeping Mavis Webb company, though he detested the woman as much as Carina did. Still, it'd be the sociable thing to do, and he'd want to keep an eye on Callie Mae besides.

Carina climbed the back steps, opened the door and went inside. Juanita, her housekeeper, wasn't in the kitchen, but a pot of spicy chili simmered on the stove. Voices from the front room confirmed the presence of visitors. Carina dumped her saddlebags on the table, washed up as best she could, then braced herself to go in and join them.

But she stopped short in the archway. Mavis sat on the couch, looking as elegant as usual in an olive-green dress featuring a fashionable bustle. A straw bonnet trimmed with an ostrich feather perched on a nearby side table. She chatted animatedly while she shared the open book in her lap with the young girl beside her.

A child Carina hardly recognized.

Her own.

Chapter Two

Callie Mae wore a party frock that had enough shiny, peach-colored fabric draped in gathers and ruffles to make two of her plain calico ones. Delicate pin-striped hosiery covered her legs; shiny patent leather shoes sheathed her feet. Her cinnamon hair was arranged in perfect coils around her head, a wide taffeta bow perched on top, and she looked more like a child of royalty than the daughter of a cattlewoman.

Her grandmother's doing, and a gully washer of resentment shot through Carina. "Hello, Callie Mae."

Callie Mae started in surprise and bolted to her feet, as if she'd been caught doing something she shouldn't.

Which maybe she had. Like enjoying the spoiling she knew she'd never get from Carina, and until Carina could decide what Mavis was up to, she couldn't help feeling disgruntled that Callie Mae had gone along with it.

"Hello, Mother."

Carina banked a reaction that she hadn't called her "Mama" as she always did. "Mother" sounded formal, grown-up. What possessed her to start calling her that?

Carina strolled into the room, managing a smile along the way. "I'm back, sweet." She held out her arms. "I've missed you."

Callie Mae grinned, then, and rushed toward her. Carina bent to take her slender body against her, relishing the embrace she'd looked forward to for nine long, hard days. Her daughter smelled faintly of rosewater, Carina noted, though neither of them owned a single drop.

Abruptly, Callie Mae gasped and pushed away. She held out the dress's full skirt, giving it a worried inspection. "Don't hug me so tight, Mother. You'll make wrinkles."

Carina straightened slowly from the rebuff. "You'd best take it off anyway, Callie Mae. You've got some unfinished chores to tend to."

"Chores!" She looked aghast, as if she'd never done one in her life. "But I don't *want* to do chores. I want to wear my new dress and stay here with Grandmother."

Carina's patience slipped; she tugged it back into place. She was reluctant to ruin her homecoming with a scolding the minute she walked in the door, but the matter needed addressing. "You've got weeds to pull, and Daisy's standing in the yard. She needs to be corralled and brushed down. You're responsible for her, and I shouldn't be reminding you that you are."

Mavis set aside her book and stood with a condescending smile. "Isn't there someone who can do this work for her, Carina?"

Carina stiffened. She didn't bother to attempt a sociable greeting. "No. There is not."

"Certainly one of the ranch hands around here is quite capable."

"My daughter is capable."

"My *grand*daughter should not be forced to work like an adult. She's only a child."

"A child who is not allowed to be lazy," Carina shot back. "She's accustomed to chores for her age and abilities, and she's well aware they must be done."

"It breaks my heart to see her toil so. Pulling weeds, Carina. Really." Mavis clucked her tongue in disapproval. "She's a Webb, after all."

"She's a Lockett more." Carina clenched her fists. "A *Lockett,* Mavis."

Clearly loath to quarrel about the subject which had embittered their relationship from the time Carina refused to marry her conniving son, Mavis pinched her lips closed. Carina gave her credit for it. Callie Mae was listening wide-eyed to their every word.

And from the time she'd been born, Carina wanted to spare her the ugliness. She smiled down at her daughter and hoped her effort looked genuine. "Go on to your room, sweet. Change your dress, like I said."

A pout formed on her heart-shaped mouth. "I don't want to."

"Callie Mae," she said in warning.

"I'll do it later. I *promise.*"

Carina was determined to quell the rebellion her

child showed more and more often. "You'll do it now. And for being disobedient, you'll not ride Daisy anymore today or tomorrow. Do you understand?"

"Carina."

Mavis stepped forward and slipped a thin arm about Callie Mae's shoulders. Sensing the ally she had in her, Callie Mae flung her arms around her grandmother's waist and buried her face against the olive-green bosom.

Hurt rippled through Carina. Her daughter didn't appear concerned with wrinkling her dress *now*. And the way she was clinging, as if she'd never let go...

Mavis lovingly smoothed the shiny red-brown ringlets. "Carina, please." Her cultured voice turned cajoling. "Let her wear the dress. We've spent the morning curling her hair and dressing her up. She's enjoyed it immensely."

"She has, has she?"

"She looks beautiful, too." Mavis beamed proudly down at Callie Mae.

Carina swallowed. Yes. As beautiful as a princess with her eyes the color of a summer sky, and her hair streaked from the sun. She looked as rich as one, too.

But she wasn't a princess, Carina reminded herself firmly. She was a young girl who lived on a ranch, who wore plain cotton dresses with boots and braids, and she could get as dirty as any boy when she put her mind to it.

While Carina was gone, Mavis had shrewdly targeted Callie Mae's feminine side, the woman in her just beginning to develop. She'd filled Callie Mae's head with foolish ideas of being pampered, tantalized her with gifts sinfully expensive, and just what did the old witch hope to gain by all of it?

"Can I wear my dress a little longer?" Callie Mae asked, peeping at her from beneath long lashes, her cheek still pressed against Mavis. "Grandmother brought it all the way from New Orleans. It'd be rude of you not to let me."

Carina remained unmoved by the accusation. She pointed to the couch and the book still lying on the cushion. "I'd like you to read quietly for a few minutes while I speak to your grandmother."

Callie Mae drew back and glanced upward at Mavis, as if to seek her permission. Carina glared at both of them.

"Go on, darling. We'll be right here." Mavis smiled gently.

Callie Mae released her then. Skirt hems swishing, she headed for the couch, settled herself primly on the cushion and opened the book.

Carina grasped Mavis's bony elbow and pulled her firmly to the far side of the room. Her nostrils flared. "Get out."

"Believe me, Carina. There's nothing I'd like more."

"You've no right to sway her against me. You've manipulated her to play favorites between us by bribing her with things she doesn't need and will never have."

"And isn't that a shame." Mavis drew herself up and gave Carina a contemptuous once-over, from the top of her wide-brimmed hat down to her mud-caked boots. "Look at you. You're filthy. You smell of manure. You've left your daughter alone for nine full days with a teetering old man while you ride off into the middle of nowhere to work with your precious outfit. All men, of course." Her lips tightened. "What kind of mother are you?"

As boss of the C Bar C, she'd had her share of criticism. Rebukes. Disdain. She'd heard language at its foulest, threats at their blackest, but *this*, this stinging slew of insults cut deep.

Mavis Webb had struck a raw chord, stirred up a heap of guilt, but damned if Carina would allow her to see her bleed.

"Callie Mae is mine," she hissed. "I'll raise her in the best way I know how. And until you learn to respect my way of doing it, I forbid you from seeing her again."

"Don't be naive, Carina."

"Ever," she added vehemently, thinking of the men on her payroll who would help her enforce the order.

"Callie Mae is an intelligent child. She deserves more than you can give her out here."

"You're wrong."

"She deserves the finest education. The privileges of being a Webb."

Carina clenched her teeth. The Webb bloodline was her daughter's one flaw, the single *worst* thing Carina could have given her.

Mavis fastened a cold, hard gaze over Carina, like a hawk homing in for the kill. "I'll be leaving soon for a trip to Europe. I want to take Callie Mae with me."

Carina drew back in shock.

"By the time we return, it'll be time for her to start her studies," she continued. "New Orleans has an excellent finishing school for young girls. I insist she be enrolled. I'll see to the costs of her tuition, of course."

"No." Carina gave a vehement shake of her head. "Absolutely not."

"We've talked of it at length while you were gone, Carina. She wants to go."

The little schoolroom where her daughter went with the rest of the C Bar C children flashed through Carina's mind. Callie Mae enjoyed school. Excelled at it. She came home every afternoon, *every single one,* and if Mavis assumed she could just whisk Callie Mae hundreds of miles away to another state and keep her for months without a care to what Callie Mae would leave behind, her mother most of all…

"The C Bar C is her home," Carina grated. "Damn you for trying to convince her otherwise."

"I didn't expect you to agree readily." For the first time, something like desperation appeared in the woman's expression. "Callie Mae is my only grandchild. She's like the daughter I never had. She means the world to me, and I assure you she'll have the best attention and care possible."

"Get out." Carina had been a fool to listen to the witch. She should've sent her packing the minute she saw her sitting on the couch with Callie Mae. "Get out now."

"You don't have time to raise a child. Admit it. You're so consumed with this blamed ranch that she's only a diversion for you at the end of your day. You're not being fair to her. Or to me."

Mavis would never understand why Carina worked

so hard to give her daughter a legacy to be proud of. The Lockett legacy. Her inheritance. The snooty woman had probably never worked a day for anything in her life.

"You don't believe I'm serious, do you?" Mavis taunted coolly.

"I don't care if you are."

Carina refused to continue the discussion. She'd given an order. Mavis was too stubborn to obey it. She'd overstayed her welcome, and it was long past time to throw her out.

She pivoted away to grab the woman's feathered hat—and noticed the suitcase sitting near the door. A rag doll lay on top, along with a new coat Carina had never seen before.

Callie Mae stood beside the heap, her book clutched in one arm. By the set to her jaw, she'd heard everything. By the tempest brewing in her expression, she was fired up plenty from it.

"I want to go with her, Mother," she said. "Why won't you let me?"

Carina glowered. "That's a ridiculous question."

"But it's *boring* here." She stomped her foot, her temper building. "We never go anywhere, just stay on this stupid ranch all the time. Grandmother showed me lots of beautiful pictures of Europe, and I want to see those places for real!"

"Another time, Callie Mae," she gritted. "Maybe when you're older. Grown-up."

"I want to go now! And I won't be gone that long. Please, Mother." She took a pleading step closer. "I'll write you every day, I promise, and I'll buy you something really special. Grandmother says I can."

When had her daughter turned so shallow? So self-centered? Had she always been that way, and had Carina been too busy to notice? Or had Mavis been grooming her during each of her visits, turning her into a younger version of herself?

Pain burned with frustration and a good dose of anger, too. Callie Mae needed to know there were things far more important in life than travel and money, like her home and family, and—

Her thoughts came to a screeching halt.

"Where's Grandpa, Callie Mae?" she asked. "Or Juanita?"

Stormy blue eyes rolled. "How would I know? I haven't seen them for a while."

The first stirrings of alarm prickled. Juanita had left chili simmering. And it wasn't like Wesley Lockett to be far from his great-granddaughter, not with Mavis in the house.

Reckon you'll want to know you got visitors, Miss Lockett. TJ's words thudded in her memory. *Callie Mae's grandmother, for one.*

Someone else was here. Someone she hadn't yet realized.

The alarm pounded. She thought of Woollie, not yet back from the roundup. Her men, all of them too far away to help.

Footsteps sounded in the hall near the bedrooms. Callie Mae's gaze shifted, her pout disappeared and a bright smile creased her face. "Hi, Daddy."

Carina's heart stopped.

She swung toward the male shape filling the doorway. The man who had fathered her baby, who had caused her enough pain and heartache and *hate* to last a lifetime.

Rogan Webb.

"Hello, Carina," he said.

His voice, drawling and amused, yanked her backward in time to when she was an impressionable young woman, swept off her feet by his devilish charm and big-city ways. She'd met him at a dark time in her life, when she was struggling through the grief of her parents' death, when Grandpa's love and affection wasn't enough. She'd turned a little wild, hungry for distraction, something—or someone—to help her forget....

Rogan had been in Dallas that year she'd gone with her grandfather to buy horses. Son of a New Orleans businessman who'd made his fortune in cotton, Rogan was looking for a little distraction, too. Of the female type.

Carina had been an easy conquest.

Not anymore.

She was smarter, tougher, now. And it rankled he'd taken her by surprise, that it showed, clear as rain, on her face.

"What are you doing here?" she demanded.

"I've come to see you and my dear Callie Mae, of course." His gaze tumbled leisurely over her body, making her forget her argument with her daughter and become acutely aware of how dirty and disheveled she looked. His amusement deepened. "Too bad we meet again under less than flattering circumstances. At least for one of us."

She stiffened. Refused to give him the satisfaction of knowing his slur pricked her pride, especially when he was as well dressed and handsome as ever. Maybe more so, considering the confidence and maturity the years had given him. Years when he'd stayed away, leaving his mother to love his daughter in his place, as if he refused to acknowledge she existed.

Until now.

No doubt Mavis brought him along as her weapon to convince Carina to let Callie Mae leave the C Bar C with her. A clever ploy to dangle her son's fatherly rights in front of Carina's defiant nose.

Rights he didn't deserve.

They'd both learn she wouldn't be maneuvered so easily. Carina wasn't young and vulnerable anymore, and she had a few weapons of her own to dangle.

She laid her hands on two of them, strapped to her hips.

"You should've saved yourself the trouble of coming, Rogan," she said coldly. "You're wasting your time, same as your mother is."

He leaned against the portal and crossed his arms over his chest. Unfazed, his arrogant glance touched briefly on her holster.

"Now, Carina, dear. You're not going to do anything rash, are you?" he murmured. "You might upset our daughter if you did."

She fought to hold her rage in check. *Our* daughter? As if he'd been a part of her life and had a hand in raising her the past ten years?

Her finger curled over the trigger. Much as she itched to pull it, she couldn't let Callie Mae see her shoot the bastard in cold blood, no matter how sorely she was tempted.

"Are you mad at Daddy for coming to see us?" Callie Mae asked.

Carina strove for composure. If there was one thing she'd valiantly accomplished from the day her daughter had been born, it was keeping her contempt for Rogan to herself.

But Callie Mae had to know things were serious right now. Carina didn't like that Grandpa wasn't around. And she didn't like the way Rogan had been keeping himself hidden in the bedroom part of the house, either. Her instincts warned he was up to no good, and she could use a little help in throwing both him and his mother out before trouble set in.

"Go outside, Callie Mae," she ordered. "If you see Grandpa, tell him to come up to the house as fast as he can. Stay outside until I tell you different, understand?"

"She's not going to find him," Rogan said amiably.

The certainty in the words raised the hair on the back of Carina's neck.

"Where is he?" she asked past growing fear.

A man appeared at his side, then. From the bedroom hallway shadows. Blond-haired, dressed in a dark suit and well-heeled.

A gunslinger.

"He's sleeping," he said.

"Peacefully," Rogan added.

Carina's heart stopped. "What?"

"I'll take Callie Mae outside." Mavis already had her feathered hat pinned to her head. She reached for the child's hand.

Callie Mae took it willingly. She didn't seem surprised at the stranger's presence, which meant he, too, had been there a while, and oh, God, what had gone on while Carina was at the roundup?

Mavis headed with Callie Mae toward the door, and Carina took a frantic step after them, the dread in her building, the gut-wrenching conviction that if she didn't go after her daughter now, they'd take her away for a long time, maybe forever, and a part of her died, knowing it.

"No!" she cried. "Callie Mae, wait!"

Her daughter's stride faltered, but Mavis kept her moving out the door. Carina bolted in their direction. A long arm hooked around her waist and jerked her back with enough force that her booted feet kicked up from the floor. A revolver's barrel pressed into her back.

"Shut up, Carina!" Rogan snarled in her ear. "You'll have to listen to me if you want to see her again, y'hear?"

She stilled instantly. A moment passed. His arm tentatively loosened, and she swung around, her hand yanking out a pearl-handled Colt, but too quick, his hand gripped her wrist and tightened. Hard. Hard enough to break each fragile bone if he wanted, and she cried out from the pain. Unable to keep her hold on the gun, it fell from her grasp with a loud thud.

Rogan flung her away with an oath; she stumbled backward into the side table and knocked it over. A lamp crashed to the floor. She scrambled to keep her balance.

"Take off your hardware." He aimed the revolver square at her heaving chest. "And don't try anything stupid when you do."

Her mind raced. She considered her chances of defying him. A quick glance toward the door confirmed Mavis was gone, her precious child with her, and dear God, the suitcase, too.

But the blurred shape of the carriage through the front room window curtains assured her Callie Mae wasn't gone—yet. With both men's weapons trained on her, Carina had no choice but to comply, but she had to find some way to stop her daughter from leaving.

Her fingers shaking, she managed to unbuckle her holster and toss it onto the couch cushion. Unfettered hate burned through her.

"What do you want from me, Rogan?" she grated.

He dragged his attention off her long enough to gesture to the blond-haired stranger.

"The door, Durant. Don't let anyone in," he commanded.

"You'll never get Callie Mae." The desperation built in Carina like a range fire out of control. "Not without fighting me and the entire C Bar C outfit."

His eyes, as blue as Callie Mae's, swung back toward her. With the gunfighter standing guard, Rogan seemed to grow calmer. More in control. "Funny you should mention the C Bar C."

She'd been so sure he'd threaten her with kidnapping her daughter that his mention of the ranch threw her off-kilter.

"Word around here is you're making a name for

yourself. Carina Lockett, Texas cattle queen." He regarded her, his gaze unwavering. "Every year, you buy a little more land, and your herd gets a little bigger."

"My affairs are none of your business," she snapped.

"Just coming off your roundup, your herd bigger than the last…well, when you take them to market, you'll make a very nice profit, won't you?"

She stilled.

But her heart speeded up….

"You think I haven't been keeping an eye on you and my daughter all these years, Carina? You think I don't know how much all that cattle is worth?"

The horror speeded up, too. Deep in her veins.

"Mother's got Callie Mae." His expression turned hard. Cold. "She'll take her so far away, you'll never find her again."

Carina could hardly breathe.

"You know that, don't you, Carina?"

She knew. Oh, God, she knew Mavis could go anywhere she wanted. She had the money, the determination, the absolute devotion to Callie Mae to steal her away, and oh, God, oh, God.

"Your cattle will get her back," he said, his voice like ice. "Ransom for Callie Mae."

The blood pounded in her throat. The absolute horror of what he was doing…

"I'll make sure Mother cooperates." A corner of his mouth lifted, making him look charmingly evil. Lucifer himself. "After you pay me first."

His words pelted her brain, left her numb, stricken, her choices chillingly clear.

If she gave him her herd, she'd lose the ranch. She'd lose everything. The legacy she'd worked day in and day out for, for more than a decade. Callie Mae's heritage.

Or else she'd lose Callie Mae.

From outside the front room window, the faint sound of wheels beginning to turn, of harnesses jangling, penetrated her numbness.

She whirled. Mavis's carriage began to move, pick up speed. Carina screamed her daughter's name and lunged toward the door, not caring that she could be shot, or killed, because without Callie Mae, she'd have nothing, nothing at all…

Rogan shouted. Durant, too. They both came at her, one from behind, one from the front, and she fought them both, kicked and screamed and clawed, until it took their combined strength to tackle her to the floor.

But still she fought. Writhed and bucked and bit. Each man swore. Savagely. One of them produced something white, a handkerchief, and pressed it to her face while the other held her down.

A sweet smell surrounded her. She tried not to inhale, to breathe, but she couldn't help it. Dear God, she couldn't help her need to breathe, and the dizzying drug stole into her body, her muscles, and pulled her deeper into the blackness.

"You're not the only one who needs the money from that herd, Carina." Rogan's voice slithered into the last wisps of her consciousness. "But there's only one of us who's going to get it."

Chapter Three

Sometime after Midnight

A jagged, raucous sound dragged Penn out of the velvety-black caverns of sleep. The functioning part of him hinted the sound was familiar. He didn't move, didn't open his eyes, but his head said the noise was close.

From his own mouth.

His sluggish brain finally recognized it as…snoring.

Damn. He was going to have to quit drinking so much.

He inched himself upward out of the cavern. He wasn't sure he could move if he wanted to. Which he didn't. Cold, hard sensation crept into his face. His chest. The stone floor he sprawled on in the new Mobeetie jail.

His brain flexed, replayed the brawl that landed him

in here. The woman involved, too. A dance hall girl who looked like Abigail…

He groaned. But it wasn't her. It was never her. She was dead. Shot to death after she'd double crossed him and the United States government. Killed by her son-of-a-bitch partner, Rogan Webb.

Webb was going to die next for all he'd done. If it was the last thing Penn ever did.

He tried to sink back into oblivion again. To forget. Wished for more whiskey so he could. But the desire for revenge made him burn, turned him restless, ate at him from the inside out.

The need for it never left him. It was what brought him down to this part of Texas. To find the kin he'd discovered Webb had. Penn had hoped to learn Webb's whereabouts so the revenge could be satisfied.

But Penn had failed at that, too. As he'd failed with Abigail…

"Look at him, Woollie. He's still all roostered up."

The female voice jolted him. He strained to identify the source. The direction. Close, a few yards away. Outside his jail cell.

Penn managed to squint up at her through slitted eyes. He hadn't known she was there. Or the man with her. But he knew who they were, even with the lantern shining behind them, throwing their faces into shadow.

Woollie Morgan, foreman of the C Bar C. And his boss, Carina Lockett herself.

Penn didn't move. Didn't have a clue why they'd be here in the middle of the night. He'd finished the job they hired him to do. After the roundup was done, he collected his pay and headed to Mobeetie with the rest of her outfit for a night of women and drinking.

That much he remembered. What happened after, he didn't. Not much, anyway. He was all but sure whatever trouble he got himself into had nothing to do with either of them.

Did it?

"Damn him."

The she-boss crossed her arms. Paced the length of his cell, then back again.

"Easy, Carina," Woollie said. "He just needs some time to come to. Not going to be any good to you until he does."

"But I don't have time to wait," she snapped.

"I know."

"Where's Sheriff Dunbar? Get me his key ring, and I'll wake McClure myself."

"Here I am, Miss Lockett." Boot soles scraped the stone floor. "I went and fetched a bucket of water. That'll get him a-goin' for sure."

Penn swore. Rolled to his side and half lifted his head.

"What the hell?" he growled.

The Lockett woman turned toward him. Even through the shadows and his own bleary state, Penn could tell she was coiled tight as a spring.

"Let me in there, Sheriff, so I don't have to talk to him through iron bars," she ordered.

"Reckon he's harmless enough now that he's slept some of his whiskey off." The lawman set the bucket down, plucked his ring of keys from his pocket. Metal clinked, and the cell door creaked open. "But I'll keep an eye on him, just in case."

She swept inside, her foreman close behind. Tension kept her stance rigid.

"Would you care to stand, McClure?" she asked coolly. "I'd like to see if you're able."

He frowned at her low-voiced challenge. Well, a man had his pride, didn't he? Penn figured he'd give it a go, considering his curiosity about why she was here.

He heaved himself to a sitting position. Had to wait some to get his world to stop spinning before he made it up onto his feet, but he did. Except he swayed right after, had to catch himself and brace his arm against the rock wall to keep upright.

Main thing was he got the job done, and he glared at her for his trouble. He couldn't recall being this close to her since he'd hired on to her outfit. She was taller than he'd expected. Slender-built. She wore a riding skirt and blouse and appeared more desperate than he'd ever thought the imperious Carina Lockett could be.

He waited for her to make the next move, watched her through heavy-lidded eyes. And kept a good hold on that wall.

Her chin lifted. "I'm in need of your help, McClure. I'm hoping we can strike up a deal."

"Yeah?" His voice sounded rough as sandpaper. "What kind of deal?"

"Sheriff Dunbar tells me you were in a brawl tonight. There was damage to the saloon, for which you were responsible."

Hell. He couldn't have brawled alone, but he declined to argue the point. It was all he could do to stand there and follow the conversation as it was.

"I'm prepared to post your bail to get you out of here," she continued. "I'll also take care of restitution to the saloon on your behalf."

He wasn't so drunk that a little suspicion didn't curl through him at her offer. "You don't say."

"On the condition that you work off all fees incurred by me by returning to my employ."

He thought of Rogan Webb, of the hate for the man simmering inside him. But mostly he thought about the revenge he couldn't satisfy if he kept on playing cowboy for Carina Lockett.

"No deal," he said.

"Let me explain further." The slender column of her throat moved. "I must drive my cattle to Dodge City. Immediately. I need men capable of helping me do that."

"So find 'em."

"You don't understand." She drew in a breath, as if striving for the control she seemed to be losing. "I've seen you work. You're good. You're the kind of ranch hand I need to get my herd north." She hesitated. "I need *you,* McClure."

Penn clenched his jaw. He wasn't just a "ranch hand." He was a government agent who'd quit his job to satisfy a case of festering revenge in the way he wanted to satisfy it, and dear God, she wanted him for a *cattle drive?* Weeks on the trail with too little sleep and too much hard work and enough dirt and dust to choke a mule?

"Forget it," he said.

She exhaled slowly. "Please."

"Not interested."

From beneath her wide-brimmed hat, her gaze spit sparks. "There'll be repercussions if you refuse."

"Carina," Woollie said, frowning.

His voice held some disapproval in it, and she swung toward him in frustration.

"I'll force him if I have to, Woollie!" she said sharply. "I'll use the saloon or the sheriff or—or—"

"Why don't you tell him the truth?"

She grew deathly still. Obviously, the idea hadn't occurred to her. "Why? It's none of his business. It's no one's business but mine, and—and yours, and we're wasting time in here arguing about it."

"Reckon it's only fair so he'll understand what's driving you like this. You won't make it easy for him, or any of us, once we're on the trail. If he agrees to come, that is. And not that I'm complaining, considering the circumstances."

Her pride kept her mouth shut while she debated his logic. Penn found himself intrigued, now that his head had cleared a little.

She shot a glance at Sheriff Dunbar. Penn guessed the lawman knew the story behind her coming to his jail this time of the morning, too. The sheriff just nodded, showing his agreement with her foreman.

Finally, she turned back to Penn.

"Blackmail," she grated. "I'm being blackmailed to get my daughter back."

He blinked. Replayed the words in his mind to make sure he got them right. And was pretty sure he did.

"With your herd?"

"Yes."

"As ransom?"

"Yes."

A slow pounding began in his temples. "She's been kidnapped, then."

"Yes. I mean, no." She halted, as if to tamp down a welling of emotion. "She went willingly, if you must know. With her grandmother."

Sounded like the she-boss had some serious family problems. Too bad her daughter was stuck in the middle of them. "Where'd she go?"

"If I knew that, I'd go get her, wouldn't I?"

Woollie flinched at the snap in her voice. "The woman said she wanted to take her to Europe for a spell. Trouble is Carina refused to agree, but they took off anyway."

"And we don't know which way any of 'em went," the sheriff added.

Penn's gaze swung to the man. "You're the law around here, aren't you?"

The sheriff glowered, clearly offended at Penn's accusation. "They got a good head start on Miss Lockett. Made sure she wasn't in no shape to go after 'em. Going to take a while before we can scrape up any leads, McClure. Helluva lot of country out here, if you haven't noticed."

Carina Lockett's face was angled away from him, but her shadowed profile, her silence, showed her pain. Penn couldn't help but be affected by it. What had happened to keep a mother from letting her child run off the way she did?

"They used chloroform on her," Woollie said quietly, his regard over Penn intuitive. "Then tied her up and locked her in a bedroom. Did the same to her grandpa and housekeeper. Took us some time before we found 'em, let me tell you. By then, the bastards were long gone."

Penn couldn't keep from watching her. She pulled at him, even with the whiskey still in his blood, his temples throbbing from its effects. Carina Lockett needed help, and she needed comfort, and she was too damn proud to ask for either one.

He didn't know why he felt the need to give her both. Pulling her into his arms would satisfy it, but she'd likely shoot him where he stood.

And wasn't that a hell of a shame?

He reminded himself he had his own life to live, and it didn't include her. He had to douse the flames of revenge burning inside him, see it done or die trying. Helping her drive her cattle to Kansas was a distraction he didn't want, need or care about.

He opened his mouth to refuse her request. But a single strand of curiosity remained.

"The child's grandmother was working with someone," he said. "Who?"

Carina Lockett's head lifted. She faced him, then, her full lips twisted with contempt.

"Her son," she said. "My daughter's father. Rogan Webb."

Slowly, Penn straightened from the wall. The whiskey cleared from his veins, and of all the names, every single one she could've said, Rogan Webb's was the absolute *last* he expected to hear.

"You know him, McClure?" she asked coolly.

Penn's brain shifted gears, filtered through a plan, forming fast. A plan that dropped into his jail cell like manna from heaven. And the woman standing in front of him would help him see it through.

"Yeah. I know him."

Penn intended to stick with Carina Lockett like red on a rose. Webb wanted her herd for the ransom money it would pay. Desperate as she was, she was going to give it to him.

Penn intended to see he wouldn't get a dime. She didn't know it yet, but she would soon enough. Main thing was she'd be hearing from Webb at some point along the way, and Penn would be there when she did.

Deep in his ruminating, he'd forgotten they were waiting for his answer. All three of them, their expressions grim in the shadowy light.

But it was the woman's gaze he sought and held.

"You just cut yourself a deal, Miss Lockett," he said finally. "I'll help you drive your herd to Dodge City."

Three Days Later

Dawn crept upward into the Texas sky and smeared hazy shades of color along the horizon. It was cooler than usual for a spring morning, the air damp and heavy, and Carina shivered in the chill. She lifted the tin cup she held to her lips and sipped. Strong coffee laced with canned milk slid down her throat, warming her, helping her think.

It'd been pure hell since Callie Mae left. Three days of endless worry, no sleep and constant work to get ready for the trail.

Thank God for Woollie. How would she have managed without him?

He was hurting as much as she was. He'd always favored Callie Mae. Called her Tea Cup and teased her to no end. His children were grown and gone, but he treated her like his own little girl. Callie Mae adored him.

How could she leave?

How *dare* she?

Carina had run the gamut from anger, to blinding hurt, to panic and all-out hate for Mavis and Rogan.

Now there was only desperation left. The hellish fear Callie Mae would never return, at least not for a long time. Or that when she did, she'd be a different child, her head turned to city life and high-society thinking.

And worse. That she'd not love the C Bar C anymore. Or the family she had there.

Carina's eyes burned, and she lowered her gaze to the brew in her cup. She was alone, sitting on the Appaloosa out here on the range. Her men and the herd were sprawled out in the valley before her, yet it appalled her someone might see her grief. She didn't want her men's pity. She wanted them as driven and committed to get to Dodge City as she was.

Only Woollie had seen her pain. And Grandpa.

She'd spent as much time with him as she could the past several days, leaving the bulk of the organization of the trail drive to her foreman. Grandpa needed caring after Rogan and the gunslinger, Durant, roughed him up, damn them both. An old man, trying to keep his granddaughter safe.

But the doctor from Mobeetie assured her he

would heal, and he would. It'd take some time, that's all. Time Carina couldn't spare. Juanita could nurse him in her place, but it'd been hard to leave him just the same.

Getting a better hold on her emotions, Carina lifted her head. Blackmail kept a person on edge, for sure. She hated feeling this desperate, this out of control. Hated it more that she was at Rogan's mercy. He'd cut her deep, at her most vulnerable. And there wasn't a damn thing she could do about it.

Yet. Getting her herd to Kansas had to be her main focus in the coming weeks. She'd do nothing, *nothing,* to jeopardize getting Callie Mae back.

She swallowed the last of her coffee and shut down her thoughts. The itch of impatience took their place. She was set to ride. The outfit was, too, thanks to Woollie. And most important of all, the cattle, already road-branded and grazing their breakfast in the pasture.

They were the best of what she had, strong enough to withstand the long walk to Dodge City and to fetch top price once they got there. All three thousand head were pointed north; they'd pull out as soon as Woollie gave the word.

Carina rose up in the stirrups and searched for him. She found him down by the chuck wagon talking to Sourdough with a stick in his hand, drawing in the dirt, likely giving last-minute directions for a place to meet later this morning.

Penn McClure was there, too. She eased back down into her seat, and her gaze lingered. He was easy to look at, she admitted. Tall and lean with his thumb hooked into a hip pocket, his Stetson pulled low, a coffee cup in one hand.

She'd not spoken to him since she bailed him out of the Mobeetie jail, but then, she'd hardly spoken with any of her men. It'd been easier to leave explaining the matter of Callie Mae's absence to Woollie. Worry over her and Grandpa had been consuming, to say the least.

But she saw them from her office window. Woollie and McClure, together. Her foreman spoke highly of the man, and Carina appreciated that he did. McClure was one of the few strokes of good luck she'd had since the nightmare with Callie Mae began.

Which was why he intrigued her, she supposed. She'd never bargained to keep a cowboy before and that set him apart. But just because McClure was good with a horse and a gather of cattle didn't mean she should be sitting here, thinking about him like she was.

As if he sensed her doing that very thing, his gaze lifted and caught her, here on the hill. For a moment, she felt suspended in time. As if it was only the two of them in all of Texas. And her heart did a funny, unexpected flip.

Guilt rushed through her. She was his boss, not a pink-cheeked schoolgirl, and resolutely, she took the reins in her hands. McClure said something to Woollie; he glanced up, too, and lifted his hand in greeting.

But only McClure mounted up to ride toward her. Carina nudged her Appaloosa into an easy lope, meeting him halfway.

"How much longer before we head out?" she asked.

"As soon as Sourdough's ready."

The low timbre of his voice sounded different now that he wasn't drunk. Smooth, husky. Richly masculine. She dragged herself back from noticing. "Good. Shouldn't be much longer then."

The cook would leave first, she knew. He needed the time to get ahead of the herd to arrive at the location Woollie designated. By the time the outfit met up with him about midday, Sourdough would have dinner hot and waiting.

But it seemed neither he nor Woollie were going to leave just yet. They stood at the back of the chuck wagon with the table down while Sourdough rummaged around in one of his possible drawers.

"Woollie wants to make camp tonight at the Washita," McClure said. "It'll be a long day to get there."

"That's all right."

She pulled her attention back to him, and her concentration wavered again. A stubble roughened his cheeks, and with the Stetson riding low on his forehead, his features were thrown into shadow. He had an air about him she couldn't figure. An edge. Untamed and wild.

She steeled herself against it. Another time, she might have given in to this fascination that continued to sway her. But not now. She couldn't think about anything except what lay ahead.

"Making it to the river would be a good head start for us to get to Kansas." Carina was grateful for the cool authority she managed to infuse into her voice. "I'll ride at the front with Woollie."

Carina knew her limitations. Woollie had always

been the C Bar C's trail boss, not her. He'd be the one to make the decisions in the coming weeks, but her place would be right beside him when he did.

McClure reached into his pocket, pulled out a rolled cigarette. "Ever been on a cattle drive before, Miss Lockett?"

"Of course I have," she said.

But not since Callie Mae had been born. Even then, only once back in '73 when her father gave in to her pleadings and let her tag along. The spring and fall roundups kept Carina away from home long enough. And what business was it of his if she had or not?

"No place for a woman, if you don't mind me saying so." McClure tucked the unlit cigarette into the corner of his mouth.

She bristled. "I do, as a matter of fact. Mind you saying so."

"Going to be hard work. Hate to see you go through it."

Carina glared at him. It was something she'd always done. Work hard. Just like everyone else in her outfit. And he knew, he *knew,* how important this trail drive was to getting her daughter back.

"What would you have me do, then?" she asked coolly. "Sit home and knit socks until everyone comes back?"

The emptiness in the house, the silence, would be her undoing. Not hearing Callie Mae's chatter, her boots clomping on the wood floors, and seeing her empty chair at the dinner table night after night would be harder than any cattle drive could ever be.

He regarded her, his eyes as brown as saddle leather, his expression as tough. "If you had to."

She stared in disbelief. "You seem to have forgotten I'm the boss of this outfit, McClure. The herd you're driving to Dodge City is mine. I intend to see that it gets there and that I'm paid in full when it does."

"So you can turn your hard-earned money over to Rogan Webb."

"Yes."

"And leave Kansas with nothing to show for your trouble."

The words burned right through her. "Yes."

"Damned waste, isn't it?"

Mockery threaded his low voice, taunting her with his disapproval. Carina wanted to punch him for it.

"You're not being paid to tell me your opinion of my personal matters, McClure. We made a deal to get your sorry ass out of jail. Just keep your end of it and your mouth shut while you do."

The faintest of curves softened the hard line of his mouth. He inclined his head. That mockery again. "Yes, ma'am."

She gripped the reins. It rankled he found her amusing over something so serious, but she forced herself to keep from chastising him about it. If she offended him, he could quit on her, leave her shorthanded, and she didn't dare risk it. She needed him too much. She'd gone to him with her pride in her pocket and practically begged him to come to work for her, after all.

She gestured toward the chuck wagon. "I'll go down to see what's taking Sourdough so long."

"Woollie's not feeling well this morning."

"Isn't he?"

Concern filtered through her, and her gaze swiveled toward the two men. Sourdough appeared to have found what he was looking for in the last possible drawer and handed it to Woollie, who promptly uncapped the container and took a quick swig.

"His stomach bitters," she said, dismayed. "He has a headache again?"

"Yes," McClure said.

Poor Woollie. He'd been plagued by the affliction for as long as she'd known him.

He swore by his bottle of Hostetter's, though, which claimed the medicine would cure anything from dry cough to liver ailments. Carina was convinced a good nap was really the cure, since Woollie always seemed to need one even when he didn't take a dose, but what did she know?

"We'll head out of here about nine," McClure said. "That'll give him time to rest up."

She glanced at the sky, beginning to clear from the dawn, and couldn't help feeling disappointment. "That's two hours yet."

"The grass is too wet if we leave sooner. Hooves can go soft. Best to let the ground dry some."

"A longhorn's hoof is as strong as steel, McClure. Or maybe you didn't know?"

"There's different opinions about cattle walking on wet grass. You've just heard mine."

"I see." Her chin tilted. She wasn't accustomed to being put in her place by one of her men. Did he think he had the right? "I wasn't aware you were in charge of this drive."

"Never said I was."

"I'll discuss our departure time with Woollie."

"I already have. He agrees."

"But it's two hours, McClure."

The words were out before she could think to stop them, a protest that made her sound petulant and desperate, even if she was both.

But of course, she had to do what was best for the herd. If she didn't, it would only cost her in the end.

"Never mind," she said, her tone an impatient snap. "Two hours is fine."

She didn't want to see his triumph, and she tugged on the reins to leave him. She could find plenty to do in those two hours, she supposed, despite her haste to get moving, and checking on her foreman was first on the list.

"Miss Lockett."

She turned back toward McClure. He pulled the cigarette from his mouth and studied the end he hadn't bothered to light.

"You'll get your daughter back," he said. His gaze, dark and piercing, lifted to meet hers. "If it's the last thing I do."

The grim avowal pushed a surge of unwanted emotion into her throat. She hadn't expected him to be intuitive, certainly not this determined. Maybe she hadn't given him enough credit for being either one.

"That makes two of us, then," she managed, and giving the Appaloosa a nudge in the ribs, she left him.

Chapter Four

"I'm going to close my eyes for a spell, Carina," Woollie muttered, climbing up onto the pile of bedrolls loaded on the chuck wagon. The canvas stretched over him would keep the rising sun off and the bedding would make him comfortable while he dozed. "Just long enough to give the bitters time to work."

"Take as long as you need." She watched him worriedly. She was still seated on her horse, which made it easier to see him. "We'll pull out when you're feeling better."

"Don't wait for me." He lay back and closed his eyes. "I can stay with Sourdough, then ride back to meet you and the herd later."

Carina bit her lip. From the miserable looks of him, it was the best way. But why did he have to fall ill now? Of all mornings, when she needed him most to move her herd toward the trail?

But she knew why. They both did.

"You've been worrying about Callie Mae." She reached over to pat his leg in sympathy. "That's what made you sick, isn't it?"

"Haven't been worryin' any more than you or anyone else in this outfit. And don't you go worryin' about this drive, either," he said, his words sounding tired. "McClure can do the job without me."

"McClure?"

She drew back. He was practically a stranger. What did she know about him except that he was good with a rope and a horse?

"He knows what he's doin', Carina. Going to have to trust him on that. Don't fight him so much."

"He doesn't want the cattle to get their hooves wet." She frowned. Sounded silly, just saying it.

"He told me. Some truth in it, besides."

"We could be moving out right now. Two hours closer to Callie Mae."

"I know."

Carina swallowed down further complaint. Woollie was in no condition to keep hearing them. Besides, she'd just been counting herself lucky to have McClure on the payroll only a short time ago. And it wasn't as if Woollie was leaving her for good. Only the morning, until he felt better.

He emitted a soft moan and covered his face with his Stetson. She glanced up at Sourdough, sitting up on the box, waiting.

"Have a care with him, you hear?" she said.

"He'll sleep like a baby if I can help it," Sourdough said.

She eyed her cook doubtfully. He'd drive like a bat out of hell so he could arrive at the noon rendezvous point as soon as possible and start stirring up dinner. The ride over rough rangeland would be merciless.

"I'll meet up with you later. McClure knows where," Sourdough said.

"All right. Later, then."

She nudged her horse back a few steps. Sourdough slapped the reins over his team of four, and harnesses clinking, they strained forward under their heavy load.

Carina watched them go. The iron wheels picked up speed; the wagon jostled and groaned, and she was glad for the heap of bedding that would cushion Woollie's ride.

By the time she saw him again, the Hostetter's nostrum would have had time to kick in. His pain and nausea would be gone. He'd be back to his old self.

She hoped.

Penn had to admit it was an impressive sight.

A long river of brown moving north across the Texas range. The longhorns traveled four and six abreast, guided on both sides by C Bar C riders who kept them in line with their ropes and hollers. A few seasoned steers led the cattle in a steady march toward the Western Trail, which would take them directly into Dodge City in a few weeks time.

Yeah, it was impressive all right.

And something Penn hadn't expected to take part in again anytime soon. Make that for the rest of his life. But then, Rogan Webb changed his plans. Abigail, too, and the greed they shared.

His gut tightened, as it always did when he thought of her. Of what she'd done.

Of how absolutely stupid he'd been to fall in love with her.

He clenched his jaw, fought down the pain, rechanneled his thinking to Carina Lockett and how she fit in his picture. She filled a big part of it. Driving her beeves proved a real handy way of getting his revenge satisfied and his counterfeit ring case closed, all at the same time.

Penn grimaced. But damned if the she-boss wasn't a pistol waiting to fire, prone to wound him any chance she got.

Granted, she had a lot on her mind. Having a child taken away would make anyone edgy. Being on the verge of financial ruin would, too, and her foreman being sick hadn't helped any. She was used to being in control, and this drive was out of her hands. Penn would need a heap of patience to get through the next few weeks with her.

About the only thing he could look forward to was Rogan Webb waiting for them when it was all over.

"So what makes you an expert at driving cattle, McClure?"

He swiveled a glance toward Miss Lockett, seated on her mare beside him. She had a proud profile with her chin tilted higher than most. A perfectly shaped nose and high cheekbones. She wore her wide-brimmed hat low on her forehead to shut out the sun, but her days on the roundup had already tinted her skin golden, something a woman of genteel society would've been loath to allow. By the time the drive was over, she'd be as brown as a bear cub.

She'd insisted on riding in front, though he could've used another swing rider down the line. They moved a ways ahead of the herd to inspect the range behind them. That long river of brown. Her silence up to now told him she was as impressed as he was.

"Never said I was expert, did I?" he said, knowing he hadn't.

"Woollie seems to think so."

Penn grunted. They'd become friends based on mutual respect, nothing more. The foreman was as dedicated as he could be to the C Bar C Ranch. He appreciated Penn doing the job he was being paid to do. Penn suspected the only difference between himself and the rest of the outfit was that Woollie had determined Penn was more experienced than most.

"I used to drive cattle for Tom Snyder, down in south Texas in the seventies," he said.

She nodded. "I've heard of him."

"Most cattlemen around these parts have."

"How long did you work for him?"

Penn accepted her grilling. Figured as his boss she had the right to know who was handling her herd in her foreman's place.

"Six seasons." He squinted an eye against the midmorning sun and scanned the limitless country in front of him. They were hard, grueling years. He'd started them as a kid, finished them as a man. He'd thrived from the adventure, the exhilaration that came from surviving the whole experience. "I've driven from the Gulf up to Salt Lake City and every state in between one time or another."

"My, my. You are good," she murmured.

He met the directness of her gaze. The morning sun darkened her eyes to deep purplish pools, a shade that could've been blue in a different light. Long, sultry lashes fringed those orbs. If a man wasn't careful, he could just about drown himself in eyes like hers.

But Penn wouldn't be so foolish. Or weak. Not the way he'd been with Abigail.

He pulled himself back from the past. Into the present. "Yeah. Reckon I am."

As if she disdained his scrutiny, she turned away. Her own gaze swept over the cattle, drawing steadily closer. "Why did you quit?"

"I wanted to do something different."

"Like what?"

Despite his avowal, his glance stayed on her. Drifted lower. Past her face and to the slender column of her throat. The breeze lifted the edge of her blouse beneath her jacket, presenting him with a shadowy glimpse of the curve of her breast.

His imagination stirred. Warmth strolled through his groin. Not since Abigail left him cold and bitter had a woman affected him like this.

"McClure. I asked you a question."

Annoyed she'd caught him staring, he straightened and dragged his gaze off her. Carina Lockett didn't seem to know she was a beautiful woman. Or didn't care that she was. But he couldn't let her distract him anymore.

"I wanted to do office work," he said finally, knowing she wouldn't understand why.

Her brow arched. "Office work!"

"Yep," he said, figuring her right.

He didn't expect her to understand. When he hired on with the United States government as an agent with the Secret Service, it'd been important to have a real job, with decent wages and room to climb through the ranks. He wanted to wear a suit and tie instead of a sweaty Stetson and dusty Levi's. To work with his brain instead of his body.

He'd wanted all those things. Still did. And he'd have them again once he settled his score with the low-life who took them away.

"Why aren't you, then?" she asked. "Doing office work?"

He heard the scoffing she didn't bother to hide. "My plans changed."

He declined telling her the rest of his story. The man he truly was. A former Treasury Department agent who'd gone beyond the toil of routine office work to investigate cases involving hundreds of thousands of dollars. Crimes of counterfeit. And that he'd gotten damn good at it.

Until Abigail. Until Rogan Webb.

She wouldn't like his plan to keep Webb from getting all her money, not when she was so desperate to give it to him. She wanted her daughter back, and that affected her thinking.

"Well, McClure, in case your plans include leaving this outfit to do office work somewhere, let me remind you of the deal I expect you to honor." All her scoffing was gone. She was back to being tough Carina Lockett, cattle queen for the C Bar C. "I've got money tied up in you. You're a long ways off from settling your debt."

His mouth thinned. Another stupid thing he'd done. Getting drunk in Mobeetie. Damages to the saloon had been considerable. More than he'd expected.

Maybe the saloon owner was just getting even, but regardless, the she-boss was right. Penn had cost her some bucks, and he owed her for it.

He studied the stream of three thousand head of bawling cattle, the remuda comprised of eighty horses moving alongside, the dozen men working the drive. He had a hand in organizing all of it, right along with Woollie. He'd come too far to back out now, even if he didn't have revenge to settle.

"Pull your claws in, Miss Lockett," he said finally. "I have every intention of returning to my office job as soon as I can. But I'm not going anywhere in the next three weeks except to Dodge City."

"I'm glad we're in agreement, then. I don't take kindly to a man whose word can't be trusted."

A sharp whistle kept him from a response and had both their heads turning toward the direction of it. Jesse Keller, who'd worked as her tallyman during the roundup and agreed to work the drive after, was taking a shift as point rider. He waved his hat to get their attention and indicated the horse coming at a fair run toward them.

"Can you tell who it is?" she asked.

"No."

"He's coming from Mobeetie or thereabouts." A moment passed. "It's Sheriff Dunbar."

She sat back a little in the saddle, as if she braced herself for the news he had to bring. Penn was certain her daughter was the first thing to jump into her mind. She'd think there was no other reason why the lawman would go through the trouble of seeking her out like this. And Penn was inclined to agree.

Dunbar pulled up and touched a finger to the brim of his hat. "Miss Lockett."

"This had better be good, Sheriff," she said stiffly. "My herd's not trail-broke yet. You could've set them to stampeding as fast as you were riding by them."

"I figured you'd want to know we found the carriage."

She sucked in a slow breath. "Mavis's?"

"Yes, ma'am. Found it abandoned in ol' Steve Bussell's pasture just outside of town."

"Oh, God."

"Everything all right with it?" Penn asked.

If it overturned, if the Webb woman and Callie Mae were hurt…

"Not a scratch on it. The rig was just sittin' there, stripped of its team. Just plain sinful to leave a fine rig like that behind. And no tellin' how long it'd been sittin' there before Steve came upon it and called for me to take a look."

"They switched," Penn said, grim.

The she-boss swung wide eyes at him. "For another rig?"

"One the sheriff couldn't track."

"That's what I'm thinkin'," Dunbar said. "No explanation but that."

"Oh, God," she said again.

"I'm sure you know, Miss Lockett, that second rig could've taken 'em anywhere without anyone noticin'," the lawman said. "If they escaped by stage, the Mobeetie line runs to Las Vegas, New Mexico. Or it could've taken 'em north to Dodge. Then again, they could've headed south to Fort Worth and taken the train."

"They didn't go to Mobeetie," she said with a firm shake of her head. "Folks know Callie Mae there. They would've recognized her." She turned to Penn, her expression a little desperate beneath her hat brim. "Wouldn't they?"

"Unless her grandmother disguised her."

As much as he hated to state the possibility, the she-boss needed to hear it. Rogan was that shrewd. And from the sounds of it, so was his mother.

"A disguise." Her fingers tightened over the saddle horn. "No. Callie Mae would never have stood for it."

Penn kept his mouth shut right along with Dunbar. The girl appeared determined to leave with her grandmother. If she saw the whole thing as an adventure, it'd be easy for her to cooperate, no matter what Miss Lockett thought.

He shifted his glance to meet the sheriff's. "You checked to make sure no one registered at the stage station under the name of Webb? Or Lockett?"

"'Course. First thing. No one had. But I got wires out at the other stations 'round these parts in case someone does."

"Mavis lives in New Orleans. I told you she did, didn't I?" Threads of urgency laced Miss Lockett's words. "Maybe they've arrived there by now. Did you check?"

The lawman lifted his hat, speared stubby fingers through his graying hair. "New Orleans's a big city, ma'am. It'd be like findin' a needle in a haystack."

"I don't give a damn!" she snapped. "You have to keep looking! They're going to Europe, and we have to stop them before they do!"

"Easy, Miss Lockett." Penn kept his voice low, firm. "Tracking them down is going to take some time. You have to understand that."

"Exactly. Callie Mae might even have changed her mind and be on her way home by now. Your grandpa will send word if she shows up, won't he?" Dunbar asked.

She shot him a look that said he was an idiot. "Of course he would."

"I'm doin' all I can the best way I know how. But I wish it was more for you." He glanced over his shoulder at the long trail of cattle and shook his head sadly. "I'm real sorry you have to give up your herd like this."

"She hasn't yet," Penn said.

And wouldn't, if he could help it.

Miss Lockett's throat moved. Seconds passed before she spoke.

"Herds can be rebuilt," she said finally.

But her defiance failed to sway the man's sympathy. It was there on his face, plain as paint. "I'd best be on my way. I'll be in touch if I learn anything more. You're headin' to Dodge City on the Western, ain't you?"

"Yes," she said.

"We'll get on the trail at the Canadian River. A couple of days," Penn added.

"Good enough." He touched a finger to his brim. "My best to you, Miss Lockett. Reckon you're goin' to need it."

She gave him a stiff smile and made no response, as if she didn't trust herself to make one. He rode off, and she glared after him.

"Damn you for pitying me," she muttered.

Then, as if she just realized she'd spoken aloud and Penn had heard every word, she glared at him, too.

"What are you waiting for, McClure?" she demanded. "Let's keep this herd moving."

Chapter Five

Woollie looked like death warmed over.

Carina sat on an overturned crate and kept an eye on him while she ate her supper. They'd pushed hard to make camp on the banks of the Washita River, and night had already fallen. Across the campfire, he sat cross-legged on the ground, his shoulders hunched, looking at his tin plate of beans and bacon as if he was going to throw up any minute.

It wasn't like him to have a headache for so long, and now here it was, the end of the day, and he wasn't feeling any better.

Why a nap and his stomach bitters didn't give him relief, she didn't know. She took it as a bad sign. And it didn't help matters any that he'd crawled out of Sourdough's wagon this afternoon and spent some time on the back of his horse, working right along with the other men. He'd insisted on it, even though Carina tried to convince him otherwise. All that noise from the herd, the dust and toil of the drive, well, it only made his affliction worse.

Worry gnawed at her. Between her daughter and her foreman, she'd never felt so burdened by it. With a heavy sigh, she rose and strode toward the chuck wagon, lit by the lanterns Sourdough had hung on hooks. With the exception of the men out getting the herd settled for the night, the rest had already eaten and lay sprawled around the fire, bone-weary from the day's work. She dropped her empty plate into the wreck pan, filled with soapy water.

"He'll be fit as a fiddle by morning," Sourdough said, eyeing her as he dried one of his cast-iron skillets. "Try not to fret so much."

She frowned. "Unless you've got some magic potion there in your possible drawer, I think he needs a doctor."

"Closest one is back in Mobeetie. Are you going to take him all the way back there?"

"If I have to."

"Carina."

His tone revealed his opinion of the idea, and Carina agonized over what to do. Sourdough could set bones and sew stitches, but he couldn't write the prescription for the medicine Woollie needed. Something stronger than the stomach bitters.

Having Woollie healthy again was as important as getting her herd to Kansas. He was the only trail boss the C Bar C had ever had. If he didn't get better, how would she manage without him?

"Talk to Penn about it," Sourdough said, reaching for another wet skillet. "You don't have to decide alone."

"Penn McClure?"

The suggestion startled her. He was just a ranch hand, someone she'd hired to get her through a tough spot. Granted, he was good on the back of a horse, and he was experienced with cattle trailing, but to depend on him for a decision about someone as important to her as Woollie?

No. She'd figure out what was best for him on her own. She didn't need McClure to do it for her.

Yet, of its own accord, her gaze lifted toward the beeves milling beyond their camp. He was out there, watching over them, calming them after their first hard day on the trail. He had a couple of the cowboys with him, including the worthless Orlin Fahey. Carina would never have hired Orlin to help drive her cattle, but he'd volunteered for the job, and she'd needed the extra hand. McClure had taken it upon himself to show the lout what to do to keep the animals calm throughout the night.

McClure hadn't taken a break since they made camp. His belly had to be feeling mighty empty by now. His body bone-tired.

And there she was. Thinking about him again.

Disgruntled, she found a knife and cut herself a piece of dried apple cake. By the time she slid the dessert onto a clean plate and forked a chunk into her mouth, the muffled rumble of horse hooves had her looking to see who rode in.

"Speak of the devil," Sourdough said.

McClure. Her pulse tripped a little. He drew up on the fringes of their camp, and TJ Grier, her wrangler, ran up to take his gelding. McClure said something and handed over the reins; the kid grinned wide and appeared proud as a bull. From the looks of him, Carina was sure he'd drop to the ground where McClure stood and start kissing dirt.

She scowled, took another bite of cake and couldn't peel her gaze off the man if she tried. Which she didn't. He headed to camp with a lithe, unhurried stride, his long legs sheathed in leather chaps. Yet there was a coiled power about him, too. Like a mountain cat in the wild. Untamed and free.

He pulled off his Stetson and carelessly ruffled his hair, flattened by the brim and the day's sweat. He didn't bother putting the hat back on; instead, he held it loose in one hand while the other scratched his chest, that single gesture so blatantly male that heat curled in the pit of her belly.

Damn him for it.

He approached Jesse Keller and Stinky Dale Cooper, a slick-haired cowboy nicknamed for the foul-smelling tonic he plastered on his head every morning. Both squatted on their haunches, enjoying a smoke. Without breaking stride, McClure bent toward them, and whatever he said had them guffawing loudly after him.

He kept walking toward the campfire. Toward Woollie. Determined he wouldn't see her staring, Carina stepped out of the chuck wagon's lantern light, deeper into the shadows. She hadn't noticed before how McClure had engaged her men, that in his short time with them, he'd won their friendship.

Their respect.

He hunkered down to Woollie's level, and though his low voice barely reached her, she guessed he inquired about the blamed headache. His brief, commiserating clasp on her foreman's shoulder confirmed it, and something went soft inside Carina.

The man had some good in him. Woollie appeared to perk up, just having his attention. McClure took a seat beside him, in front of the campfire, and pulled out the trail map from his vest pocket.

"Here, Carina." Sourdough thrust a plate heaped with beans and bacon at her, sending her thoughts scattering. "This'll remind Penn he needs to eat. Head over there and give it to him, will you?"

She opened her mouth to protest she was McClure's boss, not his waitress. But when Sourdough nudged aside her cake and set a cup of steaming black coffee beside it, she closed it again.

McClure was entitled, she supposed. Not that she'd ever served one of her men before, and not that McClure wasn't capable of serving himself now. But he'd put in a long day. Even longer than she had. Besides, she wanted to hear what plans he made with Woollie for tomorrow.

With a plate balanced in each hand, she strode toward them. Squatting, she handed him his supper, and he glanced at her in surprise.

"Thanks," he said.

She set his coffee in the grass carefully so the cup wouldn't tip. "Don't expect to have your food handed to you every day. Sourdough wants to make sure you're fed, that's all."

"Yeah?" His mouth curved in a knowing, crooked grin that poked at her insides. "But you're the one making sure I am, Miss Lockett."

He shoveled the beans into his mouth. There was something about the way her senses attuned to him that made it hard to think. The way the firelight threw his features into shadow, giving him a dangerous, rugged look, too.

Made it hard to concentrate, all right. She had to work at it so she could.

"Just helping you keep up your strength," she retorted. "I've got too much money tied up in you to have you go weak-kneed on me from lack of nourishment."

He chuckled around his chewing, and the sound wound right through her. His amusement was at her expense, but even Woollie managed to smile, and that made it worth it.

"Let's see the map," she said, getting down to business.

He had the paper already unfolded and spread out on the grass in front of them. A light breeze flitted at the edges, and she leaned forward to hold the nearest corner down.

McClure leaned forward, too; his lean finger pointed to their location on the Washita. She caught his scent, an appealing blend of saddle leather and tobacco, of sweat and man, and damned if her concentration didn't start falling apart all over again.

"Should be a good ford across the river," he said. "With rock bottom on the north side."

"Plenty of wood and water, too, as I recall," Woollie added in a subdued tone.

McClure took time to swallow down more beans with a swig of his coffee. "There is. All the way to the Canadian River. I figure if we started heading east about here—" his finger moved again "—we can reach the south bank by nightfall."

"We'll have to push hard," Carina said.

"But we can do it. No problem."

She nodded, pleased with the progress he intended to make. "And the weather's good. In our favor."

McClure turned toward her, their heads close enough his nose just barely missed her hat brim. She had to tilt her head back some to see him. In the golden firelight, his eyes shone like onyx, deep piercing pools of brown, almost black, and the way he looked at her, as if he could drag her right in, had her blood spinning in her veins.

"I do believe she's agreeing with me, don't you, Woollie?" he murmured.

"Sounds that way," her foreman said with a small smile.

"Not sure what to make of it."

"Best enjoy it. Might not happen again for a spell."

Exasperated, she drew back, snapping that strange pull he had over her. The two of them, teaming against her, throwing her off guard. And Woollie, as sick as he was. "It has nothing to do with agreeing with you, McClure. The facts are right there, on that map of yours."

"So it is, and yeah, it'll be a good walk." His gaze lowered to her plate. "You going to eat your cake?"

His sudden change of subject left her staring down at her dessert in confusion.

"I'll take it if you're not," he said.

His beans were almost gone. Sourdough had more at the chuck wagon, plenty of cake, too, and the casual intimacy with which McClure asked for hers instead left her flustered and without a logical thought to refuse him.

She frowned. This effect he had on her had to stop. "Go ahead."

He reached over and speared what she had left with his fork. But before he could mention his thanks or even take a bite, Carina suddenly heard the bellows of the herd. The first rumblings of hooves, vibrating through the ground.

McClure went still.

Carina's horrified gaze shot to the darkness behind them. To the herd no longer settled in.

McClure swore. Vehemently.

Oh, God. A stampede!

Penn threw aside his dinner and bolted to his feet.

"Every man on a horse!" he yelled. "Let's go! Let's go!"

They exploded into action, shouting, swearing, running to the remuda tethered beyond the fringes of camp. Every second was precious. Every head of cattle valuable. They had to move *fast*.

TJ, looking frantic, sprinted toward him, leading the gelding by the reins. "I was just taking his saddle off, but when I heard them hooves movin', I hurried right up and put it back on again. Here you go, Mr. McClure."

Penn leaped on, taking no time for the thanks he could say later.

"Miss Lockett, I'll get your Appaloosa." The wrangler ran off again.

Penn twisted. The she-boss took off after the kid. Penn slid a sharp whistle through his teeth to stop her.

Amazingly, she halted and spun toward him.

"Stay here," he yelled.

Her jaw dropped. "That's my herd out there, McClure!"

"No place for a woman. *Stay here.*"

"I won't!"

She took off toward the rope corral again, and Penn gritted his teeth. There was no time, no damn *time,* to force her to stay. He yanked on the reins, dug his heels into the gelding's ribs and took off in full pursuit of the fleeing herd.

The cattle had turned themselves around and were heading south, losing the ground they'd gained all day. He had to get to the front of them and turn the leaders so the rest would follow. Their hooves hammered against the ground, surrounded him with a deafening roar. Dust clouded his vision, thickened in his throat, but he lay over the gelding's neck and rode even faster.

In the moonlight, those three thousand head of wild-eyed, horn-swinging cattle were a dark mass of terrifying power. Penn hoped fervently none of the men would be trampled. Or gored. One wrong move, and it could happen. It'd be easy, so easy. Dangerous for anyone, but especially a woman...

He closed his mind to Carina Lockett, to the worry

that she was out here with him and the rest of her outfit. He pressed on, at last passing the thundering longhorns. Moving in amongst them, he swung his bullwhip again and again, aware if his horse found a prairie dog hole, or a hidden ravine, he'd go down, stomped to his death by those heavy hooves.

Yelling, relentless, he fought to turn the animals into the center of the herd. Then, to the side of him, there was Woollie, Stinky Dale and Jesse, and damn it, the she-boss, too, lashing her quirt, as desperate as the rest of them to get her herd to shift direction.

Finally, *finally,* the cattle began to veer into a wide circle, changing their straight run into a giant wheel of heaving cowhide. The switch got them bellowing to one another in confusion, and relief flowed through Penn at the sound, a sign their stampede was nearing an end. Gradually, they slowed and shuddered to an exhausted halt.

Penn halted, too. Breathing hard, he vowed vengeance on the night-herders responsible. Orlin Fahey was one, and he'd better have one *hell* of a good reason for those steers to run like they did.

His gaze clawed through the dusty air for a wide-brimmed hat, and he found it, the she-boss safe farther down the circle. He found Jesse and Stinky Dale, too, and the other cowboys whose darkened shapes he couldn't distinguish.

"Woollie!" Miss Lockett's voice called out. She twisted in her saddle, looking for him. "Woollie! Where are you?"

"He's here, Miss Lockett. Right here. Aw, hell, I think he's hurt."

Stinky slid from his horse, and dread rolled through Penn. If the cowboy had to get down, it meant Woollie was on the ground, and that could mean he'd been trampled. Or worse.

Penn barked orders to the others to guard the cattle. Moonlight illuminated Woollie's unmoving shape, Stinky down on one knee beside him. Penn raced toward them and dismounted. The staccato of horse hooves indicated the she-boss wasn't far behind. He hunkered next to Woollie, but his glance lifted to Stinky's.

"How bad is it?" he asked, grim.

"Not sure, Mr. McClure. But he's alive, at least," the cowboy said.

"Yeah." Woollie's head swiveled. "But it's bad enough. My shoulder, Penn. My arm, too. I think they're broke."

Miss Lockett reined her horse in hard and was out of the saddle before the mare came to a full stop. She dropped to her knees beside Penn, her breathing ragged, and reached for her foreman as if to assure herself he wasn't dead.

"Oh, Woollie. What happened?" she asked, her anguish pure.

He grimaced, held the injured limb against his chest. "My horse got hit, Carina, and I got thrown. I must've rolled across a couple of steers' backs before I landed." He sucked in a breath, seeming to get a hold on the pain. "Next thing I know, there's Stinky lookin' down at me."

"You had no business running this stampede," Penn growled, sliding a hand over the injured shoulder and finding it out of place. "Not with your head hurting like it was. Slowed your thinking." He examined the favored arm, too. "You could've been stomped into sausage."

"Reckon so," he said, looking serious.

Miss Lockett bit her lip.

"Could've been worse, I suppose," Penn said. "Easier to fix bones than sausage." He drew back. "Your shoulder's dislocated, and you broke your arm, all right. I suspect your collarbone's broken, too. Going to be hard to get you on a horse if we don't fix you up here and now. You agreeable with that?"

"Guess I don't have a choice." Woollie frowned. "My horse doin' okay?"

In unison, Penn and Miss Lockett's heads lifted, searching for the mount. Found him a short distance away, reins dragging, apparently none the worse for wear for the collision he'd had.

"He's fine, Woollie," Miss Lockett said. "Just waiting for you to climb on him again, that's all."

"Anyone got some tarantula juice?" he said, tried to move and moaned from the mistake.

Penn recalled the bottle of whiskey he had never been without since the day Abigail was killed. Old Taylor had given him plenty of comfort since then, but Carina Lockett put an end to his imbibing the night she sprung him out of jail. Everyone in her outfit knew it was one rule she strictly enforced. No drinking allowed. Ever. Much to his regret.

And now, Woollie's.

"Going to have to go through it stone sober," Penn said, commiserating. "Wish it could be different for you."

"Makes two of us. Let's do it, then."

"McClure. I'd like a word with you." Miss Lockett stood. "Stinky Dale, let the others know we'll be driving the herd back to the bed ground as soon as Woollie is tended to, you hear? Then take Jesse and Ronnie with you to look for strays. There'll be plenty."

"Yes, ma'am." The cowboy stood, too, and mounted up to follow her orders.

She moved away from her foreman in that purposeful stride Penn had learned to recognize. She had something to say, and she'd mince no words to say it.

He had little choice but to follow and hear her out. She swung toward him, her head tilted back.

"Sourdough is the next best thing to a physician this outfit has," she said in a low voice.

"So I've heard."

"He should be tending Woollie, not you."

"Sourdough is back at camp." Penn set his hands on his hips and glared down at her. She knew a cook never worked the cattle, no matter what happened, his place being to watch the camp until the rest of the outfit returned. "The stampede put a couple of miles between us. How're you going to get him here? On wings?"

"Do you have any idea what you're doing?" she demanded.

Her doubt in him rankled. "You mean about doctoring?"

"That's right."

Penn thought of his years with Tom Snyder, the injuries he'd seen, the mending he'd done, all learned from men who'd driven cattle longer and farther than she had.

"I can handle it," he said.

She seemed to war with his response, taking so long to answer, Penn began to wonder if she would.

"What if you can't?" she asked.

The night's shadows hid her expression, but the words sounded wrenched from her. Penn knew her foreman meant a lot to her. She was scared to death of seeing him hurt.

She'd already had Callie Mae taken from her. She had to know she'd lose Woollie, too, from this drive, that he'd be in no shape to herd cattle one-armed with a painful shoulder and collarbone in the grueling weeks ahead. Right now, he couldn't even sit a horse.

"You'll just have to trust me, Miss Lockett," he said softly. "Won't you?"

At some point, it'd become important to him that she did. Trust him. In getting her cattle to Dodge City. In leading her men. In preventing her from handing her hard-earned money over to Rogan Webb, most of all.

"I learned a long time ago trust is something that must be earned, McClure. I don't give mine at will, and certainly not to a man. At least, not one I hardly know."

Her contempt made it clear she allowed no one but a prized few into her private, self-reliant world, and he sure as hell wasn't one of them. He had to change that, or it could cost him his chance for revenge. His jaw hardened.

"Like it or not, I'm all you've got, Miss Lockett," he taunted. He indicated Woollie lying behind them, full

out in the grass. "Unless you want to tend to him yourself, here and now." He glared at her. "What's it going
to be?"

Her throat moved. A moment passed. The trust she
struggled to wrest into place.

"Just do your best with him, McClure," she said finally. "You'll do that, won't you?"

Despite the command in her tone, the persistence of
her worry showed through. It moved him, that worry,
coming from the tough Carina Lockett. She'd had more
than her share of it of late.

"My best, yes," he grated.

"I'll help you."

She took a step around him, heading back to her
foreman.

Penn's hand shot out, snatched her elbow, stopping
her. "No."

The shadows couldn't hide the tempest quick to brew
in her features. "The hell I won't."

He intended to spare her the experience. Some men
took their hurting in stride. Others screamed like a baby.
Penn didn't know which category Woollie would fit in,
and the she-boss shouldn't have to witness either one.

"There's a few things I'll need first," he said.

"Like what?"

"Something for a splint—a couple of tree branches,
sturdy and straight. And bandannas to tie them on with."

Her gaze darted to Woollie, then back to Penn. She
nodded once. "All right. I'll get them."

He didn't let her go, engrossed instead with how his
grasp revealed the slimness of her arm through the

sleeve of her blouse. If he tried, his fingers would almost touch around it. Somehow, she should be bigger than that, he mused, the thought dropping into his mind. Her power, her resilience, gave the impression of it.

She was tall, too. Taller than Abigail had been, and most women besides. Without her hat, her head would be level with his nose, something he didn't often find when he stood next to a female like this.

It shouldn't matter what Carina Lockett felt like, he told himself firmly. Or how tall she stood. What had to matter was knowing if he wasn't more careful from here on out, she'd get him to thinking of her more as a woman, and less as his boss.

And that would be a mistake. A distraction he couldn't afford. Carina Lockett was the ticket on his journey to revenge, he told himself firmly. His inside track to Rogan Webb. Nothing more.

He released her then. She stepped back.

And they both braced themselves for what lay ahead.

Chapter Six

It was nearly dawn by the time things were said and done. Strays gathered up. The herd driven back to camp. Each man present and accounted for.

Except for Woollie, no one had gotten hurt. Carina had found a quiet place for him to rest, on the edge of camp. He slept quietly wrapped in his bedroll, his arm in a sling, his pain relieved from the healthy dose of laudanum Sourdough had given him.

Her stomach tightened just thinking how close she'd come to losing him. Those long horns, spread five, six feet wide, could rip bark off a tree. Only divine intervention spared him from dying a gruesome death.

He'd given her the scare of her life, for sure, and she'd hardly left his side since. What would she have done without McClure to take care of him? The man had slipped Woollie's shoulder back into place and reset the arm with a skill she'd been afraid to hope for—using an efficiency she couldn't have matched to save her soul.

Woollie bore it with remarkable stoicism, but now, he'd have to leave the trail. Just for a while, until he was fully healed, and the knowledge left her feeling empty inside.

Carina rubbed her forehead. Driving three thousand head of cattle was a gargantuan task for anyone, rife with problems and hardship, and daunting for even the most seasoned of drovers. Times like these, she wished she was a man. Wished she had the tenacity and experience to handle it herself.

But she didn't.

McClure had the ability, however, and she had to depend on him now. There was no one else.

But it was unsettling, McClure having that much power over her. He was a stranger, a drifter Woollie had hired right off the range. What did she know about him really? Enough to entrust him with the job of getting to Dodge City in the shortest time possible? Enough to ensure her ability to pay the ransom for Callie Mae once they got there?

"Miss Lockett?"

Her musing ended at Jesse Keller's approach, and she glanced up at him expectantly.

"Mr. McClure has a few things to say to the outfit," the cowboy said. "He sent me over to ask if you'd like to join him."

Her gaze slid across the camp. The men began to collect around the chuck wagon. More specifically, Sourdough's coffeepot. The stampede's aftermath had kept them in the saddle all night long. No one had had any sleep yet.

Including McClure. Whatever he intended to talk about was sure to pertain to the near crisis. He'd want to get to the root of it.

"I would," she said.

Thanks to the laudanum, Woollie still slept quietly. She reached over and tugged his quilt higher over his shoulder.

Jesse extended a hand. "Let me help you up, Miss Lockett. Reckon you're as tired as I am."

Another time, she would've deplored looking so helpless, so *female,* but she had to admit her tired muscles appreciated the gesture. She took the young cowboy's hand and allowed him to assist her to her feet.

"Thanks, Jesse."

She fell into step with him. Jesse was close to her age and had worked for the C Bar C for the past six years. She trusted his loyalty. And she'd noticed how he and the rest of her men had begun to think of McClure more as "Mister" and less as "Penn." The shift of authority evident.

"A real shame about Woollie getting hurt and all," Jesse said. "Is Mr. McClure going to be boss for him from here on out?"

She was sorely tempted to remind him exactly who was in charge. As owner of the C Bar C, those three thousand head of cattle were hers, and hers alone, at least until she turned them over to Rogan.

"Can you think of anyone better for the job?" she asked.

"No, ma'am. He knows what he's doing, no doubt about it. That's important to drive a herd the size of yours."

"Does the rest of the outfit like him well enough?" she asked, not sure why she did, except to assuage her own weary worries.

"Yes, ma'am." He hesitated. "Well, at least most of us."

His glance touched on Orlin Fahey, looking morose as he stood off to one side, all but ignored by the rest of the hands. He was one of the night-herders assigned to watch over the herd, Carina recalled, and her mouth tightened. He had to know he'd be held responsible for any wrongdoing.

"Seems to me Mr. McClure's doing all he can to help you move your herd on Miss Callie Mae's account," Jesse continued. "Guess that says something for him."

Carina declined to mention the bargain she'd struck with McClure in his jail cell. That shackled him to her right there. But her gut instinct insisted the man had integrity. Jesse's impression of him—Woollie's and Sourdough's and just about everyone else's—confirmed it.

They reached the chuck wagon, and Jesse took the cup of Arbuckles' coffee Sourdough handed him. Lifting a finger to his hat brim, he left Carina to join the others at the campfire.

"Best give me one, too, Sourdough," Carina said. "I can barely keep my eyes open."

But her eyes found McClure just fine, hunkered next to the fire.

"He looks mad enough to eat the devil." Sourdough shook his head while he poured a dose of milk from the Borden's can into her brew. "He ain't takin' the stampede lightly."

McClure stared out over the herd, which was bedded down, chewing their cuds and so peaceful no one would know they'd spooked and run only hours before. His Stetson rode low on his forehead, and the shadow of a beard roughened his cheeks, giving him the look of a ruthless outlaw.

She accepted the cup from Sourdough. As an afterthought, she asked for another, and once obliged, she headed toward the fire.

McClure roused at her approach, and their gazes met. He stood slowly and watched her come toward him, that simple uncoiling of his body lithe and so full of unleashed power that the blood fluttered in her veins.

She sensed the anger in him—untamed, barely restrained. Warranted, but dangerous, too, and a slow heat curled inside her.

He appealed to a primitive side of her she didn't know existed. Why this man was capable of affecting her, she didn't know, couldn't comprehend, and she did her best to hide the way he made her feel. She halted in front of him and offered him the cup, steaming in the chill of the dawn.

"It's fresh, and it's strong," she said.

Beneath the brim of the Stetson, those dark eyes smoldered, like embers stirring into fire. She sensed the fading of his fury, as if he'd banked it for something else.

"Just what a man wants to hear," he murmured.

His fingers closed over hers while she held the tin, a deliberate ploy to keep her from stepping away. She felt their strength, yet there was a gentleness in them, too, and for a moment, a single, wild moment, she thought he misunderstood what she said. That he'd guessed the effect he was beginning to have on her more and more, this attraction building inside her. That he thought she spoke of *that* instead of the Arbuckles' in her hand, and oh, God—

She couldn't let him know. This blamed weakness. If he knew, he'd use it to his advantage, as Rogan had done....

Her chin lifted. She schooled her features into an impassive mask. Rechanneled her thinking into a logical response. "A woman, too, McClure. When she's been up all night."

He nodded, agreeing. He still hadn't released her.

"How's Woollie?" he asked in his low voice. Smoky, intimate, controlled.

"Sleeping. Doing as well as can be expected."

"There's a farmhouse a few miles back. We'll see if he can stay there a while."

"Nothing else to do, I suppose," she said, hating it.

"He'll catch up with us later. You mind if I send a cow along?"

Their gratitude for the privilege of Woollie's recuperation. The farmer would appreciate having the beef.

"Of course not," she said.

She tugged against his grasp. Her men were surely watching. What would they think, his fingers bold on hers like this? As if there was something between them. McClure and her.

"If you have something to say to the outfit, you'd best get a start on it," she said coolly. Which was nothing like how she felt. Cool. "They're tired, and they're waiting on you."

A moment passed, as if he debated obeying her order just yet. But he released her. Finally. She took a discreet step back. Covered her awareness of him by taking a sip of the coffee in her cup, the pathetic side of her needing something ordinary to do, when he made her feel anything but…ordinary.

Yet with maddening ease, he turned his attention from her to the cowboys sprawled on the ground. The tension shimmered from him, a return of the anger he held inside. Bleary-eyed, unshaven, and tousle-haired from the night's work, her men talked in somber tones while they kept themselves awake with the Arbuckles'.

"What happened to cause the stampede last night?" McClure demanded. "Anyone know?"

Their talking ended; expressions shifted toward him.

"Could've been a lot of things, Mr. McClure."

His gaze swung to Billy Aspen, a veteran cowboy who'd put in his share of years working with cattle. One of the assigned night-herders, Carina guessed he wanted to make sure he didn't get blamed for them bolting.

"No storm rolled in that I could see. No lightning, no thunder." McClure propped a booted foot on a boulder jutting from the ground. "Haven't seen a tumbleweed since we left the C Bar C. Of course, it could've been a fox or a coyote that spooked the cattle. Maybe a rabbit. Anyone see any or hear any?"

Heads shook. Faces were grave. Their moods as serious as McClure's.

"Real quiet night last night," he said. "But this soon

out from their home range, the cattle were a long ways from being trail-broke. Wouldn't take much to spook them."

Agreement rippled through them.

"That stampede had something to do with the fire someone lit," McClure snapped.

Carina nearly spewed coffee. A fire? What fire?

"You know anything about it, Orlin?" he demanded.

All heads swung toward the ranch hand.

Including Carina's.

And he looked as nervous as a prostitute in church. As if he'd rather be anywhere but here, with McClure and the entire C Bar C outfit glowering their disapproval at him.

"Now, listen up, McClure. Ain't no way you can pin that fire on me," he sputtered, jowls quivering.

"When you went on herd, you were stationed at the rear while Billy and Ronnie guarded the front. That's where I found that fire, Orlin. At the rear and still hot."

"Yeah? Don't mean I started it."

"No one else out there but you," McClure shot back. "What happened? Did you get cold? A little bored, maybe? Did you decide to get a fire going to warm yourself?"

Orlin's mouth puckered, as though he was gathering up the words to deny it.

"To start the fire, you had to strike a match," McClure said before he could. "As quiet as the night was, it could've been the match that spooked the herd you were supposed to keep calm. Might've been the wood you were burning, too. Popping and crackling, like wood does."

A slow boil stirred inside Carina. The implications of what he'd done…the negligence, the risk.

"You couldn't have made the fire while you were still in the saddle." Unrelenting, McClure kept on. "You had to get down off your horse to start it. You probably stayed down a spell, too. Just so you could get warm all over."

How could the man be so thoughtless? So utterly stupid?

"No one gets off his horse when he's guarding the herd." McClure's voice rumbled. "No one."

And now, because of Orlin, it'd take even longer to get to Dodge City. To get to her little girl.

"A man gets distracted when he's not in the saddle, ready to ride if the cattle get spooked and bolt. He loses time when they do. By then, it's too late."

Did the lazy lout think of Callie Mae at all?

"You've cost us a night without sleep and a day off the trail. But even worse, Woollie got hurt. Did you think about any of that when you struck the match, Orlin?" McClure grated.

"Look, I'm sorry, all right?" he snapped. "I didn't start the stampede on purpose. It was an accident. A pure accident."

At the admission, a muscle leaped in McClure's cheek. Grumbles of head-shaking disgust went through the others.

"Damn you, Orlin," Carina fumed.

Had she ever hired a man more worthless?

McClure straightened. "All right. The rest of you, get some sleep. We'll pull out in a few hours. Orlin, get your sorry ass over here."

Reproving glares shot from the men like arrows from a Comanche's bow, but they were quick to cover the ground with their bedrolls, clearly more interested in following McClure's orders than seeing him make Orlin suffer for his sin. Each of them more forgiving than Carina.

While Orlin lumbered reluctantly toward them, McClure angled his body in front of her, keeping their conversation from drifting.

"I know you want to fire him, but don't," he said, his voice low.

"He's got it coming."

"Probably."

"So why the hell wouldn't I?"

"If I have to tell you the answer to that, then it's a good thing I'm trail boss." He leveled her with a hard glance. "And not you."

He stepped back and left her mind working through his words while her pride worked through his arrogance. Orlin shuffled up, and Carina swallowed down a scathing reprimand to them both. McClure might have let his respect for her authority slip, but at least he had the courtesy of not doing it in front of the ranch hand.

"Now before you get all set on sending me packing, McClure, I want you to know I'm needin' this job real bad," Orlin said.

McClure nodded, took a sip of coffee gone cold by now. "Reckon that's why you hired out with us."

"I shouldn't have done what I did. I know that now. And everythin' that happened, it was an *accident*."

"So you said."

"I've never been nothin' but a sheep farmer till I

came over to the C Bar C. Ain't never trailed cattle before, so how the hell was I supposed to know what I should and shouldn't do?"

"Because I told you."

A moment passed while Orlin did some recollecting. "Well, I must've forgot."

Carina rolled her eyes. Despite her stewing, she kept her mouth shut.

"The damage is done, Orlin," he said. "Main thing is, you 'fessed up to the mistake. Next time you do something wrong, just let me know. Don't go making me hunt down the truth."

"No, sir."

"I'm good at it," McClure said, his voice rough. "Finding out the truth."

"Yes, sir." Clearly relieved at his continued employment, Orlin's cheeks quivered from a vigorous nod. "Seems you are."

"We'll go on from here. Miss Lockett and I, we're going to give you another chance. But it's going to be your last. Understand?"

"Yes, Mr. McClure. I do."

"Good enough, then. Get some sleep."

"Guess I will." He hesitated. Blew out a breath. "Thanks."

Then, he hurried off.

Carina's lips thinned. Well. As much as she hated to admit it, McClure was fair. Considering the consequences of the stampede, losing Woollie and having a frustrating delay to get Callie Mae back, she wouldn't have been as reasonable.

"We're shorthanded. We need him," McClure said simply, reading her thoughts.

"How long do you suppose he'll be licking your boots?" she asked, recalling the deference which had slipped into the word *Mister* when Orlin addressed him.

"If he's smart, until we get to Dodge City. After that, it doesn't matter."

Her lip curled, revealing her skepticism that the lazy lout would make it so far. "He doesn't deserve to stay on with us."

"I disagree."

"Doesn't matter if you do."

"You're thinking of Callie Mae. That's personal. I'm thinking of trailing your herd north as fast as we can, any way we can. That's business."

Yes. Her perspective was skewed. Another time, another year, driving the beeves to market would have been routine. A financial necessity scores of other ranchers would do, too, for all the same reasons.

This year was different.

This year was worse.

A nightmare she'd never conceived of living.

"It's not that simple, McClure," she said.

He narrowed an eye over the dawning horizon, and a faraway look stole into his rugged features. It seemed he returned to a world different than where he was, here on the Texas range. A place in his past. And forgot Carina was there.

Then, he pulled himself back. Inclined his head with a sardonic glint in his eye. And smiled coldly.

"You're right, Miss Lockett," he said. "It's not."

Chapter Seven

◦◦◦◦◦◦◦

Afternoon, Day Two

Rogan watched the huge mass of bellowing longhorns ford the Washita River with extreme satisfaction.

A beautiful sight, that herd.

They swam with their heads just out of the water and their broad horns pointing to the sky. The C Bar C riders kept the cattle's momentum going, slow and steady, with persistent yips and yells.

From his place on a ridge, Durant beside him, both of them hidden in the brush, Rogan's gaze swept the riders for one familiar, wearing a wide-brimmed hat. Carina. He found her in the water with the rest of her men, looking slender and out of place as she added her voice to theirs to get those longhorns crossed over to the river's north bank.

"Any idea who the man next to her is?" Durant asked.

Rogan shifted his study. Compared to the other riders spread out point and flank, this one kept close to her side. As if he was afraid she'd get caught in a swift undercurrent and be swept away if he wasn't there to keep her from it.

"No."

The distance separating them prevented Rogan from getting a good look, but the man rode with confidence in the saddle, as if he forded rivers every day. He called out orders, and the men listened.

"Maybe her trail boss, eh?" Durant said.

Rogan didn't know what happened to her precious foreman, Woollie. Or why this man took his place. But he took note of him, just in case. "Maybe."

"He's acting like her shadow. He must think she needs protecting."

Rogan grunted. "She doesn't need a man to protect her from anything."

"Except us." Durant grinned.

Rogan scowled. "Not even then."

The woman was tough. Driven. But he'd enjoyed her company once. A decade ago. She'd been young, hot-blooded. A firestorm in bed. Even now, she made him hard from the remembrance.

Only thing that softened her up these days was Callie Mae.

The daughter he never wanted.

His lip curled in disgust. Carina had been foolish to let herself get pregnant. He'd made it clear their time together in Dallas would be just for fun. Without attachments. She should've known he had no intention of being any woman's husband. Or any child's father.

He returned his scrutiny to the river and those beautiful cows that would be his salvation. His ticket back to the life he'd had before that damned government agent took it away from him.

Hate stirred, the way it always did when he thought of Penn McClure. Abigail had warned him of the man's determination to make him pay for his counterfeiting crimes. If McClure found him, he'd throw him in jail. Mother would disown him for sure. And then where would he be?

She didn't know about his counterfeiting, and she wouldn't. Ever. Not if he could help it. Mavis Webb controlled the purse strings to the Webb fortune, slowed the flow of money into his account to a pathetic allowance and constantly nagged him to be a success like his father.

Rogan did a slow seethe. She should know how much he'd tried. All she saw was how he'd failed.

She'd despise his illegal activities and any scandal they brought to the high-and-mighty Webb name. But she wasn't above agreeing to a little blackmail to get what *she* wanted. And she wanted Callie Mae. It'd been easy to convince Mother to force Carina to bargain with him. She'd been desperate enough to go along with the ploy.

"Carina Lockett will want to get even," Durant said.

"What if she does?" he demanded, dragging his thoughts from the past. "She won't get Callie Mae back until she pays us first."

"Maybe your old lady won't give her up."

Rogan opened his mouth to argue. Then closed it again. It was something he'd considered, Mother wanting to keep Callie Mae for herself. Taking her somewhere far away where Carina couldn't find her.

She was selfish enough to do it. Rogan was convinced she'd always been secretly disappointed he wasn't born smart and female.

Which was how Callie Mae got to be so important to her.

The daughter Mavis Webb never had.

And that made him more determined than ever to go through with his plan. Rogan glared at the gunslinger. "Having second thoughts, Durant?"

"Without her cattle, Carina Lockett's ruined. She won't give that herd up without a fight."

Rogan considered what she could be capable of, and involuntarily, his glance fell to the man riding at her side. If he was as protective as he looked, he could be a problem, too.

Rogan squared his shoulders. He couldn't let Durant's paranoia affect him. They'd come too far to start second-guessing themselves now.

Besides, that big, beautiful herd was heading due north. Carina wanted her daughter back. That would keep her cooperative and trailing right on schedule.

A few weeks, Rogan reminded himself. They'd be in Dodge City.

And then, finally, he'd have the money he needed.

After Midnight, Day Three

Carina couldn't sleep. Again.

The agony of being away from Callie Mae kept her awake. Every minute of every grueling day, her daughter was there. In her mind, filling her thoughts, pushing her onward through the hours until she should've dropped like a rock from exhaustion at night.

She didn't.

She tossed and turned in her bedroll. Stared up at the canvas roof of her tent. Fought tears of frustration and fury and terror at Rogan, his mother, and yes, Callie Mae, for what they'd done.

This worry, no mother should have to endure it. The haunting agony from not being with her child, not knowing if she was safe. Happy or sad...

Mavis could have booked passage with her on a ship by now. From where, Carina could only speculate. New Orleans? New York? She didn't know a thing about their plans, which direction they were headed, or who they were with.

Carina groaned. Callie Mae had never stepped beyond Texas state lines in her life. Was she homesick at all? Crying? Frightened?

The nightmare of having her so far away, maybe already on the great Atlantic Ocean, surrounded by hundreds, *thousands,* of miles of water turned Carina's stomach into nauseating mush. What if the ship sank? Or a storm rolled in and blew them off course? They'd be stranded, helpless, even lost in the horrendous depths of some part of the ocean only God knew where.

But Carina wouldn't know. Until it was too late.

If only she could find out. She'd take after them, fast as greased lightning, and then, Mavis Webb—

The old witch deserved to be shot.

Carina rolled to her side, jerked up the quilt. And fumed.

If she was a man, Rogan wouldn't have succeeded at blackmailing her. She would've had the physical strength to fight both him and Durant off and prevent them from zeroing in on the one thing that set her apart from being male.

Being a mother.

Her one weak spot. Rogan had blindsided her with Mavis's help, betrayed her trust, hit her hard where she expected it least.

Frustrated, eyes brimming, Carina tossed aside the quilt and sat up. She'd been so stupid not to have seen through their scheme. Mavis with her spoiling of Callie Mae, turning her head to extravagant fripperies.

Damn the woman for being so clever. So calculating.

Carina covered her face with her hands and fought the sob welling in her throat. Did her little girl enjoy running away? Had the allure of traveling to faraway places turned her forever from the C Bar C? Her legacy?

Or did she want to come back? And couldn't?

The endless questions pelted Carina's heart until she bled. Until her surroundings turned suffocating. She needed air, the freedom, the peace of the late night.

She had to get out.

She flung the tent's canvas flap open and slipped through. The camp was quiet except for the scattered snores of the men splayed around the fire. Beyond its flickering light, the cattle rested, calmed by the faint croons of the night-herders. Somewhere beyond, a coyote howled.

Carina stood, breathed in deep, held the air in her lungs. For long moments, with her eyes closed, she didn't move.

Then, she exhaled, slow and deliberate. And her anguish faded in degrees.

She'd get through this, one day at a time.

Her eyes opened. The night's dark serenity gathered her in. Air slid cool through the thin cotton sleeves of her nightgown, raising the flesh on her skin. Rough range grass prickled the bottoms of her bare feet.

After supper, in the privacy of a stand of cottonwoods, she'd bathed in Sourdough's big metal tub. Washed her hair, too, and left the tresses loose to dry. Feeling clean again and donning a fresh nightgown had been heaven after the afternoon's rigors of fording the Washita River.

Now, Carina gave little thought to her dishabille. It was late, and the exhausted outfit slept like stones after another day of hard work. No one would see her. She was far from being shy, but she was their boss, and she was the only woman on this drive. She had to keep the boundaries clear.

They were the only family she had right now, her men. This far from the C Bar C, circumstances being what they were, where would she be without them?

And yet…she needed McClure most.

Her gaze lifted toward the herd. He'd taken the worst of the shifts as night-herder despite having gone almost a full day without solid rest, an offer the others were only too glad to accept.

The man had the stamina of a bull, for sure.

She was grateful for all he did. More than he knew. His focus on getting her to Dodge City and everything he did in between stirred up a growing dependence on him that she couldn't ignore.

The fire had withered down to glowing embers. Wanting to keep away pesky critters, Carina stepped gingerly over the bristly grass, making her way toward the chuck wagon and the leather sling beneath where Sourdough kept a supply of cow chips. She'd only need a few to build the fire again, and bending, she reached toward the pile—

Strong fingers clasped over her wrist and jerked her away.

"Don't reach under there bare-handed," McClure said in a rough voice.

A startled gasp rushed from her throat. He'd pulled her back so fast, she had to grapple for balance.

"You could get bit," he said.

Releasing her, he struck a match, and the flame's light revealed the curly-tailed scorpion perched on the heap of cow chips. Repulsed, she yelped and leaped backward, right into McClure's chest. The awful-looking scorpion skittered deeper into the pile and disappeared from sight.

McClure blew the match out. "Wear the gloves next time."

She knew where they were—on top of the water barrel. A pair was always kept there for that very reason, and she shuddered at her carelessness. "Oh, God. They're disgusting, aren't they? Scorpions, I mean."

"Venomous, too."

His arm had wound around her after she'd careened into him, holding her steady, and she didn't even realize it until now. In pure reflex, she twisted away, her nerves so frazzled, she could barely think straight.

She drew in a breath, raked her fingers through her hair, pulling the weight of it off her cheek.

"You okay?" he asked, watching her in the dark.

She wasn't sure. She could still feel where his arm had been, strong around her waist. Warm through her cotton nightgown.

"Of course I am," she lied.

A moment passed. As if he was skeptical. "What are you doing out here? Couldn't sleep?"

She hesitated. She debated lying about that, too, but it was obvious she couldn't, since she was standing here with him, outside, in the middle of the night.

"No," she said.

"I'll listen if you want to talk."

"No." When before had she opened herself up and confided in any of her men, besides Grandpa or Woollie? "Thanks, but it won't be necessary."

But the offer touched her. He had to be bone-tired.

"You're worried about Callie Mae," he said.

Just hearing her name caused instant tears to well. Carina strove for control, glad for the dark that would keep the tears from showing.

"What kind of mother would I be if I wasn't?" To her horror, her voice quavered.

"I know you don't think so, but she's fine. Try to believe that."

Carina turned her head away, refused to look at him. How would he know if her daughter was fine or not? No one knew, except that witch Mavis. And maybe Rogan.

McClure moved, just out of her range of vision, and

before she could even think he'd dare to do such a thing, he slipped an arm behind her knees, the other at her back, and scooped her up against him, as easy as if she was a child.

She squeaked in surprise, grabbed for his shoulders and hung on. "McClure! What the hell are you *doing?*"

Her voice sounded loud in the quiet, but she couldn't help it. Over by the campfire, Stinky Dale stopped snoring, frowned and rolled over.

"You'll feel better if you get some of that worry off your chest," McClure said in his low voice. "And this is as good a time as any for me to say a few things myself."

"Put me down. Now."

"Can't." He began walking, beyond the chuck wagon. "You're not wearing your boots. You want to step on a rattlesnake?"

She didn't. Not a snake or anything else she couldn't see. He continued past her tent, which she should never have left in the first place.

"Where are we going?" she demanded through gritted teeth.

"Far enough away where we won't spook the herd while we're talking."

He left camp and headed toward the cottonwood trees where she'd taken her bath earlier. He halted and set her down.

She took a quick step back and straightened her nightgown over her hips. The grass was softer here, at least. And the night deeper.

"All right, McClure. What do you want to say?" she snapped.

She sensed a hardening in him. A palpable determination she could almost reach out and feel.

"Rogan's not going to get away with what he's doing to you," he said.

Her chest hurt with a sudden stab of pain. "In case you haven't noticed, he already is."

"No. He's not. You haven't paid him a dime."

"Yet. But I will. I have to."

McClure clenched his jaw, as if he struggled to control the argument simmering between them.

"Why are you making it easy for him to destroy you?" he demanded roughly.

"Easy?" She gaped at him. "Easy? Damn you, McClure, he's not giving me a choice."

"You'll lose everything."

"I'll have nothing without Callie Mae."

"Years of hope and hard work," he persisted, ruthless. "Land, cattle, the outfit who'd lay down their lives for you if they had to."

She pressed her fingers to her mouth in a sudden rush of emotion. The stark truth in his words dug deep.

"What about them?" he demanded, driving his point home with cold precision. "Where will the men on your payroll go when you give away the C Bar C?"

Tears stung her eyes. The responsibility she wore on her shoulders had never felt heavier.

"You give in to Rogan, you give up your daughter's heritage, too," he grated.

Her control came to the edge of breaking. "Damn it, yes. The Lockett legacy." The words were wrenched from her. "I should have been a better mother, McClure.

Then none of this would be happening, would it? But I wasn't, and it is, and Callie Mae's gone. She'll have nothing to come home to, and I'll have nothing to give her to—to make her happy."

"Don't underestimate her," he shot back. "Give her some credit to figure out what matters most to her."

"She's only a child. She's impressionable, and vulnerable, and I'll give Rogan and Mavis what they want so I can have her back again."

"Not if I can help it."

Her eyes narrowed at the fierceness in his tone. "I don't recall you having a say in the matter."

"I'm giving myself one."

She studied him. A tall, dark shape in front of her. Loyal, she'd learned in the short time she'd known him. Now, determined to get involved in her affairs. Protecting her for reasons of his own.

"Why?" she asked.

He seemed to ponder the simplicity of her question, as if his response was too complex to explain.

"There's no law out here, except us," he said finally. "And I've always had a strong sense of justice."

"Sheriff Dunbar is the law, and he's doing what he can to stop Rogan. He's contacting railroads, stagecoach lines, sending wires out to other lawmen. Giving them all descriptions of Callie Mae and Mavis. You know he is."

McClure shook his head slowly, a cool dismissal of her logic. "Like finding a bee in a blizzard."

"But there's not much else he can do, is there?" Carina said, fighting off a rise of hopelessness. "I have to give Rogan what he wants. I refuse to do anything to jeopardize my daughter's return."

"What makes you so sure he'll keep up his end of the bargain?"

Carina's breathing quickened. It was always in the back of her mind that he wouldn't. Rogan was capable of it. Double-crossing her. Taking her money and her daughter and leaving her with nothing.

Nothing.

She crossed her arms over her breasts and shivered. From fear. From the night's chill. From the awful certainty that if she wasn't very, very careful, Rogan would win.

"Justice, Miss Lockett." McClure reached out and slid his fingers through the hair falling along her shoulder, slow and easy. "He'll have it. I swear."

She wanted to believe him. More than anything. So much she didn't even protest he took the liberty of touching her hair. A boldness which another time, with another man, would've caused her to pull her Colt and burn some powder on him.

But not now. Not with McClure. He had the ability to soothe her with the words she needed to hear. To fill her with hope of the justice she craved. The justice Rogan deserved.

She shouldn't be here with him. Alone, in the middle of the night. In her nightgown and feeling miserable and in sorry need of having his arms around her.

Because it'd been so long since a man held her.

And she was so afraid.

He stepped closer, a slight shift of his body, moving

toward hers. Anticipation coiled through her, the knowledge of what he might do. The comfort he seemed to know she needed.

His fingers curled around her neck, rough-skinned but gentle. Sure. Carina couldn't have resisted him if she tried. And she didn't. She should have. His head lowered, and hers tilted back.

A moment of stillness hovered between them. As if McClure debated the wisdom of what he was about to do. Their breaths mingled, their heat. His scent filled her, saddle leather and sweat, and damn it, it didn't matter he was one of her men or that she was about to break the most important rule she'd ever made regarding them.

She took his lips against hers with a tentative hunger that set down roots. Then burst inside her. He cupped the back of her head and hardened the kiss. Her mouth opened. His arm circled her waist and crushed her against him.

A moan came from her. The feel of being held by him like this…

Their tongues mated with wet, frenzied strokes that left her knees weak, her body all but boneless. Penn McClure's strength, his power, would be her undoing. Or her salvation. She didn't know which, and she didn't care, but he filled her, this awful need in her which needed filling.

He opened a part of her she'd closed up tight ten years ago. Rogan had her denying herself what McClure got her to wanting again. A man, and the things he could make a woman feel. Deep down, hidden things. The physical, ache-clear-down-to-her-toes ones, too.

And that's what he made her do with his kisses and his sheltering embrace. Ache. For more. To forget and to feel. To believe that, with him, everything would be right again in her world.

He turned her shameless. Shameless enough to want to take him down to the grass and sate this lust burning through her, but before she could, he ended the kiss and slowly drew back.

His breathing came rough. Hers was no better, and when she could think again, open her eyes and comprehend what had just happened between them, his mouth curved into a slow, sultry smile.

"Justice, Carina," he murmured. "You've just gotten my vow on it."

Then, before she could convince herself she shouldn't have kissed him as she did or allow him the liberty of using her given name, he scooped her into his arms and carried her back to her tent.

Chapter Eight

One Week Later

Penn had pushed the cattle hard those first few days to wear them out and keep them from trying to turn back toward their home range. Because of it, they'd made good time out of Texas and arrived at Fort Supply, a military post deep in Indian Territory, safe and a little ahead of schedule.

He was ready for a break. So was the rest of the outfit.

Carina, especially.

Funny how he'd begun to use her name like that. Carina. Not Miss Lockett. He thought of her different, too. As a woman. A desirable one. She was still his boss, was still hard as nails when she had to be, but he'd gotten a glimpse of her softer, vulnerable side. Something the rest of her men had been denied.

Because of their kiss.

Yeah, everything was different now.

She'd all but turned a cold shoulder on him since then, but Penn figured it had more to do with her being mortified at letting her guard down than anything improper he'd done. Now, she worked hard at keeping things all business. Avoided getting too close, making sure her men knew that nothing personal was going on between her and the trail boss.

Not that there was. Something personal.

And there wouldn't be.

Penn wasn't going to let anyone steer him off course from his revenge against Rogan. Not even an intriguing woman who could kiss a man the way Carina Lockett could. He had to keep his head straight, his hate focused.

Yet despite his resolve, Penn couldn't shake her out of his thoughts. She'd been a willing participant in that kiss, for sure. She fit in his arms, and no matter what happened after they got to Dodge City and settled the score with Rogan Webb, he'd always remember that about her.

How she fit.

Carina Lockett was a hot-blooded woman. Meant to pleasure a man. Hell of a shame she didn't have a husband in her bed at night. He'd be one lucky son of a bitch if she did.

Penn's gaze sifted over the herd, corralled in massive pens outside the military fort. Might be Rogan had something to do with her not having a husband, and Penn could relate. Betrayal left scars that took a while to heal.

Abigail and Rogan. They belonged in the same category with one another.

Penn put the woman he'd almost married from his mind. Deserving or not, she'd never betray a man again.

Rogan was a different story, though. Carina had her hands full with him, but she wouldn't fight him alone. When it was all over, she wouldn't like learning Penn had used her and her herd to get his revenge, but there was no help for it.

Might be she'd even thank him for it.

Then again, maybe she wouldn't.

Troubled, he found her at a mud hole beyond the corralled cattle. Orlin Fahey was with her, frowning at a cow caught in the mire, her bawling calf on the edge. The cowboy was off his horse, but his rope was attached to the cow's horns. He stood there, feet braced, rope straining, trying to get her out while fighting to keep her worried calf from going in.

Carina looked none too pleased at his ignorance. Penn leaned forward, rested his elbow on the saddle horn, and waited to see what she'd do about it.

After an exasperated snap of her fingers, Orlin quickly handed his end of the rope over, then dropped to one knee and kept a secure hold on the fidgeting calf. Carina wrapped the hemp around the saddle horn, and twisting to keep an eye on the stranded cow, she carefully nudged the Appaloosa forward. Bellowing, the cow inched higher out of the mud until all hooves were on dry ground again.

Orlin released the calf to reunite with its mother. He stood, his mouth tight and his face red, and Carina tossed him his rope. Whatever she said to him next had his head bobbing in terse and repentant agreement.

Amused, Penn moseyed his gelding closer. Orlin might need saving himself about now, and Penn figured he'd do him the favor. Since his blunder with the stampede, the cowboy had been trying hard to do his job right. Up until now, at least, Penn couldn't fault him for his work.

"Looks like you needed some help there, Orlin," Penn said, drawing closer.

Carina's glance darted to him, then flitted away. She busied herself adjusting her lariat, coiled just fine against her saddle.

"Yes, sir," Orlin said. Looking grim, he mounted up. "But Miss Lockett here set me straight."

"Did you really think you could pull that cow out with your own strength?"

"Never pulled one out before, so I didn't know otherwise."

"Always use your horse for the hard work. That's what you've got him for."

"Guess I didn't think of it just then."

Carina gestured toward the muddied mother, nuzzling her baby. "Put 'em back with the herd, Orlin. We'll be here for a few hours yet. If you want to spend some time down at the fort, you're welcome, but be back before supper."

"Yes, ma'am." The cowboy gathered up his reins. On an apparent afterthought, he darted his glance between them. "We'll be all right out here, won't we?" Penn saw his unease. "Bein's we're in Indian Territory, I mean."

Carina appeared startled. "Why wouldn't we be?"

"I've heard stories, that's all."

And he must've been spooked by them. Easy to tell he needed some reassurance.

"We've paid our tolls for crossing their land," Penn said. "The tribes around here have no reason to come after us."

"The army does a good job patrolling the area, besides. Herds come through on this trail all the time. We'll be fine," Carina added.

"Hope so." He looked a mite pale, but he touched a finger to his hat and rode off.

"He's scared," Penn said and wondered at it.

"He'll get over it. We won't be in the Territory much longer." Carina dragged her gaze off the cowboy. "The veterinary surgeon is inspecting the herd now. I'll settle up with him and meet Sourdough, then go into the outpost with him. He's got a long list of supplies to fill."

After the diversion with Orlin, she was back to business. It was all she knew, Penn mused. Her cattle business.

Did she ever make time for herself?

"I'll go with you," he said.

Her eye narrowed. "Why?"

His mind sifted through a few reasons, working fast.

"Thought maybe we could check at the telegraph office," he said. One of the most important of the reasons. "Might be you have a wire from Sheriff Dunbar."

"You think I will?"

She looked so hopeful, Penn did some fervent hoping of his own she'd have one waiting. "Won't know until we check."

"All right. That's what we'll do."

"Maybe you can find a private bath somewhere, too. Then do some shopping." A couple of his other reasons.

"Shopping!" Obviously, the idea hadn't occurred to her. "For what?"

"I don't know." He shrugged. Thought of Abigail and how she used to shop for herself any chance she got. Lord, but the woman could spend money. "Female things."

Carina scowled. "This trail drive isn't a pleasure trip, McClure. I've got all I need right here."

She patted her saddlebag. Which held necessities and not much else. Penn knew without looking there wouldn't be a single frippery included.

His gaze slid to her mouth. Their kiss had taught him the softness of her lips. Since then, they'd gotten chapped from the wind. Her skin browned from the sun. Though she kept her hair in a prim braid at her back, wild wisps escaped from beneath her hat. Her fingernails were chipped, her knuckles callused and dust covered her down to her muddied boots.

A trail drive was no place for a woman, even one as tough as Carina Lockett. She lived her days and nights with men, did a man's work with them, and Penn couldn't help wondering if there weren't times she forgot she was female.

And that just plain wasn't right.

Because he knew for a fact she was, through and through. She kissed like one, and she felt like one, and for some inexplicable reason, it became important to remind her.

Fort Supply would help him do that.

* * *

The herd passed the veterinary surgeon's inspection. Even though Carina was sure none of her cattle carried the dreaded Texas fever, having the obstacle removed, even if it was an unlikely one, was a relief. She didn't want anything to delay their arrival in Dodge City.

She rode with Sourdough and McClure to the military post with a lighter mood. Sourdough's supply list warranted bringing a couple of extra horses along to pack their provisions, and after tethering the mounts in front of the post store, Carina succumbed to a curious look around.

"A busy place," Sourdough said.

"Takes a lot of military presence to keep the peace around here," McClure agreed.

"And a lot of supplies to keep folks like us happy," Sourdough finished. "Speaking of supplies, I'd better get to it."

"We'll meet up in a couple of hours," Carina said. "In front of the store."

"See you then."

After he left, Carina scanned the people around her, all of varying races and stations in life. Civilian merchants mingled with soldiers dressed in flat-brimmed hats and dark blue coats. Long-haired, buckskin-clad hunters traded with blanket-wrapped Cherokee. Freight wagons lumbered through the streets; officers' wives and their children scurried from their path. The aroma of baking bread hovered in the air.

Fort Supply was self-contained, efficient and bustling. A thriving complex of officers' quarters, soldiers' barracks, stables, hospital and jailhouse. In addition, rows of frame buildings were used for everything from ordnance stores to icehouses to a butcher shop.

"Something to see, isn't it?" McClure asked, head tilted back toward the flag waving over it all.

"Yes." Her moving gaze caught on a Cheyenne squaw with a papoose tied to her back. The black-eyed baby grinned at her, and Carina smiled back.

McClure squinted up at the telegraph lines that made Fort Supply a communications hub, too. Perused the roads crisscrossing on the horizon which connected the garrison with the other forts, reservations and settlements in this part of the country. He shook his head, clearly amazed.

"Impressive what the government has done out here," he said.

Carina heard the pride in his voice. "It is."

"There's the telegraph office."

Carina tried not to anticipate a message that might not be there, but it'd been so long since she'd heard anything about her daughter, it was impossible not to hope for one. Surely, Sheriff Dunbar had something to report by now.

They headed toward the plain front frame building, a match to the others in its row. McClure reached around her to open the door at the same moment she did. Then, together, they drew back.

"Do you think I can't open a door by myself?" she asked, expecting him to step back so she could.

He didn't. He scowled down at her instead.

"It's time you got off your high horse and let a

man show you a courtesy now and again, Carina," he growled. "That's what I think."

"My high horse!" she said, taken aback.

"We'll try it again," he said, his voice low. "I'm going to reach over and open the door. You'll wait politely until I do. Then you'll go through it like a lady should, and I'll follow." He paused, letting his words sink in. "When we leave, it'll be the same thing all over again. Understand?"

Her fists clenched to keep from smacking him. "You're being ridiculous."

"Go ahead and think so, but we're standing right here until you agree."

What made him decide he could talk to her like this? Had he forgotten she was the boss? She reached for the doorknob, but too quick, he angled the breadth of his body so she couldn't.

"I mean it, Carina," he said in warning.

She glared. "I'm well aware of how a woman behaves in polite society, McClure."

"Are you? Funny. You don't act like it."

The barb stung. She ignored it. "This is a damned fort out in the middle of nowhere. There's no reason—"

"Doesn't matter where we are. You're still a woman, and I intend to treat you like one."

His persistence poked some hidden part of her she'd kept banked for so long she had trouble identifying it. A soft spot too frivolous to contend with when she had more important matters to take care of.

Besides, the shuffle of boot soles on the boardwalk reminded her they weren't alone and that they blocked the path of anyone strolling past. Even the telegraph operator inside eyed them curiously through the window.

"Fine," she snapped. "Open the damn door for me."

"That's better." But he didn't move. "One more thing."

"What?" she demanded.

Hinges creaked. "Ma'am? Is everything all right out here?"

Carina swiveled toward the telegrapher, a young soldier barely in his twenties, wearing a uniform adorned with chevrons and brass buttons. Concern marred his features.

"Yes," she said. And strove for patience. "Everything's fine."

"If there's a problem, just say so. I'll call for an officer, and this gentleman will be escorted from the post promptly."

"That won't be necessary." She arched a brow at McClure. "Will it?"

McClure inclined his head agreeably toward the soldier.

"Just teaching her how to go through the door, is all," he said. "She's ignorant of the right way to do it."

"Ignorant!" she gasped.

Confusion replaced the concern in the soldier's face. "Sir?"

"We'll be in directly. But I appreciate you checking on her just the same," McClure said, his smile disgustingly charming.

The young man turned toward Carina. "Ma'am, if that's all right with you?"

"It is, I suppose." She forced the aggravation from her voice to assure him. He wouldn't leave if she didn't.

"Well, I'll be close by if you need me." The hinges creaked again. "Call if you do."

"She won't be. Calling, that is. While you're in there, check to see if you have any wires for her, will you?" McClure asked. "The name's Carina Lockett."

The soldier pondered a moment. "Of the C Bar C?"

"Yes!" she exclaimed.

His glance swept over her, as if seeing her in a new light. And not a particularly favorable one, either. "Have you been trailing *cattle,* ma'am?"

His surprise carried a vein of censure, and knowing how she looked to him, how she must smell, too, Carina stiffened.

"Yes. No other reason why I'd be here," she said in a frosty tone.

"Hard job for a woman." He shook his head, as if he considered it a shame she had to endure it.

"Yes, well, we all have a job to do, don't we? And I believe yours is to check to see if I have a wire waiting."

He took the rebuke with a hasty nod. "Yes, ma'am. I'll do that."

The door clattered behind him, and renewed hope swelled through Carina. This far from her ranch, the soldier would have no reason to associate her name with it unless he'd received a telegram for her. Her mind raced through possible senders—Sheriff Dunbar, most likely. But maybe Grandpa. Mavis or Rogan?

Or Callie Mae.

Carina all but leaped toward the door, but McClure's

arm shot out, a band of steel, and kept her right there. On the boardwalk.

"Whoa," he said, as if he was trying to slow a high-stepping filly. "Not so fast."

This time, she did smack him, a good stiff punch on that muscled arm.

Which barely got a flinch out of him.

"Out of my way, McClure," she ordered.

"I'm not finished laying a few ground rules first," he said.

"I'll let you open the damn door for me. Didn't I say I would?"

"But you're not going through it until you promise to keep from cussing."

She blinked at him. "Why?"

"A lady shouldn't cuss as often as you do."

Was he serious?

"It's one thing to talk that way around your men," he went on. "Another in polite society."

"This isn't polite society," she grated. "It's a fort with soldiers who can cuss the air blue. And Indians and hunters who could care less about the way I talk, and McClure, damn you, let me by."

A muscle leaped in his cheek. He didn't move. "Of course, asking you to call me 'Penn' might be too much for you to manage, considering all I'm throwing at you right now, but I'll mention it anyway."

Her fists clenched. She debated darting around him like a rabbit around a fence post. If she was quick enough, she'd succeed in getting inside that telegraph office before he could stop her.

But she didn't. He'd only find a way to best her on it.

She threw up her chin and choked down her impatience. She had her pride. Two could play his game, even if she had to be an unwilling participant.

"It seems there's a message waiting for me," she said, striving to keep her tone even. "I'd be much obliged if we went inside to see who it's from and what it says."

"Promise me you'll put a lid on your can of cuss words, and we will."

Her teeth gritted. The promise was as absurd as his expectations. "Fine."

He inclined his head with a satisfied nod. "That's better."

Carefully, his arm lowered. He reached for the door and pulled it open. She whisked past him with a disparaging sniff which let him know he wasn't doing anything she couldn't do herself, and that, against her better judgment, she let him do it anyway.

He followed her in and closed the door. Their footsteps echoed over the wooden floor and sounded loud in the tiny, barren office. An instrument desk occupied the far wall; above it, the switchboard, and not much else.

But next to the set of sending keys were several envelopes. The soldier riffled through them until, triumphant, he held one up. "Here it is. Carina Lockett, C Bar C Ranch, Texas."

Suddenly, half-afraid of what she'd read inside, she blew out a breath. "Is the news good?"

"Don't know, ma'am. I didn't record the information. The night operator did, and it's been here—" he consulted a small calendar pinned to the wall "—five days now."

Carina endured a sinking feeling. So much could've happened since then.

"All communications are private, if you have a concern," he said. "We're bonded, you know, to keep from disclosing information relayed from station to station." He glanced down at a scribbled notation. "Your wire is from the New Orleans police department."

Her breath hitched. Where Mavis lived.

Sheriff Dunbar had informed the law officers the old witch might head there after she fled the C Bar C, and their wire could only mean they knew something about Callie Mae. Carina snatched the envelope from the soldier's grasp, ripped the paper open and scanned the cryptic contents.

"Mavis and Callie Mae arrived in New Orleans by train six days ago." Her glance lifted, verifying the date on the telegrapher's calendar. "The police want me to advise them what to do next."

And with that, except for the telegraph operator's initials, the transmission ended. Carina flipped the paper over, just to be sure, but there was nothing else.

She'd suspected Mavis would do this. Take Callie Mae to her home, almost two states away.

And so long ago, too. Six days' worth of long. Were they still there, in Louisiana? Were Rogan and Durant with them?

Or had Mavis taken Callie Mae onto a ship to Europe by now?

The possibility scared her spitless. Both alternatives filled her with cold resolve. And gave her a plan of attack. Her gaze met McClure's, watching her.

"I want Mavis hunted down and arrested," she said.

He nodded. "I'm sure you do."

"I'll bring charges against her and have her thrown in jail." The fury built in Carina. Hot and quick and as fresh as the day the old witch kidnapped her little girl. "I'll wire the police and demand it."

"And then what happens to Callie Mae?"

The query dragged her thoughts off vengeance. "We bring her back!"

He shook his head. "Think it through, Carina. You put her grandmother in jail, where will she go? Who will take care of her?"

Carina thought fast. And failed to come up with a perfect answer. "I don't know yet. But I'll think of something."

"She's too young to travel so far alone. She'd have to stay with strangers until you got there. Could take weeks by the time the law caught up with you," he said. "By then, she could've been sent to an asylum or an orphanage somewhere. Or maybe she'd stay with friends of the Webb family."

Carina bit her lip. Her thinking began to follow his.

"Those friends might even take Callie Mae into hiding until Mavis posted bail," he went on. "No telling what would happen then. But you can be sure as hell the woman won't sit idle in her parlor and wait for the scandal of a trial if you press charges against her."

Carina's need for vengeance withered. Mavis detested scandal. She'd escape to Europe for sure to evade putting herself through it. And she'd take Callie Mae with her.

"Know what I think?" he asked.

She swallowed hard. Her brain had gone numb. "No."

"We need to keep on doing what we're doing, Carina." He reached out and knuckled her chin, saying without words that she had to buck up and be strong. "Callie Mae is in good hands with her grandmother. As long as they're together, nothing will happen to her. You have to believe that."

"Maybe." She released an uncertain sigh. Mavis loved Callie Mae. Had always loved her.

"We have to concentrate on getting to Dodge City." McClure's voice was low, firm. As methodical as his thinking. "Rogan will be there, waiting for us. We can be all but sure he's keeping in touch with his mother. As long as he knows we're cooperating, he won't let anything happen to Callie Mae." His mouth hardened. "He wants your money too much."

"Yes." His daughter's heritage, damn him.

"And you know what else?"

She peered at him. "What?"

"That puts you in control."

Carina turned and strode to the window. She stared through the panes, off into the distance, toward her herd corralled beyond the boundaries of Fort Supply.

Carina didn't want control.

She wanted Callie Mae.

But, unfortunately, McClure was right. They could do nothing to jeopardize getting her back.

As much as it pained her, Carina couldn't send a wire to the New Orleans police, pressing the charges that would get Mavis arrested. She didn't dare.

A couple more weeks, she told herself. They'd be in Dodge City. Then, she'd turn the money over to Rogan.

But afterward, she'd find a way to make him—and his conniving mother—pay for what they'd done.

Chapter Nine

Penn could tell the telegraph operator, Private Bekins, put two and two together and came up with trouble for Carina. His sympathy was genuine for what she was going through, and he'd been quick to offer help, any way he could.

Penn took him up on it by asking for a place where Carina could enjoy a relaxing bath. She'd been startled at his request, tried to refuse for its foolishness, but he countered that Sourdough wouldn't be ready to leave Fort Supply for a while yet. What else did she have to do?

Private Bekins joined in the argument, insistent she have one, as well. Penn suspected the soldier's sympathy had been compounded by the fact she was trailing cattle, which he was clearly of the opinion she had no business doing. He'd gone out of his way to enlist his wife's help in making sure Carina received a little female pampering and generously gave her the use of their bathhouse, located behind the Married Men's Quarters.

Now, after making a quick stop at the dry goods store, Penn found himself waiting for her to come out. He hunkered in the grass and indulged in a leisurely smoke while his thoughts stayed busy wrapping themselves around her.

Which is where they seemed to be lately. On her. On what she'd endured. What lay ahead. And how important it'd become to get her through it.

After it was all said and done at the telegraph station, she'd wired the New Orleans police with a firm request that they keep Mavis under discreet surveillance to the best of their ability and to notify Carina immediately if the woman attempted to leave the city with Callie Mae.

It was a long shot, Penn knew. She didn't even know if Mavis was still *in* New Orleans since the news of her arrival there was six days old. The woman could've moved on, and no telling when if she did.

Besides, once the C Bar C outfit hit the Western Trail again in a few hours, they'd be miles from a telegraph station. Any attempt to contact Carina would be delayed until they reached the town of Ashland, in Kansas. A week from now at best.

But it was something, that wire. Carina seemed to feel better after sending it.

Some of the starch came back in her, if only for a little while. He preferred her hate for Rogan and Mavis over the haunting despair she'd been wearing since the ordeal started. Having a child kidnapped would scare any parent into an early graying, but Carina Lockett was too much of a fighter to lie down and play doormat for long. The fact that she was fired up and ready to file charges against them was a good sign she still had some spunk left.

Too bad Penn had had to talk her out of doing it. If not for the revenge he craved, he would've filed them himself. Mavis deserved justice as much as her son did. Neither could get away with what they were doing to Carina, no matter how willing Callie Mae had been to go along with their scheme.

Hell, she was just a kid. Naive and impressionable. Penn doubted she had a clear picture of the whole deal even now. She'd been swept away by the novelty of all her grandmother could give her. What kid wouldn't have been?

In time, that would wear off, and she'd begin to see things she didn't see before. Like how she'd hurt Carina by running off, for one. Might be she'd gotten to missing her, too. And the ranch, her grandpa and Woollie and everyone else in the C Bar C.

Penn had never met the girl, but if she was anything like her mother, she'd be smart as a whip. Wouldn't take long, and she'd start to see through the Webbs' greed and selfishness and want to fight them on it.

He frowned. Unless she was more like her father.

And wouldn't that be a shame if she was?

Penn couldn't see Carina tolerating behavior of any kind that might show similarities to Rogan's way of doing things, but what did he know? It was none of his business, besides. He just wanted his revenge from the man. Stop his counterfeiting activities.

Throw him behind bars for a good long while, most of all.

And Penn would, soon enough.

Reshuffling his thoughts, he pulled his watch from his vest pocket. Sourdough would be back at the General Store, waiting for them, in a few minutes.

Penn's glance slid toward the bathhouse door, still closed. Carina should've been done in there by now. Strange she hadn't come out yet.

His mind dallied over an image of her lounging in the tub, naked and beautiful with her skin glistening wet, her hair a brunette waterfall that shimmered down her shoulders and back. An image so strong, so clear, his groin tightened with a rush of heat that all but knocked the breath right out of him.

He ground his cigarette in the weeds with a curse. He couldn't think of Carina Lockett like that. Naked and beautiful. He couldn't get involved with her. Not mentally. Not physically. Not at all. She'd only knock him off course in his determination to get even with Rogan.

Hadn't he learned *anything* from Abigail?

Oh, yeah. He'd learned plenty.

Penn straightened with renewed resolve, taking his package with him. He didn't know what was taking Carina so long in that bathhouse, but as late as it was, he'd have to find someone to go in and do some prodding on her.

Unfortunately, he wasn't sure where Private Bekins's wife was, if she was home or went shopping, and he had no desire to scour the post looking for her.

Nor did he want to go knocking on barracks doors

to ask the favor of someone else's wife. A quick glance around the area didn't yield any other female who might be willing to do the job.

Well, hell. He strode toward the bathhouse and knocked on the door himself. When Carina didn't answer, he knocked again. With the same result.

Concern had him turning the knob and pushing the door open a space.

"Carina," he said.

She didn't respond. Frowning, he widened the opening and peered inside.

He found her all right. Sound asleep in the metal tub. And his groin heated up all over again.

He couldn't have kept from going inside if he wanted to. And he would've been crazy if he didn't. She drew him, like a thirsty man to water. Like a *pathetically* thirsty man who should know better than to intrude upon a woman's private bath. When she was sleeping, no less. Completely unaware he was there.

Staring. Lusting. Wanting things he shouldn't.

But, Lord, the sight she made, reclined against the back of the tub with her long, brunette hair falling over the edge. Her knees were drawn up and resting at the side. Soapy water barely covered the mounds of her breasts, just enough to tantalize him with a glimpse of their rosy tips. To fill his head with ideas he had no business having.

He was tantalized all right. He moved closer, quietly set aside his package and eased down into a squat beside her. Her hand curled loose on the tub's rim, and he was struck by the sight of it, the thought of all that hand had to do.

Too much, every day. Whether roping an ornery steer or cuddling an anxious calf, Carina worked her hands harder than any woman should have to. Regret tugged at him, and he slipped his finger beneath hers, gently lifted their limp weight and dropped a kiss to her knuckles.

She didn't move, her weariness that deep. Penn never claimed to be perfect, and this unexpected availability of her nakedness to enjoy at his leisure reached in and latched onto the healthy male in him. Carina Lockett was a wondrous vision of long-legged, full-breasted womanhood. If he were a weaker man, he'd peel himself naked, too, then climb in with her.

And wouldn't that get her good and riled?

A corner of his mouth lifted. Too bad he had to choose the honorable route. He dipped a hand into the water, drizzled some over her bare shoulder. A lone trickle disappeared into the valley of her breasts, captivating him, compelling his gaze to linger over their glistening, rounded shape.

And damned if he didn't long to cup one in his palm and savor the feel of her supple flesh. Experience what Carina had to give. Which she allowed no man to have.

Sighing, he slid his wet finger down her cheek in a light caress.

"Carina," he said softly. "Hey, wake up."

She stirred, then. Finally. A slight shifting of her dark head toward him. Her long lashes fluttered open; her mouth moved into a languid smile.

"McClure."

The sultry sound of her voice shot instant heat into

his blood. She'd sound the same way in the morning, he knew, and some day, some lucky man would get to hear her, see her, warm and slumberous, just like this, for the rest of his life.

The idea of seducing her then and there had never been more appealing. But before he could convince himself it would be the absolute most stupid thing he could ever do—Carina Lockett was his *boss,* for damned sake—her eyes flared wide. She yelped with a flail of those willowy legs and slapped her arms over her breasts.

"What the hell?" Water sloshed over the edge of the tub. "McClure, damn you! What are you doing—oh, get out of here! *Get out!*"

He reached for the towel. "There you go, cussing again. You promised you wouldn't, remember?"

"I'll have you shot for this."

"Yeah, well. Right now, I think I have the advantage." He rose, shaking out the towel. "Stand up."

"I'll order Private Bekins to have you locked up in jail *forever.*"

"For what?" he asked, feigning innocence.

"For—for violating my privacy, and—and—"

He'd never seen her so flustered. For once, the she-boss didn't have control, and wasn't that something to behold?

"Trust me. Nothing happened," he said.

"But you *looked.* That's worth getting you arrested right there."

Her ire amused him. "Go ahead. Trump up charges against me, Carina, but that herd of yours isn't going anywhere without us while you do."

He waited, still holding the towel open.

She peered up at him, blinked, and breathed a curse. This time, at least, she had the sense to keep it lassoed to a whisper.

"I forgot about Sourdough," she groaned.

Penn nodded. "He's waiting for us."

"How late is it?"

"Late," he said, cutting her no slack.

She swallowed. Her pride in shreds, she stood, water sluicing down those long, slim legs. He stepped closer, draped the towel around her shoulders. She clutched it closed with both hands, and he helped her climb out.

Dripping on the wood floor, she stood before him. But Penn didn't step away. When again would he have an opportunity like this? Carina Lockett, naked under the towel, at her most desirable. Purely feminine, more than that. He drew her against him, his grasp both firm and gentle, and amazingly, she didn't resist.

Her forehead sank onto his chest, as if she was too mortified to look him in the eye. Bathwater soaked into his shirt. She smelled like soap, like woman, and a sudden, fierce protectiveness slid through him.

"Don't be shy with me, Carina," he murmured, his jaw pressed into the wet mass of her hair.

"None of my men have ever…seen me like you did just now."

"No one?" he asked, teasing.

But she was gut-twisting serious. "Not since Rogan, I mean, and that was so long ago, he—he doesn't count."

Hearing the name, Penn's teasing died. "He never deserved you, even then."

Her head came up. "You won't tell them, will you? The others?"

He stared into those violet-blue eyes, dark with worry about her prized station in life. Head of the C Bar C outfit. That her reputation with them might be tarnished from a little scandal with the trail boss.

Something deep in his chest moved, a need to assure her she could trust him, in the bathhouse and out. His head lowered, and he touched his mouth to hers. The sensation of the fullness of her lips rolled through him, warmed his blood, tugged at his restraints. Her mouth fit itself to his with a provocative ease, as if she'd kissed him a hundred times before, naked under a towel, and if only she had, and could keep on kissing him....

But she couldn't, and slowly, his head lifted. Her languid gaze met his. He dragged himself backward to the reason why he'd kissed her in the first place.

"You really think I'd tell them?" he demanded in a rough whisper.

"Men gossip, same as women do," she said, her voice husky.

"I told you, Carina, nothing happened between us." His mind lingered on what she'd said earlier. What transpired ten years previous. "You're a beautiful woman. It's not right you haven't found someone to bed you since Rogan."

She stiffened, cheeks pinking. "That's none of your business."

Penn had poked a raw spot he suspected had been gnawing at her a good long while. "Just doing a little ruminating on something you brought up first, that's all."

"I don't need a man, so don't go feeling sorry for me that I don't have one, all right?"

Yet that raw spot told him she did, more than she wanted to admit. Even to herself.

"Yeah, well, it's a good thing you had one to get you up from your nap just now, wasn't it?" he countered smoothly. "Otherwise you'd still be snoring."

She gasped, still keeping a tight hold on that towel. "I wasn't!"

He couldn't help a grin from getting her hackles up so easy. "No, you weren't. I'm just stirring your oats, that's all." He released her. "Now go on. Get a wiggle on it. Sourdough will be wondering what's happened to us."

"I'm not getting dressed until you leave."

Hell, she couldn't show him something he hadn't already seen when she was lying naked in that tub, but he declined to remind her.

"Five minutes," he said. "If you're not out of here by then, I'm coming back in."

He turned to leave, and his attention caught on the package he'd laid on the floor. Retrieving it, he extended the bundle toward her.

She eyed the thing with suspicion. "What is it?"

"It's for you. Here."

"Me?" Her gaze dropped to the package, then lifted back up to him. "You bought me something?"

"I did."

"Where? When?"

"At one of the shops on Washington Avenue. A dry goods store. When you were sleeping. Or bathing. I'm not sure which."

She rolled her eyes at his teasing, but pivoted, presenting him with her back. She fiddled with her towel, tucked the ends securely between her breasts, and when she turned around again, her hands were free.

"Why in blazes would you want to buy me anything?" She took the package with obvious reluctance.

"Because I wanted to. Open it. Time's ticking."

Nibbling on her lip, she tore open the brown paper. The contents appeared—pink, with ribbons and lace, and tiny pearl buttons—and she stilled. The wrapping drifted to the floor.

"A camisole? And pantaloons?" Her cheeks turned rosy again; incredibly, her second blush of the day.

"It's good you recognize what they are."

Her perusal dragged from the underwear and narrowed over him. "What's that supposed to mean?"

He thought of the garments he'd seen hanging over bushes and tree branches after she washed them these past days on the trail. Her laundry, plain white and serviceable. Far from feminine. And nothing like what he gifted her with now.

"Figured you don't have much of a chance to wear pretty things on a cattle drive. I'm giving you one," he said.

"Why?" she asked, clearly taken aback.

"Because you're a woman, and women like pretty things."

A moment passed, as if the concept was beyond her comprehension. Wearing something feminine while herding cows.

"You deserve it, besides," he added, thinking of

Rogan and his blackmail, waiting for her with his accomplice at the end of the line. "Now, get dressed."

But she lingered, fingering the dainty tucks, the tiny satin bows and buttons. A faint frown tugged at her mouth.

The decision she warred with, he knew. Accept the gift or throw it back in his face.

Neither would be easy with that pride of hers.

"Say 'Thank you, Penn,'" he said gently, to steer her in the right direction.

She glanced up at the bathhouse roof. Sighed. "Thank you, Penn."

He liked the way his name sounded rolling off her tongue. "Now that wasn't so hard, was it?"

"I've never had a man buy me underwear before." She hugged the lingerie to her chest and finally looked at him.

Why should that please him, being the first?

He didn't have time to analyze the reason, but it did, he thought, as he left her so she could get dressed. It pleased him plenty. She'd be beautiful with that soft pink fabric lying close against her creamy skin.

But most important, she'd feel like a woman.

New Orleans

Callie Mae figured her life was as perfect as it could be.

She sat prim as a princess on the gold-threaded brocade settee and stared, entranced, at the fashionable, rich-looking ladies around her, Grandmother's high-society friends who came to the party to meet her. Some were young, some were old; some sitting, some standing. They drank tea from painted china cups and ate little cakes with icing flowers on top that Grandmother ordered from the bakery down the street.

And, oh, they talked enough to keep a windmill going. Gossiping, the whole party long.

But what else could they do? People here didn't have farms or ranches like folks back in Texas. These ladies didn't raise livestock that needed to be fed, so they didn't go on about market prices or the newest breeds of bulls and horses. Or the best crop to plant when.

They just talked about other people.

Callie Mae found it a little confusing. Is that what these ladies *did* since they didn't have chores? Go to parties like this and blather for hours on end?

Sighing, she stretched out her legs and admired the bows on her shiny, patent leather shoes. One thing Callie Mae knew for sure. Getting dressed in the morning took up a bunch of their time. Shoot, her new party frock had so many buttons and petticoats and big bows to tie that it took *forever* to do them, and she couldn't manage any of it without Grandmother's help.

But Callie Mae didn't really mind. Her new dresses were worth the trouble. She stroked the taffeta over her lap, loving the pretty shade of blue, like a robin's egg. Grandmother bought her dainty, striped stockings to match, and Callie Mae admired them, too. She'd never had any so fine. Why, they felt as if she wasn't wearing any at all!

Except she had to be careful not to get a hole in

them, and that was the worst part. Grandmother kept re-minding her she'd ruin her new clothes if she didn't sit still, and Callie Mae figured she was right. She would.

There were times, though, she missed going out to play, doing whatever she wanted, and not worrying about what she wore. The part of her life which wasn't so perfect. Grandmother kept her too busy meeting her lady friends and seeing all kinds of different places in New Orleans that Callie Mae hadn't had a chance to play.

A twinge of homesickness curled through her. If she was home right now, that's what she'd be doing. Play-ing. Or riding Daisy. Or having a game of checkers with Grandpa.

She grimaced. Unless she had to do her chores.

Mama—Mother, she corrected herself—would make sure Callie Mae got her work done before she could do anything fun.

Grandmother *never* made her work.

Mother wouldn't want her to wear a fancy dress like this blue party frock in the middle of the day, either.

Grandmother didn't want her to wear anything else *but* fancy dresses. Didn't matter what time of day it was or how frilly one was or how much it cost.

The confusion built in Callie Mae, and she fidgeted on the settee. Mother and Grandmother. The two women she loved most, who could keep her life just the way she liked it, perfect and fun, if they wanted to.

But they didn't.

They were too different from one another, and they just made her life complicated instead. Neither liked the other very much, and that put Callie Mae right in the middle.

If only she could talk to Grandpa about it. But he'd just take Mother's side as he always did when they got to discussing Mavis Webb. So would Woollie. She couldn't talk about it with Daddy, either, even if she dug up the courage. She hadn't seen him for a while besides; Grandmother said he was gone somewhere on business, and she didn't quite know when he'd be back.

And Callie Mae knew better than to bring up the subject with Grandmother. Shoot, she'd just get all stubborn and hoity-toity as she tended to do at times, then steer the conversation toward something that suited her more.

Which meant Callie Mae had to keep her mouth shut and live her perfect life until she could sort through her troubles later.

"Yoo-hoo! Toodeloo! Callie Mae!"

The shrill voice ended her ruminating in a hurry, and her gaze jumped to the stout woman waving a lacy hankie at her from across the crowded parlor. All conversation paused, which embarrassed Callie Mae to no end. She wasn't used to having so much attention on her.

But the other ladies just smiled indulgently and went back to their gossiping. Evidently, they all knew this woman who'd arrived late to the party; they didn't pay Callie Mae much mind as she slid off the settee to meet her.

Callie Mae put on her best face and gathered her

newly gained poise. She'd learned all the polite words to say, the right ways to act. She'd become the little lady her grandmother wanted her to be.

For now, that was enough.

Chapter Ten

Kansas, Near the Cimarron River

Rogan stared out the grimy window, drew in deep on his cigar and fought a bad case of boredom. He'd found a room at this sorry-looking ranch house that took in travelers off the Western Trail. After he and Durant choked down a mediocre supper of boiled beef and potatoes, the rest of the night stretched out before them.

They'd finally crossed the border, and there was nothing to do in this godforsaken part of the country. No gaming halls, no saloons, no women. Nothing. Just thousands of bellowing cattle, plodding over the Kansas prairie, as far as anyone could see.

He was sick of endless days breathing in their dust and the smell of their manure. The monotony of traveling in a desolate land broken only by the occasional ranch or sorry-excuse-for-a-cow town. The lack of decent food and modern conveniences as basic as clean drinking water, most of all.

How did Carina survive it?

Rogan had no idea. But she *was* surviving, and it was a hell of a hard life, even for her. Every day, while tracking her herd far enough away she wouldn't notice, he spied her on the spotted Appaloosa, working with her men to get them all north.

She was driven like the devil to get there, which was the only thing that kept him going, too.

"Are you complaining again?" Durant asked.

His thoughts dissipated. He turned toward his partner, seated at a table near the window and bent over pages of tracing paper with a fine-tipped pen in his hand.

"I never said a word." He stepped toward the bed, plopped on top, leaned back and crossed his ankles.

"You didn't have to."

"We'll never get to Dodge City."

Durant grunted, too engrossed in imitating the New York coat of arms from a $100 National Bank Note to bother attempting any commiseration. A perfectionist, the man was patient and precise as he practiced the state's intricate design on paper before repeating it on a copper plate.

Rogan continued to be impressed by the quality of his work, the imitations he was capable of producing that were so near perfect, so close to the original, that banking-house tellers and their officers were unable to tell the difference without the aid of a magnifying glass.

Rogan puffed on the cigar. Indeed, meeting Neal Durant in Denver last year had been a stroke of good luck. He had a penchant for high-stakes gambling and an unexpected skill for forgery, and with both of them looking for some easy money, they'd formed a fast friendship.

After Rogan collected the blackmail from Carina's herd, they'd both escape to the underworld back East. New York, to be precise, with its revered Wall Street, the country's financial capital and a breeding ground of opportunity to deal in counterfeit banknotes, bonds and forged checks.

Rogan couldn't get there soon enough. When he did, he'd lie low for a while, until the trail that could lead to his arrest turned cold as stone.

Until Penn McClure couldn't find him anymore.

"Are you thinking about seeing your mother again?" Durant asked.

The question startled Rogan. "That bitch? You've got to be joking."

"Tsk. Tsk." Durant put down his pen. "Is that any way for a son to speak about the woman who gave him life?"

Rogan grunted and took a final puff off his cigar. "That's how I talk about mine."

"She wants to be with you." Durant sat back in his chair, crossed his arms over his chest. "She'll be happy to see you in Salina."

"Yes." Rogan didn't know what was worse. Stalking Carina on the dirty, smelly Western Trail or rendezvousing with his mother halfway across the state. "I'll take a stagecoach tomorrow and meet her at her hotel in a few days."

From there, Mother intended to travel east with him and Callie Mae to Kansas City and then north to Boston, where she'd already booked passage for them on a ship to Europe.

As if they were a happy little family.

Which they weren't.

And Rogan had no intention of going. She'd find out he had plans of his own soon enough.

Plans that included ditching them and heading to Dodge City, where Durant would be waiting, right along with a fat check from Carina.

What happened to Callie Mae after that, Rogan could care less. Carina would just have to find the girl and fight Mother to get her back. By then, Rogan would be long gone.

"Your daughter will be in Salina, too, won't she?" Durant said.

His mouth tightened. "Yes."

A moment passed. Durant regarded him with eyes hard as flint.

"You're not excited about seeing her," he said. "Why does that continue to disgust me about you?"

The chill in his voice cooled the air in the room. Rogan had felt veiled disapproval from him before, but this sudden shift toward animosity was something new.

"Why should I be excited?" Rogan demanded. "She means nothing to me."

"She's your flesh and blood."

"I was there at her conception. That's it."

"She's a beautiful child. You should be proud to be her father."

Rogan stared. Why would Durant care a rat's ass about Callie Mae? Or Rogan's relationship with her? Especially now, when they were almost to Dodge City?

"I don't *want* to be her father, so shut up about it," he snarled.

Durant narrowed a cold eye, lifted a hand and stroked the curled ends of his mustache with slender, smooth fingers.

An artist's fingers.

A gunslinger's fingers, too.

Quick and dexterous. The tools of his trade.

That slow, methodical stroking made Rogan uneasy about what the man was thinking.

"Look," he said. "I never wanted a kid. They try me. They always have. Callie Mae should never have happened."

"So now you're using her to get back at her mother."

"You know damn well why I'm using her."

"She's an innocent."

"She wanted to leave—" Rogan clenched his teeth.

He refused to continue the argument. The ashes built on the end of his cigar, and he impatiently flicked them onto the threadbare carpet.

And then, from out of nowhere, realization dawned.

Durant was jealous.

"You'd like a daughter, wouldn't you?" Rogan asked in a soft voice.

His accomplice straightened, returned to his tracing papers.

"What makes you think so?" he asked, but the sting had disappeared from his voice.

"You're taking her side. You've been thinking of her." Rogan shook his head, struck by the irony. "*You'd* like to be a father."

Durant grunted, fiddled with his pen, which had yet to be set to paper. "There'd be worse things I could do." He smirked. "And I have, too."

"So why aren't you?" Rogan asked.

"Because with every child, comes a mother, and I have no need of a woman clinging to me and trying to change who I am," he snapped.

"Ah." Rogan grinned and felt better. A woman like his own mother.

He and Durant were back on common ground again. He rose from the bed, headed toward the rickety dresser where a brand-new bottle of Old Fitzgerald whiskey sat. Bought fresh off a traveling solicitor, just this afternoon, along with a box of decidedly expensive Caribbean cigars.

All paid for with a beautifully counterfeit C-Note, of course. Compliments of Bill Brockway's talent, of which the salesman was oblivious.

Unfortunately, it was Rogan's last bill, and he'd split the change with Durant. Rogan had to use the difference to get himself to Salina. Once he did, he'd have to sweet-talk Mother into giving him a little cash to tide himself over.

Just until he made it back to Dodge City.

Rogan poured himself a glass of Old Fitz and another for his partner. They'd drink the night away, then part ways in the morning.

When they met up again, he'd soon have all the money he needed.

Two Days Later

Carina emerged from her tent with her hat and bandanna in one hand, her mirror, tooth powder and hairbrush in the other. She paused to breathe in the crisp morning air. The bright, cheerful sun scooted steadily higher over the horizon, while seeming to paint a blanket blue and call it a sky. The brilliance glinted on the dew still heavy on the prairie, and the range grass sparkled as if every blade had been sprinkled with fairy dust.

That's what Callie Mae would have called it, inspired by the whimsy of her girlish imagination. Fairy dust.

Carina's heart squeezed. She'd never be able to show her daughter the Kansas prairie like this if the Lockett legacy was lost. The prairie and so many other things besides.

A deep resolve surged through her to hang on tight to Callie Mae's heritage, no matter what. To fight for her daughter and give herself a chance to return to the motherhood she'd failed so miserably at before.

She did her best to rise above the worry. To keep going. They'd finally made it to Kansas, she told herself firmly. Dodge City wasn't so far away anymore. They'd be there soon. Next week, if all went well, and she had to hope it would.

Her gaze swept the camp as she strode toward the chuck wagon. Some of the men were just beginning to stir in their bedrolls. Others had already pulled on their boots. The scent of wood smoke and fresh Arbuckles' coffee hung strong in the air, prodding them awake.

Yesterday, they'd reached the banks of the Cimarron

River. They wouldn't find water again for several days, until Bluff Creek, on the other side of Ashland, the next cow town on the trail. The herd would graze and drink their fill here for the duration of the morning before they had to cross the river this afternoon.

Strange to have the privilege of sleeping late. But it felt good. A luxury they didn't often have. She propped her small mirror on the coffee grinder Sourdough had nailed to the side of the wagon, the height she needed to see while she brushed her hair and cleaned her teeth. Strange, too, to have enough light to see with; she was accustomed to the blur of early dawn.

After braiding her hair into a long plait down her back, she gave herself a quick once-over in the mirror to make sure she didn't miss any strands. Her attention snagged on McClure, striding into camp from the direction of the remuda.

Hating herself for it, Carina angled the glass to see him better. He wouldn't notice her watching him like this, not with her back to him and the rest of the camp. He'd only think she was doing what she looked like she was doing. Grooming herself for the day.

But, really, that part was already done, so she had to pretend. She'd barely spoken to him since the afternoon in Fort Supply when he saw her as naked as the day she was born. It'd been all she could do to walk out of the bathhouse and act as though nothing unusual happened, when they both knew it had.

Her belly did a funny turn, just thinking of it. Again. Penn McClure seeing her, kissing her, the way he did.

Of course, in her quieter moments, that got her to

wondering what *he* looked like without a stitch on, and if *that* didn't get her imagination going. He was as much a man as one could be. A fine package of male muscle and power, lean grace and rugged attitude, and damn him for making her think about him all the time.

And feel things she wasn't used to feeling.

Carina resolutely turned the mirror facedown with a thump. She took the bandanna, folded it in half and knotted the ends behind her neck.

Different. That's how he made her feel. Nothing like her usual self. But soft inside, like Sourdough's raisin pudding. Warm and achy and indistinct.

Bemused, she put on her hat, then gathered up her toiletries. If nothing else, she supposed, he was a good diversion from worrying about Callie Mae so much.

She picked up the mirror again and gave herself a final inspection....

A diversion. She couldn't help it. Her gaze shifted. McClure was still there. Behind her. He'd opened the trail map, spread it on the ground. Squatting beside it, his elbow on his knee, he studied the markings, the area beyond the Cimarron, most likely. Planning the drive for the next couple of days.

Her gaze lingered. The man was a sight to see, for sure. Broad-shouldered, long-limbed, his Levi's stretched over his thighs and buttocks, his skin bronzed deep from the sun. He hadn't shaved yet, and the night's stubble shadowed his cheeks, giving him that untamed look again, and there her belly went. Curling and twisting and tickling her insides.

He'd become the center of her world. The one she

depended on most to get them all to Dodge City. A man she'd grown to trust.

What would happen when they got there? When the terms of their bargain had been met and the ugliness of Rogan's blackmail was done?

Would she see him again? Ever?

Penn McClure. Drifter, cowboy, and now her trail boss. But who was he really? Where would he go when she didn't need him anymore?

Carina didn't know, and she had no right to wonder. He had his own life to live, with family, friends, waiting for him somewhere. If she hadn't bailed him out of the Mobeetie jail and forced him to work the cattle drive for her, where would he be right now?

Well, she couldn't keep speculating about it. She'd barely gotten her morning started, and already, she'd spent just about her every thought on him. What would that get her but a full load of wasted time?

Carina pivoted to return her toiletries to the tent, but a fleeting glimpse of something unusual in the mirror stopped her.

She studied the glass again. There. In a stand of cottonwoods beyond the camp. A horse and rider, their shapes tiny but distinct. Strange how the man didn't move, just stayed there. Hiding. Watching them.

"Wagon comin', Carina," Sourdough said.

Distracted, she dragged her glance toward him. "What?"

"Over there, from the east." He stood over the fire and gestured with a spatula. Two cast-iron skillets sat over the flames. Beside them, the two-gallon enamel coffeepot. "You want one flapjack or two on your plate this mornin'?"

She ignored him, twisted direction, found the rig he spoke of. A supply wagon of some sort, lumbering toward them at a leisurely speed.

But instinct told her the man in the trees was more important. Her gaze returned to the mirror, but she couldn't find him again. She swung around and stared outright at the cottonwoods.

He was gone.

She frowned.

The supply wagon drove toward them. Curiosity had the cowboys awake and straining their necks to see who was coming. It seemed no one else noticed they were being spied on, and Carina tried to shake off a growing sense of unease.

And failed.

Short of riding over to those trees, she had no way of learning who the rider was or what he found so interesting about Carina's camp. But she couldn't deny Rogan's had been the first name to jump into her mind.

Logic told her she was wrong, that he wouldn't be out here, in the middle of the Western Trail, something his pampered existence wouldn't have prepared him for. A hard life, even for those accustomed to it.

He'd be with Mavis, wouldn't he? And Callie Mae?

All this time, she'd assumed they were together...but what happened after they fled the C Bar C?

They might have split up, after all. The telegram she received in Fort Supply never mentioned Rogan's arrival in New Orleans. Still, Carina found it hard to believe he'd follow her all the way to Dodge City. What did he think she'd do? Take her herd somewhere else?

Assuming he stayed behind in Texas while his mother and Callie Mae returned to Louisiana didn't make sense, either. Rogan wouldn't risk being seen with Durant. He'd know the law around these parts was looking for them both, and if he was smart, he'd be lying low somewhere until he met up with her in Kansas.

This man was alone in the cottonwoods.

If it was Rogan, where was Durant?

If it was Durant, where was Rogan?

Carina scanned the cottonwoods again, a slow and thorough sweep, and found no sign of the rider, whoever he was.

In spite of the swarm of questions buzzing in her head, she knew one thing for sure. It wasn't a coincidence he was out there, watching her herd over all the others trailing along the Western this season.

Troubled, she headed back to her tent, bringing her toiletries with her.

Chapter Eleven

By the time Carina came out again, the wagon had pulled up on the edge of camp. A jovial solicitor held the reins, and clearly he delighted in the interest her men showed in seeing his wares.

"Mornin', boys!" he boomed and set the brake. The bowler he wore looked small for his round, balding head. Carina marveled that he managed to keep it on. "What brand are you with?"

McClure approached him, folding the trail map along the way, and returned the greeting.

"The C Bar C." He slid the map into his shirt pocket and extended his hand. "Name's Penn McClure."

Salesmen like this one were tagged "drummers" for the business they solicited for employers located in towns too far away for the outfits to reach. He hastened from his seat, a rather awkward dismount considering the breadth of his belly. By the looks of his dusty, rumpled suit, he'd been on the road a spell.

"Theodore Farrell, sir. I'm with the Wichita Whole-sale Grocery Company." He shook Penn's hand heartily. "Just runnin' this part of the Western in case outfits like yours are gettin' low on supplies. If you're in need of somethin', I might have it for you."

Penn hooked a thumb in the waistband of his Levi's. "We made a stop at Fort Supply a few days ago. Bought some provisions then."

"Did you now? Well, I'll be your last tradin' point until you get to Dodge City."

Undeterred, Farrell headed toward the back of the wagon bed and unbuckled the straps holding in his cargo. He rolled back the tarp, opened a crate, pulled out a couple of bottles of Old Fitzgerald whiskey and several sacks of Bull Durham, then held them all out to Penn.

"Here you go, Mr. McClure. On me. I'd appreciate a few minutes of your time to show you what I have."

Amusement grew in Penn's features. He made no attempt to take the proffered goods. "Thanks, but I'm not the purchasing agent for this outfit."

"You're not?" He drew back, perused the unshaven faces of the men and evidently didn't find one who looked as though he might have some authority. "Who is?"

"I am. The name's Carina Lockett." Carina strode forward and extended her hand. "Pleased to meet you."

The drummer blinked, turned to McClure and suddenly guffawed with laughter. "You boys are always tryin' to pull a fast one on us greenhorns, aren't you?"

"It's the truth." McClure leaned an elbow on the wagon bed and smiled.

"A woman boss, out here trailin' cattle. That's just too rich." He laughed until his shoulders shook.

The rest of the outfit cleared the tucker from their throats and found something else to look at. Like the toes of their boots. Or that blue, blue sky. Their respect for her, Carina knew, kept their mouths shut.

She lowered her hand, the opportunity to shake Farrell's hand gone. The desire for it, too. He had an engaging way of showing his merriment. Could've been contagious if she hadn't been so annoyed with him.

"Do you think a woman isn't capable of trailing three thousand head of cattle, Mr. Farrell?" she asked coolly. "Because if you do, you'd best turn around and drive off my bed-ground. I won't be doing any business with you."

The amusement sputtered. He threw a fast glance at McClure, checking his reaction to her threat.

McClure simply nodded. "She's Carina Lockett, like she said. Owner and boss of the C Bar C Ranch outside of Mobeetie, Texas."

A short, choking sound stomped out the laugh for good. The blood drained from Farrell's round face, but then it all rushed back again to flame his cheeks red.

Muttering a strangled oath, he scrambled to bundle the whiskey bottles under the arm that already held the tobacco. He whipped off his hat and crushed the thing to his chest.

"Forgive me, ma'am. Oh, forgive me. I thought—I was sure—"

Carina had gotten the same reaction so many times it didn't matter anymore. She knew who she was and what she could do. If a man had trouble believing it, well, she couldn't care less.

The drummer looked as uncomfortable as a bear in a bramble patch, though. She took pity on him for his blunder. Most likely she'd have made the same mistake if she'd been the one to pull on his boots this morning.

"I know what you thought. Forget it," she said and found a smile to reassure him.

"Then these are for you, Miss—" He halted, looked uncomfortable again. "Or is it Missus?"

"Miss," she assured him.

Another glance at Penn suggested the drummer found that baffling, too. A female alone on the trail, with near a dozen men. And no husband with her.

"She hasn't found a man who can handle her yet," McClure said.

"Nor do I want to," she retorted so fast she didn't have time to admit to herself it wasn't always true.

Like lately. At night, in her bedroll, when she was alone and worried and in sorry need of strong arms around her.

She blamed McClure for planting the seeds of foolish womanly longings inside her. They'd begun to sprout after he kissed her up good and right. Until then, she'd never been so bothered by them.

"I hope you'll accept these blandishments, Miss Lockett," Farrell said, covering his bald pate with his hat again. "I've gotten off on the wrong foot with you, I'm afraid, but I'm still hopin' you'll take a few minutes to see what I've brought with me."

He waited for her acceptance of the whiskey and tobacco. She didn't condone liquor on a trail drive, but she fervently hoped they'd all have an opportunity to enjoy some soon.

In Dodge City. To celebrate Callie Mae's return.

The tobacco would be welcomed by the outfit until they got there, however, and she inclined her head in agreement.

"Thank you, Mr. Farrell. My men will put your gifts to good use."

He looked relieved and handed her the pair of Old Fitzgeralds. "The whiskey's fine, from Kentucky, you know, and well, I'd give you some of my best cigars if I wasn't fresh out. Had some real nice Caribbeans, but a pair of gentlemen bought my last box the other day, down by the border."

"Did they?" she asked, turning the tall bottles over to Stinky Dale with a quiet order for him to give them to Sourdough for safekeeping.

"Yes, ma'am. Paid for 'em with a crisp C-Note." After he handed her the sacks of Bull Durham, he rooted around in the wooden crate and pulled out bibles, the cigarette papers to go with them. "Strange to see a couple of men like that, carryin' new money and not herdin' cattle like everyone else."

"What were they doing if not that?" McClure asked, a frown forming.

"Don't know. They were out there, off the trail, oh, a quarter mile or so. Just ridin'." He shrugged. "They weren't cowboys, that's for sure. Didn't have so much as a single little dogie with 'em."

"Didn't happen to get their names, did you?" he asked as Carina took the bibles, too.

The drummer thought a moment. "I sure didn't, Mr. McClure. They didn't stick around to talk much. But I can tell you they had on suits and string ties. One of them had a mustache, curled and waxed. Dandies, for sure. And well-armed. I thought that was strange, too."

Carina's fingers tightened around the tobacco. Her alarmed gaze found McClure's. Her thoughts jumped to Rogan and Durant and stayed there, same as, she knew, his had.

The sound of a wooden spoon banging on a cast-iron pot had them all swiveling toward Sourdough.

"Chuck's on!" he yelled. "Come and get it if you want it hot!"

Farrell sniffed deep. "Are those flapjacks I'm smellin'?"

"They are. Have you had your breakfast yet?" Carina forced herself to think of the ordinary, the courtesy she was obliged to give a visitor.

"Well, yes, ma'am, but nothin' which smells as good as what your cook's stirrin' up."

"Go on over, then," she said. "Fill a plate. Your wares will wait."

The drummer grinned. "You sure you don't mind, Miss Lockett?"

"Not at all. There's plenty. The outfit might be inclined to spend more once their bellies are full."

"Yes, ma'am." He chuckled. "Thank you, ma'am."

He took off with the rest of them and left her alone with McClure. She pivoted toward him.

"I think Rogan and Durant are following us," she said in a low voice.

His nod was grim. "Seems so."

"I saw one of them. Just a few minutes ago."

"You did?" Eyes, dark as saddle leather, sharpened over her. "Where?"

"In the cottonwoods." She gestured across the prairie, to the stand of trees that showed no movement.

His head angled to follow where she indicated. "Who did you see?"

"I couldn't tell. He's gone, though. I think Farrell scared him off."

"No." A muscle leaped in McClure's lean cheek. He turned back to her again. "Whoever it was is still out there, Carina. If he's been following us since we left Texas, he has no reason to stop following us now that we're in Kansas."

Her gaze drilled through the cottonwoods, willing the branches and leaves to part so she could see what their shadows might hide.

"I'll ride over there, see what I can find," McClure said.

"No," she said.

His eyes narrowed. "If Rogan's hiding, I'll get him now. Save you the trouble of turning your herd over to him later. Same goes for Durant, if it's him."

"We'll do nothing to jeopardize Callie Mae, you hear me?" Her voice grated with a rush of desperation, the terrible certainty that if they didn't cooperate fully with Rogan and Durant, she'd lose her little girl. "They're holding all the cards, McClure, so we have to play by their rules."

"You're wrong." His expression turned hard. "We've

got the aces they need to win their game—that herd of yours out there. They're following us to make sure we're playing right. No other reason."

"Maybe." She took comfort in his use of *we* and *us*. The knowledge that he'd be with her to the end, no matter how the cards landed. "But don't you see, Mc-Clure? If it was anyone else, or a whole different bunch of circumstances, I'd go after him myself and fillet him alive for what he's doing. The bastards, both of them."

"Nothing to stop you from it now, is there?"

She blinked up at him. Why did the man have to be so stubborn?

"Yes!" she snapped. "Callie Mae is stopping me."

He studied her in that dark way of his. He had an air of danger, of mystery, about him. She'd sensed it before. Sensed it now. And was reminded again of how little she knew about him.

"I know," he said finally, his features not so hard anymore. "But it still won't hurt to ride over there and see what I can find."

She set her jaw and stopped fighting him on it. "Go, then. But I'm telling you, he's gone, whoever he is."

"I'd like to know why they split up, too."

"You won't find out looking in the trees."

"Maybe I will before we get to Dodge City."

Carina couldn't fathom how he would, but did it matter? Rogan and Durant would be there, waiting for them, and *that's* what mattered most.

But afterward, the uncertainty of what would happen tortured her. The risks…

God, she wanted it to be over. Her temples took on

a dull ache. She needed coffee, strong and hot. She'd yet to have her first cup of the day.

Carina thrust the drummer's gifts at McClure. "Here. See that these are distributed fairly."

"Please." Eyes narrowed, he took them.

"Please." Impatience spiraled through her. "And let's start moving the herd across the river no later than noon."

She turned on her heel to head for the chuck wagon, but his strong arm hooked around her waist. He all but lifted her off her feet, twisted and pressed her back against the wagon, all in one quick, unexpected motion.

"Not so fast, Carina." He tossed the Bull Durham and bibles onto the tarp behind her.

Her surprise warred with indignation. "What are you doing?"

"You've been avoiding me."

Her chin lifted. He stood so close, instant awareness shot through her. The breadth of his shoulders, the heat of his big body reaching toward hers. "I hadn't noticed."

"Ever since we left Fort Supply you have been."

A damning warmth bloomed in her cheeks. The memory of how completely vulnerable she'd been in the bathhouse.

The bloom caught McClure's attention.

"Don't tell me you're still embarrassed," he said, his gaze brimming with amusement.

"I'm not," she lied and pushed against the unyielding wall of his chest. "I never was."

"The hell you weren't."

She didn't waste time denying it further. "You caught me unaware, McClure. You *know* you did."

"So I got lucky," he said and chuckled.

Which distracted her. The pleasantly male sound wound its way through her, found a place somewhere inside her chest.

"I should have climbed in with you." The chuckle died, and his voice turned husky. Blood-stirringly intimate. His gaze settled over her mouth. "A thousand times, I've thought of it."

Never would she admit she'd thought of it, too. When she least expected it. Their nakedness together in that tub. Arms and legs tangled, their skin soapy and slick against the other's…

"You shouldn't be thinking such things, McClure." She hated how the words came out, soft and shaky. "They won't get you anywhere because it'll never happen." She forced herself to say the words they were both thinking of. "Us in a tub with one another."

A part of her knew she should end their silly conversation and walk away. Her men could see them, standing close and talking hushed, even though McClure kept his body angled to shield her.

She didn't walk away, though. The foolish female part of her wanted to stay.

His hand lowered to the buttons of her blouse.

"Can't help thinking of us like that." A corner of his mouth lifted. "You wearing your new pink underwear this mornin', Miss Lockett?"

His voice, so husky it could've been a whisper, contained an outrageously charming amount of male curiosity. She pressed her lips together to hide their treacherous curving.

A button flipped open.

And this time, she dared to play his game. What was a little pink fabric and lace, after all? Nothing he hadn't already seen.

A second button opened. He parted her blouse wide, and the morning air swirled over her skin.

"Well, well, well. What do you know? She is," he murmured.

"I ought to plug you with lead for the liberties you're taking with me," she said, not moving, letting him look.

"But you're not going to shoot me. 'Else you would have by now. Isn't that right, Miss Lockett?"

She bit her lip and refused to admit the truth. He took his bold curiosity another step further. By untying a narrow snip of ribbon. He undid the camisole's top button, and parted that, too.

But he stilled when his attention snared on the photograph she was never without. Lifting one corner, he pulled it from its place against her breast.

He studied the image pressed to the paper, then lifted his glance to hers. The playfulness was gone; in its place, a somber darkening of his eyes.

"My daughter," Carina said quietly. "Taken last year on Daisy, her horse."

"She looks like you," he said.

"You think so?" She didn't have to see the photo to recall the sun-streaked curls and wide, mischievous smile flirting with the camera. "Her eyes are as blue as the sky, and her hair is the perfect shade of…cinnamon." Callie Mae had delighted in the photographer's attention that day. But then, what child wouldn't? Carina frowned. "There are times she reminds me of her father."

"Can't be helped, I suppose. She's half Webb."

"To my everlasting regret."

Times had been simpler back then, when the traveling photographer stopped by the C Bar C. Carina had never questioned if Callie Mae was happy, had always thought the photo was proof.

But her daughter wanted more than Carina could give her and took off in pursuit of it, with no thought to the repercussions on those who loved her most.

And wasn't that just like a Webb?

Her throat tightened. Did Callie Mae miss her at all?

McClure gently tucked the photograph inside the camisole again. But he didn't step away, lingering instead to trail his knuckle along the swell of her breast. Her flesh tingled, and she hung on tight to her composure. His touch, the exquisite simplicity of it, its tenderness and caring, delved inward and stroked something deep, something buried, something Carina was afraid to feel.

Or enjoy.

Except she was.

Feeling and enjoying. Needing, most of all.

Yet her fingers curled around his strong wrist, the boss in her insisting she must stop him immediately for what he was doing.

The woman in her didn't.

For her weakness, he could seduce her so easily.

There, against the wagon, if he wanted. This power he had over her had gotten too complicated to comprehend.

She didn't bother trying.

But it was there. Stirring, sprouting, stretching. A yearning, a reawakening of her femininity.

Then, almost before she realized it, McClure tied the ribbon on her camisole and refastened her blouse.

The moment gone, her fingers fell away from his wrist, and he stepped back.

Yet his gaze lingered over her, a fathomless pool of unspoken things between them. Desires and promises. Curiosities left unsatisfied.

For now.

He touched the brim of his Stetson, turned and walked away.

And though he hadn't told her so, Carina knew one thing for sure.

Penn McClure wasn't finished with her yet.

Chapter Twelve

"Mr. McClure? Mind if I ask you a question?"

TJ Grier ducked under the rope corral holding in the remuda and sprinted toward Penn. He looked troubled.

Penn threw the saddle blanket over his gelding's back. "I'm listening."

"It's about Callie Mae."

He straightened the corners, made sure they hung straight. "What about her?"

"What if we don't get her back?"

Penn lifted his glance. He didn't tell the young wrangler it was a question he'd asked himself once or twice. Or a thousand times. "Don't you think we will?"

"I'm hoping, for sure. But Mavis Webb, well, from what I've seen, she's all wire and no cotton. She ain't one to mess with."

"So I hear."

"I don't trust her." He kicked the dirt with the toe of

his boot, as if he wished it was the woman's scheming fanny instead.

"You think any of us do?"

"No, sir. But folks like her, why, they've got so much money, they always get what they want, no matter what."

"Scary, isn't it?" Penn said and meant it.

"She wants to keep Callie Mae all for herself." TJ frowned at the ground. "I think she'll find a way to do it."

"I'm going to do my best to see that she doesn't. We all will," Penn said. He kept his voice firm. The kid had to know it was the truth.

TJ's head came up. Distress showed in his face, barely old enough to need a razor.

"But her son ain't no better than she is, Mr. Mc-Clure," he protested. "Worse, I reckon. With them two in cahoots with that gunslinger, hell, Miss Lockett don't have a chance against any of them."

The wrangler's words hit a raw nerve. An ugly reminder to Penn that if he hadn't failed in Denver, if he hadn't been so *stupidly* duped by Abigail, Rogan wouldn't have escaped him at the Brown Palace, fled to Texas and ended up on Carina's doorstep.

But Penn *had* failed. Now, because of it, Carina was being blackmailed.

"And you know what else?" TJ demanded.

Penn dragged himself out of the guilt. "What?"

"Trailing this herd is a waste of time," TJ said. "Ain't no way the Webbs are going to give up Callie Mae. I just got a feeling they won't."

Penn thought of the revenge that would be waiting

for him in Dodge City. He bent to retrieve his saddle from the ground. "I'm going to prove you wrong, TJ."

"I hope you do, Mr. McClure. Truly, I do."

TJ stepped forward and took the saddle. Though Penn had every intention of saddling his own horse, he let the kid do it for him. TJ seemed to have a need to stay busy and work off some of his suffering.

"Going to be real hard on Miss Lockett if she can't get her little girl back," TJ muttered and buckled the cinch.

"She will," Penn said. And vowed it. Again.

"Going to be just as hard on her if she loses the C Bar C," TJ added.

Jesse Keller strode toward them with a loose-hipped swagger. "Aw, quit your fussing, TJ, will you? No one wants to hear it."

Stinky Dale strode with him. "You got to stop thinking like you are. Where's it going to get you?"

TJ stiffened. "We'll be in Dodge City next week. Can I help it if I'm scared about what's going to happen when we get there? Miss Lockett thinks the world of her little girl and the C Bar C, too, and she stands to lose 'em both."

"You don't know for sure. None of us does," Jesse said.

"Damn shame Callie Mae has such rotten kin." Stinky Dale shook his head in regret.

The spicy smell of his cologne sailed toward Penn on a current of air. The scent was always stronger in the mornings, after he slathered his cheeks with the stuff. Penn had learned not to grimace when he was in the cowboy's company.

TJ opened his mouth to keep his place in the discussion, but Penn held up a hand. He slid a concerned glance toward Carina, standing near the chuck wagon with the drummer, who, Penn learned over breakfast, could talk the hide off a cow.

"That's enough, boys. Your voices will carry," he said. "Miss Lockett doesn't need to hear you ruminating about her affairs."

They kept their silence, then, but their expressions revealed their troubles. They'd stand by her through whatever happened, Penn knew. Ready to fight for her and Callie Mae, if necessary.

He hoped they wouldn't have to. Spilling their blood wasn't in the plan.

"Go on now," he said. "Miss Lockett will want to pull out as soon as the drummer leaves."

From the looks of him, TJ didn't feel much better about her situation, but he obediently headed back to the remuda with the other two following. Penn wished he could've found the words to assure them Carina would find happiness in the end.

But he couldn't. Because she stood to lose a lot.

Her men didn't fully understand what drove Rogan and Durant, besides, or that greed was only a part of it. Rogan's need to avoid arrest, Durant's partnership, and their certain escape into hiding with Carina's blackmail money stuffed in their pockets...hell, Penn didn't know himself how it'd all turn out.

He'd sleep better at night if he did.

His scrutiny found her again. She took the drummer's breakfast plate and dropped it into the wreck pan with the rest of the dishes waiting to be washed, then took his elbow and urged him toward his supply wagon.

Penn's gaze clung to the soft sway of her hips while she walked. Lord, but she was something to look at. Tall, slender, always in control. She had presence, even out here on the desolate Kansas prairie, an aura about her that kept a man interested.

And Penn was interested, all right.

An image of those long legs twined with his formed into a fantasy that stirred up a slow heat in his groin. A sudden longing to have her arms wind around him, pull his body to hers. He imagined the feel of her rounded breasts pressed to his chest, her skin smooth and warm, her lips full and deliciously wet, and how she'd sheath him, slick and hot. Little sounds would come from her throat, female sounds, wild and on the edge of control….

The fantasy was so damned real and always there, on his mind. This wanting that didn't go away.

It shouldn't have happened, but Carina had come to mean something to him. More than she should. Different than her being a mother, desperate to meet the demands of her child's conniving father. Or a woman, forced to endure the rigors of a cattle drive for weeks on end.

She couldn't have been more different than Abigail. Yet Abigail had meant something to him, too. In ways opposite, but no less troubling.

Penn shook off the thoughts. That blood-heating fantasy. He had no business dwelling on either woman, not when he had revenge to win against the man who stood between them both.

But he couldn't help wondering how he'd walk away from Carina when it was all over.

Salina

Callie Mae propped her chin on her hands and stared out the Metropolitan Hotel window into the dirt street three stories below. A light afternoon rain dripped off the edge of the roof and spattered onto the glass. The gray clouds covered up the sun like a dirty blanket and left her spirits feeling as dismal as the day.

Sighing, she dragged her stare down one side of Iron Avenue as far as she could. Then, because there wasn't anything new to see from the last time she looked, she did the same thing to the other side, with the same result.

Her mouth tilted into a pout. There was nothing to do here except watch a few horses and rigs go by. Folks who didn't mind getting a little wet moseyed along the boardwalks so they could do their shopping or go to a restaurant, but mostly, Salina was boring.

Grandmother said the place was a wicked cow town, and she wouldn't let Callie Mae go outside, even if it wasn't raining. And if she *could* go outside, well, there wasn't any place for girls like her to play except at Oak Dale Park maybe, which was only a few blocks away, but Grandmother didn't know anyone, so she said Callie Mae couldn't go there, either.

Blast it.

Callie Mae didn't want to be cooped up in the hotel, like a dressed-up chicken in a fancy henhouse.

She didn't want to go to Europe anymore, either.

She wanted to go home.

Really bad.

Except she didn't know how to tell Grandmother.

At first, Callie Mae had been excited about traveling on a big ship across the Atlantic Ocean. She'd never done anything like that before, but that was days and weeks ago, and now Grandmother would be very disappointed she'd changed her mind.

Callie Mae didn't want to hurt her feelings, especially since she'd been about as nice as she could be, buying Callie Mae whatever she wanted. Like ice cream, every day. And there were so many new dresses and shoes and hair ribbons in her trunks, why, Callie Mae couldn't remember them all. Books and games and the latest toys…

Sometimes, Callie Mae felt guilty having them. Maybe because none of her friends back home did. But mostly because Mama would frown and call them an extravagance.

Which they were. Callie Mae *knew* they were.

Mama…her throat tightened. Oh, she missed Mama a whole *bunch*. More and more every day, so much it made her heart hurt.

And she'd go on missing her if she didn't do something about it. Callie Mae knew that, too. She'd just have to find a way to tell Grandmother she'd already had plenty of fun, and now she wanted to go home.

The scary part was that it had to be today, and soon, because she didn't have much time left. Rogan was coming. When he did, they'd all go to Kansas City, where they'd take a train to New York. Getting on the ship would come after that, and by then, she'd be so far away from Mama, she might never get back.

Well, not for a really long time, anyway.

Callie Mae had been gone long enough already.

A carriage appeared, and her thoughts drained away, like the rain on the windowpane. The rig appeared alongside the Opera House on the corner, turned onto Iron Avenue and finally drew up in front of the Metropolitan. The carriage door opened, and a man, dressed in a dark suit, stepped out.

She drew in a breath, straightened and turned toward her grandmother, sitting at the desk, her reading glasses perched on her nose. A lamp illuminated the papers spread out before her, the itinerary for their upcoming travels. On one side of the desk, her pocketbook sat open with her fine leather wallet beside it, left there after she'd paid the beautician for curling their hair.

"Rogan's here," Callie Mae said.

Grandmother looked up, her brow arched in surprise. "Rogan?" She removed her glasses. "He's your father, darling. You should address him as such."

Callie Mae remained silent. He didn't act like a father, so she'd stopped calling him one. She knew how babies came, and that he'd been with Mama a long time ago, but ever since, he acted as though Callie Mae was a stranger. Even after they left the C Bar C.

No wonder Mama didn't like him very much. Callie Mae didn't, either, and sometimes, that made her sad. Other times, though, like now, she just plain didn't care.

"I want to go home," she blurted.

Grandmother stilled. But slowly, she smiled and set her glasses on top of her papers. She held her arms out. "Come here, darling."

Callie Mae's petticoats rustled beneath her dusty-rose silk dress, her step silent on the thick carpet as she obediently drew closer to her grandmother, but halted just beyond her reach.

Because if Grandmother hugged her and smoothed her hair and said loving things as she always did, Callie Mae would give in and do anything Grandmother wanted her to do.

"Please send a wire to Mama and have her come get me," she said.

Grandmother's arms lowered. "The weather's dreadful, and it's making you restless, isn't it? Have I told you I have tickets to see a champion roller skater in Kansas City? Why, he's a boy just your age, and he'll be great fun to see. I'm told he's all the rage right now. That will give you something to look forward to, won't it?"

Callie Mae shook her head. She'd already been to a magic show and a Chinese acrobat performance in New Orleans. A children's opera, a comedy and a puppet show, too. So what if she didn't get to see a roller skater?

"No, thank you. I'd rather go back to Texas." Callie Mae strove to be polite, but it was hard when Grandmother tried to distract her like this. "Will you go with me to the telegraph office?"

Grandmother cocked her perfectly coiffed head. "Are you missing Daisy again? Perhaps we can find a stable in Kansas City—"

"I'm missing *Mama*," Callie Mae said and barely kept from stomping her foot from frustration. She didn't like it that Grandmother wasn't listening to her. "I'm missing Grandpa, too. I've been gone a long time from home, and I want to go back to see them."

"But arrangements have already been made to go to Europe, darling. You know that."

Callie Mae bit her lip. Yes, and the tickets were really expensive. Besides, Grandmother had spent a lot of time planning this trip across the ocean, and she was looking forward to it a bunch. Now, everything would be wasted.

"I'm sorry," she said. "Will they give you your money back?"

"It's not about the money." Grandmother leaned forward and reached for her again. "I just want to be with you, that's all. It means so much to me when we're together."

Callie Mae took a step back. Rebellion she hadn't felt for a good long while stirred. It meant a lot to *her* to be with Mama and Grandpa. "I'll go to the telegraph office by myself, then."

Grandmother looked alarmed. "No, you won't. A beautiful child like you, alone on those streets out there? Absolutely not." She sat back in the chair and regarded her. "How about we write a letter instead? You can tell your mother all about the wonderful things you've seen and done, and we'll mail it, first thing in the morning. I promise."

Callie Mae had already sent letters. Almost every day. Grandmother should know—she'd posted them for her at the post office.

Still, mail could be slow in getting to Mobeetie, and even slower out to the ranch. Maybe Mama hadn't gotten the letters yet.

But if she had, she didn't answer. Every day, Callie Mae waited for word from her, and it never came.

She always found that disappointing. And strange. Why wouldn't Mama write her back?

A knock sounded, and her glance jumped toward the door, the dismay building inside her that with Rogan's arrival, the opportunity to convince Grandmother to let her go back home was lost.

"Let your father in, won't you?" Grandmother asked, tidying up the papers strewn in front of her. Clearly, she considered their discussion finished.

Callie Mae debated disobeying until she got the answer she wanted, but in the end, she did as she was told. Rogan entered the room, unbuttoning his overcoat. His brief nod acknowledged her; he removed the garment, shook off the rain and hung it on the rack.

"Hello, Mother," he said, adding his hat.

"Rogan." She smiled, happy as always to see him.

Callie Mae rolled her eyes and shut the door. She didn't bother to greet him, and he didn't appear to notice. She glowered at them both.

He bent and kissed his mother's cheek. "A dreary day, isn't it?"

"The worst. Come, sit here beside me. I trust your trip went well?"

"As well as can be expected, I suppose." He took the chair she offered, his glance touching on her purse, her wallet, the papers stacked in a neat pile. "The roads in this godforsaken part of the country are wretched. I've never seen so much mud in my life."

"Indeed." She nodded, sympathetic. "We've been

spoiled by life in the city, haven't we? I don't believe I'll ever take a paved street for granted again."

"I can't wait to get back to civilization," he muttered.

"Tomorrow. When we arrive in Kansas City. Conditions will be better for us there." She smiled again.

Rogan shifted in his seat, indicated the papers on her desk. "Do you have everything arranged?"

"Of course." Her smile wavered, as if she recalled her conversation with Callie Mae. She reached for her pocketbook, withdrew several pieces of wrapped candy. "Darling, your father and I have some things to talk about. Here's some caramels. Why don't you read one of your books while you eat them? You'll feel better, and then we'll write your mother a letter. Like I promised."

Callie Mae made no move to take the candy. Considered the merits of flinging herself to the floor and throwing a full-blown tantrum right then and there from being ignored.

And discarded the idea.

If she'd never understood how selfish Grandmother was before, she did now. It was one of the things Mama had never liked about Grandmother. Her selfishness.

Like a fog melting in the sun, Callie Mae began to see things different. Clearer. Like a grown-up.

Like Mama.

Rogan watched her with eyes as blue as her own. She didn't like the way he looked at her with his lids lowered all secretive. As if there were things about him he didn't want her to know.

He didn't care one blasted whit about what she

wanted. He never had. He wouldn't help her get home to Texas, so she'd just have to get there on her own.

Putting on her polite face, she stepped forward, took the caramels from Grandmother's outstretched palm, then went into the adjoining bedroom and shut the door.

Chapter Thirteen

"She wants to go back to Texas," Mother said. She kept her voice low and slid a worried look at the closed door.

Mother was too confident of herself to get worried. Which made Rogan nervous.

"You're not going to let her, are you?" he asked.

Her gaze snapped toward him. "Of course not. After we've come this far?"

He relaxed a little. "Good. Distract her, then. Buy her something expensive."

"She's not swayed so easily anymore."

"Then you must not be spending enough," he said and smirked.

But Mother wasn't amused. "She's a smart child, Rogan. She's discovering what matters most to her."

"She's just a kid. How would she know what matters? Convince her you have what she needs, and she'll get over her whining."

"She's *whining* to go back to her mother. How can I compete with that?"

His gaze hardened. "Find a way."

Her thin nostrils flared, but she inclined her head, conceding him the point. "It'll be easier to distract her once we're on the train and out of this awful place."

Rogan let her go on believing he'd be on that train with her. It never occurred to the old biddy he might have plans of his own. Ambitions and dreams. Did she really think she could manipulate him to fit hers? Did she honestly believe he wanted to spend weeks on end with her and the daughter he had no room—or desire for—in his life?

Well, she had another think coming.

"Tell me about Carina," Mother said suddenly. "Have you heard from her?"

"Of course not." Rogan wasn't that stupid. If they ever got close enough to breathe in the same air, she'd shoot him dead. "But she's getting closer to Dodge City. Right on schedule."

"Very good."

"She should be there next week," he added, counting the days.

She appeared relieved. "And Mr. Durant is prepared to meet her as we discussed?"

Anger licked at the fringes of his patience. There she was. Controlling him again. Putting her nose in his business. Not trusting him to see to the details of a scheme that would net him a small fortune.

"Neal and I are taking a great deal of care to make sure nothing goes wrong, Mother. Getting that herd sold is important to us." He gave her a cold smile.

So was his counterfeiting ring and escaping to the New York underground. Each as important as the other.

She sat back in her chair, eyed him with shrewd consideration. "Carina's money doesn't mean a thing, you know."

His smile dropped from his mouth. "It does to me."

"It's more a matter of seeing her destroyed. The idea of my granddaughter being raised on a ranch and working her little fingers to the bone galls me. As a Webb, she deserves better. Sometimes, I think you forget that."

He kept his features impassive. Refused to let her goad him into the argument they'd had again and again.

"I've decided to put the money from Carina's cattle into a hidden trust," she said.

"What?" he exclaimed, startled.

"For Callie Mae's future."

With no thought to his own. He schooled his features to hide his growing fury.

She regarded him, shrewd again. "Are you thinking of keeping it for yourself, Rogan?"

He'd learned long ago when she looked at him like that, she took on the maddening ability to read his mind when he least wanted her to.

"It's none of your business what I'm thinking, Mother," he said, his voice gritting.

She jerked, as if she disapproved of his small burst of rebellion. She drew herself up, imperious as always. "You may as well know, too, that I've arranged for a buyer to purchase her cattle and deposit the money into a special account until the trust papers can be drawn up."

Rogan's blood went cold.

"His name is Edward Lonner," she added.

"I don't care what the hell his name is!" Rogan exploded. "He wasn't part of the plan. Carina was supposed to give the money to Durant. *That* was the plan."

She eyed him sharply. "You're a fool to think we can trust him. He's a gunfighter, for pity's sake. He'd shoot us when our backs were turned and take the money for himself."

The anger simmered and bubbled, threatened to spew. Rogan had all he could do to contain it.

"No," he grated. "He wouldn't."

"Edward will see that Durant gets his cut, of course."

Rogan's brain spun through the anger. Durant's cut? What about his own?

"By then, we'll be out of the country." Her satisfied glance lifted to the window, as if she could see through the rain and into the future. "Untraceable."

Rogan needed time to control the fury. To bank it and bury it and keep her from seeing how much he absolutely *hated* her for changing the scheme he'd meticulously designed, taking control of what had been, up to now, his perfect plan for blackmail.

"Brilliant, don't you think?" she asked, her glance returning to him.

He strove for calm. Tried to think. Assured himself she wouldn't have control long. That he'd be in Dodge City, find Carina and have her money before Mother's cattle buyer ever laid eyes on that beautiful C Bar C herd.

"Indeed," he said, finally trusting himself to speak. "It's settled, then."

Far from it. Not in the way she envisioned.

But only if Rogan kept one step ahead of her.

"I've bought tickets for tonight's performance at the Opera House across the street," Mother said. As if she recalled Callie Mae in the adjoining room, she glanced at the closed door. Worry flickered again. "We'll eat dinner first. You'll have just enough time to freshen up before we must leave."

A cow town like Salina having something of merit to parade across a stage? He couldn't imagine it. "Did it occur to you, Mother, to ask if I *wanted* to go to the Opera House?"

"What else would you do?"

"I'd find something," he said and thought of the myriad of saloons he'd passed on the way to the Metropolitan.

Her pale lips thinned. Clearly, she suspected his preference for entertainment.

"You must spend the time with your daughter," she said firmly. "You have ten years of catching up with her to do, Rogan. Beginning tonight. I insist."

He swallowed a protest down. Hard.

"Have you booked your room here at the hotel yet?" she asked.

"No," he said in a crisp tone. And declined to admit he'd hoped she'd already done that for him, given his near-penniless state of affairs.

"Well, you'd best see to it immediately. Decent lodging is at a premium in this town."

It took all his willpower not to glance down at her leather wallet. "Fine." He cleared his throat. Hated himself for what he had to do. "However, the prices they charge for transportation around here are exorbitant, and I'm afraid I've miscalculated my costs. So until I can withdraw funds from my account, could you lend me a small sum? I'll repay you."

"You still haven't repaid your last loan from me," she said coldly.

"I haven't?" He gave her an innocent look.

"The allowance I give you is plenty to live on, Rogan. There's no reason why you can't. Comfortably, I might add."

"*You* wouldn't be able to live on what you give me. So why should I? I'm just as much of a Webb as you are."

"This has nothing to do with me," she snapped in frustration. "Your penchant to mismanage your finances must stop. Until you begin to show more responsibility, how can you possibly expect to carry on your father's reputation?"

"I'm not my father," he grated. The coldhearted tyrant. No wonder he and Mother got on so famously before he died. "Nor do I want to be."

"And isn't that obvious?" She sniffed. "He left me his generous estate, of which you, as his only son, are in no shape to carry on. I'm warning you, Rogan." She jabbed a bony finger at him, and the cluster of diamonds on her ring sparkled in the lamplight. "If you fail in your duties, then those duties must fall to your daughter. Sooner than you'll expect."

He clenched his teeth. Callie Mae Lockett. Heir to the Webb fortune and all its responsibilities.

At the irony, he expelled a bitter laugh. What would Carina think about that?

"She's coming to the age where she's ready to be groomed to take over your father's fortune," his mother continued. "And she will if this—this *irreverence* to your obligations continues. Let me assure you it'll only take a few minutes of my lawyer's time to draw up the papers to turn your entire trust over to her. Maybe then, you'll appreciate the Webb name more than you do now."

Alarm shot through him at this new threat. She couldn't be serious. Callie Mae was just a kid. And the money in that trust was his. Had been from the day he was born.

"Can you see why having Callie Mae with us is so important?" she asked, her voice quieter, her anger spent. "Someday, she'll be heir to all our family's holdings. She'll have earned her rightful place in society, and you must accept her as your daughter. Love her as a father should. She deserves it. Do you understand?"

Seething, he forced himself to nod. Once. Because that was what she wanted him to do.

"All right, then. Let's start over, shall we?" She managed to smile. Reached for her wallet. Rogan's gaze dropped to the bill she withdrew. "Will an hour give you enough time to prepare for dinner?"

He accepted the money she gave him. Enough to pay for his room and not much else.

He hid his disdain. Swept aside his resentment and hate. And agreed to the time she assigned him. He'd spend the rest of the evening being the son she wanted him to be, the father she hoped for Callie Mae.

But tomorrow, she'd learn that she'd never manipulate him again.

Stunned by all she heard, Callie Mae eased away from the door and rolled from her stomach to her back.

She didn't care if she crushed her dusty-rose dress while she lay full out on the floor, her ears strained toward the voices seeping in under the threshold. Her instincts had warned that something was wrong.

Her instincts were right.

The shock pumped through her in waves. She stared up at the ceiling, replayed the words in her head again.

Carina...closer to Dodge City...her money...cattle buyer...a matter of seeing her destroyed...

Callie Mae's heart pounded in horror from that awful word that stood out from the rest.

Destroyed, destroyed, destroyed.

Now, everything made sense.

Like why Grandmother made her leave the C Bar C as if their tails were on fire, distracting Callie Mae until it was too late to realize she hadn't even told Mama goodbye.

And why they changed rigs in Old Steve Bussell's pasture, even though Grandmother made it seem as if it was a perfectly ordinary thing they had to do to get to New Orleans.

And now, today, when Grandmother refused to listen to her pleas to go home.

One by one, the thoughts turned and twisted inside Callie Mae's head until they straightened themselves out, fused together and formed a clear picture. Her horror shifted into fury at what they'd done.

At what *she'd* done, most of all.

The fury skidded into full-blown remorse. She'd been nothing but selfish and greedy, and she hadn't seen the signs.

Tears prickled her eyes. Signs that had been as plain as a hump on a camel. Now she was no better than Grandmother and Rogan, and that was the worst.

Being like them.

If only she hadn't been so stupid. If only she'd listened to Mama all along, then none of this would have happened.

Stupid, stupid, stupid.

She flung her arm over her eyes and fought despair.

Yet after a long, punishing moment, the despair wavered. She wasn't stupid. She got the best grades in school. Lots of times, Mama told her how proud she was to have a daughter who could think as well as Callie Mae could, which was really important because she'd be boss of the C Bar C some day.

Callie Mae lowered her arm and sat up. A new resolve surged through her.

She was a Lockett, not a pampered Webb princess. She refused to be selfish and greedy like Grandmother and Rogan.

She was determined to be smart and tough like Mama.

Her head cleared. She had to think hard, harder than she'd ever had to think before. Her mind sifted through the information her eavesdropping gleaned, and an ugly realization dawned.

The cattle buyer Grandmother hired was going to put the money from the herd into a special account.

Which meant he wasn't going to give it to Mama.

Which meant she wouldn't be able to pay the ranch's bills.

Callie Mae pressed her hands to her cheeks in a new rush of horror. And that meant she'd lose the C Bar C. Oh, she'd lose *everything*.

It was all Callie Mae's fault. Every bit. Because her mother would never, *never,* give up her precious cattle for anything.

Except for her.

Callie Mae's breathing quickened. But she wouldn't know about the special account. She'd think her cattle would get Callie Mae back, fair and square.

Callie Mae had to warn her.

She scrunched her eyes shut. *Think, think!* She'd have to find a way. Fast. She couldn't, she just *couldn't* get on that train with Grandmother and Rogan in the morning.

Her eyes opened. She knew where Dodge City was from Salina. She'd seen the map at the train station. Both towns were railheads, busy cattle-shipping points. If she never did anything else in her selfish, selfish life, she'd do everything she could to get there.

Somehow.

Her glance caught on the wrapped caramels, scattered on the carpet where she'd dropped them. Callie Mae had fallen in love with their buttery, creamy taste in New Orleans. Of course, Grandmother bought her a whole sackful, more than any child could ever need.

An extravagance, that candy. A symbol of yet another of her grandmother's attempts to win her affections. Bribing Callie Mae with love to get what she wanted, with no thought to the consequences.

Callie Mae stared at the tiny wrapped treats, and her stomach turned.

They were a symbol of what she'd become, too.

Resolutely, she gathered up the caramels, strode across the room toward the window. Turning the latch, she lifted the sash, leaned out into the rain and threw them all into the muddy street below.

Chapter Fourteen

The Next Morning

Carina drew an admiring eye over the flat Kansas prairie. Here, the country abounded in deer, antelope, wild turkeys and an abundance of prairie dogs. Every mile they traveled netted something new to see, something wild. Like wolves or the occasional bear or an entire herd of mustangs, running free.

And of course, there was all that beautiful grass. Different than the tall blue sedge grass that grew in Indian Territory, miles of buffalo grass covered the ground here in Kansas. Short and wiry, the grass contained nutriments upon which the cattle and horses thrived. McClure claimed the herd would weigh more in Dodge City than it did now, even after walking scores of miles to get there.

Carina sobered. Not that it mattered what kind of price her fatted herd would fetch. She wouldn't see a dime of it.

She tried not to think of all she'd lose. Only what she'd gain when she arrived in Dodge City. Her precious little girl, and there was nothing more valuable than that.

Yet her glance slid down the wide channel to find McClure, who'd created his own kind of value to her. And it seemed to grow a little more every day, so much she wondered if he'd gotten downright irreplaceable.

A bemusing dilemma she found herself in, this being so dependent on one man. Except for Woollie and Grandpa, she couldn't remember herself being in such a fix.

Under the circumstances, though, it couldn't be helped. This need she had for him. She assured herself it was only temporary, that soon her life would return to normal, in spite of everything.

She sent her thoughts onto a different road, on how McClure would get the herd over this stretch of the Cimarron, a tributary flowing low and so salty no one could drink from it. Especially the cattle, which would die if they took in too much.

He'd ordered them rounded up into a compact group, a safe distance from the deadly stream, its bed reminding her of snow, there were so many salt crystals in the dry sand.

A good rain would fill the area with pockets of treacherous quicksand, she worried as she urged the Appaloosa forward. But right now, all they had to concentrate on was getting the herd across, fast, without any of them trying to drink from the briny waters.

From the grim look on McClure's face, it wouldn't be an easy task.

"We have to keep 'em moving after we cross the stream," he ordered the outfit, gathered in front of him. "They'll want to turn back to drink. Seems they know there won't be fresh water until we reach Bluff Creek in a couple of days. So run 'em hard, once we get going, you hear?"

The men nodded, reached for their ropes.

"You got that, Orlin?" McClure asked.

The cowboy glowered. Clearly, he didn't like being singled out as the most inexperienced man on the payroll. "You think I don't know what gyp water is, Mr. McClure?"

"Just making sure," he said. "A man drinks some, he can swell up so bad he can't get his boots off."

"I'm not havin' any of that poison."

"All right, then. I want you to ride drag. Use your rope, your slicker, whatever you have to to keep them cows from spreading out."

"Yes, sir."

He continued to bark out orders to the others, leaving Carina for last. His dark gaze heated over her.

"Stay with me," he said.

He had a way of making the command sound like something it shouldn't. Possessive, provocative, full of promise. Or maybe it was her mind, toying with her heart, making her think it did.

"I will," she said, that easy.

He turned away and gave his attention to setting the herd into a sudden stampede across the water.

Carina had to admit she'd gotten used to being at his side, anyway. At least during the rough spots on this drive. She'd gotten used to him giving the orders, too. Sharing the responsibility with her.

Which would get her nowhere in the end.

I have every intention of returning to my office job as soon as I can.

The words he'd declared to her at the beginning of the trail drive were solemn and clear. Unforgettable. Next week, after they reached Dodge City, he'd be moving on to things more important to him, his debt to her fulfilled.

Her mood turning glum in a hurry, she unhooked her lariat, spurred her horse forward and moved into place beside him. It shouldn't matter she wasn't important enough to make him want to stick around the C Bar C. In her life. That he had one of his own that didn't include ranching. Or her.

She stiffened her spine and refused to let it matter. She resolved to think of what lay ahead—getting her cattle across this damned briny stream—and how the cattle milled, bawling, restless, wanting the water they'd be denied.

"The sun is shining on the river," McClure said, squinting an eye toward Happy Sam, a veteran of C Bar C drives who had an uncanny skill for swimming. The old steer's esteemed place at the front of the herd gave him the responsibility of leading the beeves to the other side. They'd follow like mice. "Going to blind 'em on top of everything else. We'll have our work cut out for us."

"You haven't failed me yet, McClure," she said. "You'll get them across fine."

"Is that a compliment I'm hearing?"

At the drawled surprise in his voice, she slanted him a look. "I suppose so."

"Not often my boss gives me one." The hard line of his mouth softened.

Her mood left her lacking a flippant response. It was, she knew, the truth.

"Maybe I'll have to start," she said with a resigned sigh. "I do appreciate you. More than you realize."

"There are ways to show it, Carina."

Her mind pointed to bonus money, privileges, legions of compliments. God knew he deserved them all. "I know."

"A few more kisses like we had would be a good start."

Her gaze jumped to his. She frowned against the flutter of her pulse. "Those kisses between us should never have happened."

"Considering we both seem to enjoy them, no doubt we'll have more."

He seemed so sure, her belly curled. "I do believe, McClure, you're out of line in your thinking."

"It's the truth." His glance, vaguely troubled, held on to hers. Dark and smoldering, thickly fringed, his eyes had the power to make her forget where they were. Or why. "I want you, Carina."

Unexpectedly, he leaned toward her with a creak of saddle leather, curled his fingers around her neck and boldly tugged her closer. He found her mouth under the brims of their hats, and their lips met. Clung, for long, blood-warming moments.

Then, his head lifted. He drew back, straight in the saddle again.

"Right or wrong, I do," he said, his voice rough.

She blew out a flustered breath, the feel of his lips lingering. The power this man had over her. How could she best him on it? "You've got nerve, McClure. I'll say that for you."

He grunted, reached for his lariat and tugged his Stetson lower over his forehead. "Better that I had more sense instead, Carina. Let's get this herd moving."

What did he mean by that? *Better that I had more sense instead.* Did he dislike this growing awareness between them as much as she did? Had she become an irritating distraction? A temptation he was struggling to ignore and couldn't?

He took the reins and moved into position near the front of the gather, leaving her frustrated by his response and his ability to change his focus as easily as he changed a shirt.

He was leaving her, she reminded herself firmly. Moving on to his damned office job. If he could be so focused on this trail drive despite the temptations between them, then she could, too.

Resolute, Carina followed him and scanned the mass of cowhide and her men surrounding it—Stinky Dale and Jesse as point riders, Ronnie Bennington, Billy Aspen and Orlin as drag riders, and the rest of the outfit in between as flank. Each ready and waiting.

"Hee-yah! Hee-yah!"

McClure's yell set the cattle into motion. The prairie rumbled from the thunder of their hooves; the air filled with a noisy mix of bellows and the cowboys' shouts. Happy Sam barreled off the grass and into the sandy stream with the rest of the herd behind him, sending up a spray of river water in their wake.

It didn't take long, considering the number of beeves, their speed and the breadth of the stream. But Carina spied an ornery calf bolting from its mother's side to veer back and steal a drink, and she spurred the Appaloosa to take off after him. By the time she circled the little stray back toward the herd again, the rest had roared into the distance, driven hard by the cowboys determined to keep them moving.

She met up with Ronnie farther down the stream, rounding up a few stragglers, too, and added the calf to his bunch.

"Did we get them all?" she asked, turning in her saddle to check.

"Reckon so, ma'am, but I lost Orlin. He and I were runnin' after these critters, and then he just disappeared."

She sighed. Where could he be? She glanced at the herd, looking small in a cloud of dust, the drone from their hooves fading. "All right. You go on. Join the others. I'll see if I can find him. He's got to be around here somewhere."

"Yes, ma'am." Releasing a sharp whistle, Ronnie prodded the recalcitrant cows forward.

Carina headed in the opposite direction and battled a healthy dose of annoyance. The ranch hand had better have a good excuse for losing himself. There weren't that many places to go, in land as flat as this.

Yet, there *was* an elevated ridge of prairie farther downstream….

Suddenly, someone yelled out, startling her. Her hand went for the Colt at her hip, just as a horse and rider took off like a cut cat from within a thicket of wild plum bushes near that ridge.

Orlin. He rode alongside the streambed as if Lucifer himself was on the chase. Carina braced herself for gunshots, for someone in hot pursuit, but there was nothing, no one….

"Orlin! Orlin!" she called.

His head came up just as his horse slowed, faltered and abruptly dipped. The ranch hand screamed, lost his seat and went down. His mount flailed and kicked, and Carina realized with a jolt of alarm they'd ridden right into a pocket of quicksand.

The horse shrieked in fear, head swinging, legs stepping high. And sinking. Carina galloped toward them both, her rope ready. Finally, his strength superior, the horse stumbled out and bolted toward dryer ground.

Orlin wasn't as lucky.

"Miss Lockett! Help!"

He floundered in the sand and managed to get himself upright. Panting, panicked, he stood in the wet mess up to his knees.

"Don't move, Orlin!" Carina ordered. "You'll only go deeper."

"Get me out of here!" Eyes wild, he struggled harder.

"No one ever drowned in quicksand." Far as she knew, she was telling him the truth. She knotted a fast loop on her rope. "But the more you move, the deeper you'll sink, then the harder it'll be to get you out."

"It's sucking me in!" he shrieked.

And that it was. Wet sand, shifting, creeping up to his thighs.

"I'm going to throw my rope at you, Orlin. Grab it, understand?"

"Hurry!" The pitch of his voice grated shrill. *"Hurry!"*

She swirled the lariat high over her head and gave the loop a smooth toss. He lunged for the hemp with both hands.

"Put the rope around your shoulders. That's right." She kept talking, figured he needed to hear the sound of her voice. "I'm going to pull you out, real careful, like we did with that cow stuck in the mud, remember? Hang on now."

She tied the hemp around the saddle horn; aided by the skill of her horse, she carefully inched him higher through the sand.

"Oh, Miss Lockett, Miss Lockett."

The raw terror on his face cut her deep. This wasn't the Orlin she knew—lazy, at times belligerent, prone to foolish mistakes. This man was a stranger, his anguish born of some nightmare he alone knew. What had happened in that thicket?

"We're almost there," she said.

The sand clung to his pant legs, the tops of his boots. His knuckles turned white from gripping the rope, but at last, the pit released him with a slurp, he stumbled out, fell to his knees. And sobbed.

Carina slid off her horse, sympathy running strong through her, and knelt beside him. Had she ever seen a man cry so hard before?

"You're okay, Orlin," she said gently. "You're just fine now."

He slumped into her arms, his shoulders shaking, and she took him against her. Held him until his sobs quieted. Carina tried not to think of McClure and the herd, leaving them farther behind.

The cowboy drew back, blew his nose into his bandanna.

"I'm rightly sorry for acting like this, Miss Lockett. It all caught up with me, I guess. Thinkin' I was gonna die in that quicksand, right after I was thinkin' I saw an Injun back there in the thicket." He sniffled, stuffed the bandanna into his back pocket, blew out a breath.

"Well, did you?"

Her glance darted toward the bushes. It was possible a rebellious brave had left the reservations, she supposed. Renegades stealing cattle had been an ongoing problem for drovers for years. But this far from Indian Territory?

"I didn't stick around to find out for sure." He shuddered.

She slipped her lariat from his shoulders. "Why not?"

He stared down at the sandy ground. "I ain't never told no one in the outfit this, ma'am, but I'm plumb scared of Injuns."

She nodded, knowing it already. "Did they ever do anything to you?"

His eyes squeezed shut. Opened again. A haunted look filled them. "A band of 'em on the warpath, back in Missouri not even a year ago. Killed my wife and two little girls, then burned my cabin to the ground. I was herdin' my sheep, and heard everyone screamin'. By the time I ran home—" he swallowed "—it was too late."

"Oh, Orlin." Compassion swept through her. "I'm sorry."

"I up and left, else I would've died from pure grief. That's when I came to Texas and hired on with the C Bar C." He sniffled again. "I ain't been no good to you as a cowboy, I know. Might be I should've left after the roundup. But I didn't."

She coiled her rope, loop by loop. His scare had opened the gate to his talk-box. Carina didn't mind listening. "Why not?"

He looked at her with red-rimmed eyes. "It ain't fair what happened to you with your Callie Mae. Just like it weren't fair what happened to me."

"No." The tragedy of their circumstances different, yet similar. Her heart tugged. "No, it wasn't."

"I've been nothin' but a heap of trouble for you, but I want you to get your young'un back, Miss Lockett. That's why I stayed. To help."

Emotion pushed up into her throat. For a moment, she couldn't speak.

He'd started out as green as a greenhorn could be. The trail drive had been difficult, more for him than anyone else in the outfit. Yet he endured it for her and Callie Mae. Worse, Carina knew she hadn't made it any easier. How many times had she snapped her impatience for something he had—or hadn't—done?

Regretting it, she embraced him in a quick hug. "Thank you, Orlin. I appreciate it more than you know."

"Naw, I have to be the one doin' the thankin'. You saved my life in that there quicksand. If you hadn't come along, I'd still be stuck in it and goin' down fast."

She released him with a smile. "You wouldn't have drowned, you know."

He shivered. "Glad I don't have to find out."

She stood up with him, noted the sand caked to his wet denims and boots. He'd have a miserable time of it until they made it to camp for a change of clothes.

He retrieved his hat, pushed it onto his head. "Reckon we'd best get going before Mr. McClure gets worried."

"You go on without me." She mounted up, returned the coiled lariat to its place against her saddle. "I'm going to keep looking for strays."

"Reckon Ronnie got 'em all." He slid an apprehensive look toward the thicket as he climbed onto his horse.

"I'd hate to lose any of my cows to gyp water, Orlin. Won't take me long."

He hesitated, clearly reluctant to leave her alone. "If you're sure."

"I am. Go on."

"Keep a watch out, then." He touched a finger to his brim and rode off, calmer for his ordeal, and oblivious to the lie she told him.

Driven by a hunch that whoever had given Orlin the scare of his life was the same man she'd glimpsed in her mirror yesterday morning, she headed straight for those wild plum bushes.

She kept a hand on the butt of her Colt, her eyes keen for movement. Carina didn't appreciate being followed by someone not man enough to admit he was, and she had every intention of letting him know it.

"Take your hand off that gun, Carina. I can shoot faster than you can."

The hair on the back of her neck rose. She drew up. A horse moseyed out of the shadows, carrying a rider with his revolver trained to her chest.

Recognition hit, and she froze. She'd been all but sure she wouldn't find a warrior hiding in the thicket. She'd been sure she'd find Rogan Webb instead.

She hadn't expected his gunslinger accomplice, Durant.

"But I'm no good to you dead, am I?" She crossed her wrists over the saddle horn, keeping her hands in plain sight, giving herself the appearance of a calm she was far from feeling. "Where's Rogan?"

He smiled coldly. "With his mother and Callie Mae, I believe."

At the sound of her daughter's name, she kept her features impassive. Refused to let the man know how instant yearning shot through her, hot as a branding iron.

"You know of her whereabouts, then."

"I'm quite aware of where she is."

He said nothing more, toying with her, and damn him, what did he hope to see her do? Get down on her knees and beg him for the information she craved?

She was on the brink of it, for sure. But how was she

to know he'd tell her the truth if she did? What would he gain by it?

Nothing, she realized suddenly. There was something he wanted from *her*, instead of the other way around. No other reason why he showed himself, considering all he had at stake.

The knowledge gave her the control she'd come precariously close to losing.

"Would you like to know where she is, Carina?" he asked. He leaned forward; his thumb absently stroked the butt of his revolver. "Because if you do, I have a proposition for you."

She braced herself. "What kind of proposition?"

"Rogan doesn't give a damn about what happens to Callie Mae," he said. "But then, maybe you already know that."

"I've spent the last ten years knowing it. What does that have to do with us now?"

"It means, I can tell you how to find her. For a price, of course."

Hope quickened her pulse. "Name it."

"We split the money from your herd fifty-fifty."

She blinked. Replayed the terms of the deal again in her brain. "And Rogan gets nothing?"

"Not a dime. He'll never find out we changed his plans until it's too late to stop us."

"Don't play me for a fool!" she snapped, suddenly angry. "Why would you offer me terms like that? You helped him kidnap Callie Mae. You wouldn't do the crime unless he gave you a fair cut of the ransom. You could get the same money from him."

"Yep." He nodded, nonplussed. "But I trust you more."

Her lip curled. "You trust me more?"

"Put yourself in my place, Carina." He sighed, as if she were being obtuse. "Trust a greedy bastard with the law breathing revenge down his neck. Or a mother who wants to have her child back. Who would I think would be the guaranteed deal?"

Carina was tempted. Sorely. Could she trust Durant to reveal Callie Mae's whereabouts? She didn't know. But if she dared, if he saw the bargain done, she'd have Callie Mae *and* enough money to keep from losing the ranch. She'd have to lay a few ground rules, of course, but—

"Whatever you're thinking, Carina—" McClure's voice shattered her thoughts "—don't."

Chapter Fifteen

Penn rode closer and kept Rogan Webb's accomplice in his rifle's sights. He'd heard enough of the conversation between them to know Durant intended to double cross Rogan. His gut told him Carina's silence meant she was giving serious consideration to going along with it.

Like hell she would.

Carina's head whipped toward him. "He knows where they are. We might get Callie Mae home sooner."

"I don't think so." He halted next to her, the barrel of the Winchester pressed to his shoulder, his eye still on the black-suited lowlife who kept his gun trained on her. "Don't trust him, Carina."

"It won't hurt to hear him out."

She didn't seem to notice she could be shot any time Durant took the notion. Had she even thought Rogan might be with him, watching somewhere out of sight, conspiring with Durant for reasons Penn couldn't fathom yet?

"So why the change of heart, Durant?" Penn demanded, ignoring her.

"Who's asking?"

Penn didn't respond.

Carina moved to do it for him. "He's—"

"Trail boss," Penn said before she could say his name. "You and Rogan have a falling-out?"

Durant's glance bounced between them. "Quite the opposite. We get along famously."

"And yet you're here, talking to betray him. Why?"

"I have my reasons," Durant said.

"Care to share them with us?"

"No."

"What changed your mind, Durant? His crimes?" Penn hammered out the questions. "Are you afraid the government will throw you in prison, like they'll do to him when they find him?"

Carina sucked in a breath of surprise.

"Or do you think he'll betray you next? Steal your share of Carina's money?" Relentless, Penn continued the interrogation. "Maybe you've realized it'll be a cold day in hell when Rogan gets away with blackmailing her."

"Or maybe I've decided he's not worth shit when it comes to being a father!" Durant snapped.

Penn lowered the rifle a fraction. *That* he hadn't expected.

"Look, the girl deserves better, all right?" Durant shifted, straining the leather on his saddle and looking furious. "She should be with her mother. I didn't see it at first, but now I do. He made me see it."

"How?" Skeptical, Penn had to ask. "What'd he do that made you decide?"

"Does it matter, McClure?" Carina demanded in a sharp tone. "He's willing to—"

"McClure?" Shock drained the blood on Durant's face. "Hell. *Penn* McClure?"

Penn's muscles coiled, one after the other. "That's right."

"You son of a bitch!" Durant's lips pulled back in a feral snarl, his revolver swung toward him—

But Penn's finger was faster. The Winchester fired. Durant's body jerked from the force of the hit, and his shot went wild. Crimson bloomed stark against the white of his shirt.

Carina screamed. Durant dropped from his horse and didn't move.

They slid off their mounts. Carina rushed toward Durant and bent over him. Penn followed, his rifle aimed. Durant's revolver lay in the grass, and Penn kicked it aside, out of reach.

"You've killed him!" she gasped.

"Didn't have a choice," he said and lowered the Winchester.

"Now we won't find out where Callie Mae is." She straightened; with a frustrated cry, she planted both palms against Penn's chest and pushed, hard enough he had to take a step back to keep his balance. "Do you hear me? He would've told us where she is!"

"Not until he had the money, Carina," he grated. "By then, it would've been too late."

"If I've lost her, I'll make you regret it to your dying days. I swear I will."

"I'll find her," he said, the avowal fervent.

Her bosom heaved as she fought to control her frustration. Violet lightning sparked from the stormy depths of her eyes. "You lied to me."

He tried to remember when. And failed. "No."

"You said you were an office worker. You weren't, were you?" Her fury gathered steam. "Are you a killer someone hired to go after Durant and Rogan? Or a bounty hunter?"

"No. Nothing like that."

"Durant knew you. How? From Rogan?"

"Carina."

Penn didn't want her to find out like this. The deception he'd kept in place to satisfy his revenge. Up to now, his motives were his own. So were his methods. She had enough on her mind worrying about Callie Mae.

But Durant's death changed everything.

"I'm an agent with the Secret Service. The Treasury Department. Or at least I used to be until I resigned to find Rogan," he said. "I never lied to you about working in an office. I did."

"You're a government agent?" The fury wavered. "What has Rogan done that made you want to hunt him down?"

"He's a master thief," Penn said, giving her the truth. She wouldn't have settled for anything less. Not anymore. "He was part of an elusive counterfeit ring. He's helped bilk banks of hundreds of thousands of dollars."

"What?" Shock stole the blood from her face.

"Just like he's trying to bilk you."

"Oh, my God."

"He killed the woman I intended to marry."

The words rumbled from him of their own accord, the purging of the hate, the anguish, he'd lived with month after month. Abigail's betrayal, and the price she paid for it.

"Oh, my God," Carina said again and pressed her fingers to her lips. "He's a criminal, a murderer, and *he has my daughter!*"

Penn's mouth tightened. She didn't need to hear how much that scared him. "Yes."

"Mavis." Carina's breathing quickened. "Does she know? Or is she involved with his counterfeiting, too?"

"She's not involved. As far as her knowing of his crimes, time will tell if she does."

He'd combed through Rogan's background, investigated his activities with every resource available. Nowhere had he found evidence of the woman's involvement.

"Callie Mae is safe with her," Penn said. "If it's any comfort."

"It's not." She curled her arms and fumed into the sky. "He's such a bastard. I want to kill him myself."

Penn reached out, took her elbow, pulled her against him. "Not unless I kill him first."

She came willingly, a sign she'd gotten used to him touching her. Might be she needed him to right now anyway. Penn was happy to oblige.

Her warmth soaked into him, brought with it an awareness of the fullness of her breasts pressed to his chest, of how the hems of her riding skirt flapped against his Levi's and the bulk of her gun belt pressed low against his belly.

Yet the rigidity in her slim body revealed the tension still inside her. The fear, the worry, from Durant's death. Penn figured they both needed a few minutes to absorb what just happened.

"This woman you wanted to marry—" But she halted, her voice stiff against his shoulder.

He sensed the curiosity about Abigail her pride struggled to contain. He removed her hat, let it hang against her back from its cord, then met the violet-blue in her eyes, no longer stormy. But troubled.

"She was a government agent for the Treasury Department, too," he said. "I met her when we were assigned to Rogan's case. I never knew she was working with him until the day we were to be wed."

A faint shake of her head revealed her sympathy. "She double crossed you, then."

"I wasn't smart enough to see it coming."

"You're one of the smartest men I know, McClure. She must've been good at it to fool you."

He grunted. How many times had he tried to convince himself of that very thing?

"Are you still in love with her?" Carina asked, chin kicked high.

He held her proud gaze. She'd be thinking of the kisses he'd taken from her, the ones she gave freely and he enjoyed without guilt.

"Hard to keep loving a woman who never loved anyone but herself," he said gruffly.

The hurt was gone, he realized. Crumpled to nothing beneath the ugliness of all Abigail had done. Carina herself had shown him how deep a woman's love could be for the things that meant most to her. A child, a home and land.

Or a man...

"Once you realized she betrayed you, then what happened?" Carina asked in a tone turned commiserating.

His thoughts dragged backward to the past. To Rogan. "Things turned ugly. When the smoke cleared, I'd killed two men in Rogan's counterfeiting ring. He'd shot Abigail and escaped. He has as much revenge to exact off me as I do him."

Carina drew back. "And now my daughter is in the middle of it."

Penn hesitated. Recognized the unfairness, same as she did. "Yes."

"I won't rest until he's in jail or dead." Her gaze turned hard. "I prefer dead."

Penn admired a woman whose thinking followed his. "So do I."

As if impatient for it to happen, she abruptly stepped away. Durant, blood-soaked and motionless, lay on the grass at their feet.

She frowned. "In the meantime, we have him to take care of. And my herd is closer to Dodge City than we are."

Her urgency reached out to him. He put away his rifle, and they set to work taking care of matters while his mind filled with what lay ahead. Repercussions from Durant's death.

But Rogan's response to it, most of all.

* * *

Callie Mae sat on a wooden bench outside the Salina train station and watched her grandmother pace back and forth. The conductor had already made the first call to board for the trip to Kansas City, and there were only a few people left on the platform.

Rogan wasn't one of them.

Grandmother didn't know where he was. Callie Mae didn't, either, but she was as sure as could be he wasn't coming. Grandmother was convinced he was just late and would arrive any minute.

Callie Mae let her go on thinking it.

Rogan had been all pouty and cold as a fish last night at dinner, and later, at the Opera House. He hardly even looked at her, let alone spoke a civil word to her, so why would he want to go to Europe with her?

Callie Mae didn't care one whit what he did or didn't do. She had other things to worry about.

Like how to escape Grandmother.

Her heart pounded her ribs from being scared she wouldn't find a way. She just couldn't get on that train. If she did, she'd have a terrible time finding her way home again. By then, Mama would've given Rogan the money for her herd and lost the C Bar C.

Callie Mae couldn't let that happen.

She'd caused enough trouble already.

She didn't have much time left. Minutes, maybe. What would she do when the conductor made the final call to board?

"Oh, where is that boy?" Grandmother fussed, shading her eyes and peering down the street toward the Metropolitan Hotel. Again.

"Guess he's not coming," she said.

Callie Mae's gaze slid toward the baggage car and the last trunk being loaded. Except for the red plaid taffeta one she was wearing today, all her beautiful new dresses and shoes were in that car. If things worked out right, she'd never see them again.

"That's ridiculous. Of course, he's coming." But Grandmother bit her lip and looked worried.

Callie Mae's gaze switched direction. Toward the rail yard. Trains came through Salina all day, every day, she knew. From every direction, too.

"He never did know what a clock was for," Grandmother huffed. "How dare he be so irresponsible? And today, of all days."

One of those trains would be going to Dodge City….

"I'll insist the conductor wait for him a little longer." Grandmother nudged her satchel closer to the bench for Callie Mae's safekeeping. "Stay right here, darling, while I speak to him."

She turned and strode toward the man, her skirts swishing, her heels clomping in determination on the wooden platform.

Callie Mae's heart pounded harder.

Now. She should run now….

But she couldn't.

She was too scared.

The clomping stopped. Grandmother tapped the conductor's shoulder. He swung toward her with a smile.

Callie Mae had to think. She had to be smart. Could

she do it? Run away to Dodge City by herself even though she'd never been there before?

It was so far away….

Grandmother's thin nose lifted in that hoity-toity way of hers. She said something, and the conductor's smile faded.

Callie Mae knew she had to act soon, but she had no food, no money.

Still, she reminded herself, she was ten years old. Old enough to take care of herself if she had to…

The conductor shook his head. Grandmother's words came louder, more insistent. Demanding. He pulled his watch from his vest pocket, read the time and shook his head again.

Callie Mae slid to the edge of the bench. She stared hard at the rail yard, the trains heading west. Long trains, with empty cattle cars, big enough to hide in.

The voices fell silent. She swiveled her stare back. Grandmother removed her leather wallet from her pocketbook, withdrew a few bills, thrust them at the conductor. His face turned red with outrage.

Callie Mae's gaze clung to those bills. She'd never stolen a single cent before. Ever. But she'd give her eyeteeth for some of that money right now. Any way she could get it.

The conductor drew himself up and returned his watch to its place in his pocket. He spun on his heel and strode away from Grandmother.

"All aboard!" he shouted to the few people lingering on the platform. "Final call! All aboard!"

Callie Mae's heart jumped to her throat. No! Not

yet! She couldn't get on that train. She had to escape. She had to hide and find a way to survive, and she just couldn't let Grandmother give the conductor those tickets—

Her panic halted.

The tickets!

Grandmother had tucked all three into the side pocket of her satchel, keeping them within easy reach for their boarding. Callie Mae could see them now, the ends sticking out….

Except, Rogan wasn't coming. He wouldn't be using his passage to New York, and Grandmother paid so much money for him to go.

Money Callie Mae could use to get to Dodge City.

Money that would go to waste if she didn't.

She didn't take time to ponder if it was right or wrong; she just bent down and plucked his ticket out, then quickly stuffed the slip of printed paper into the pocket of her red plaid dress.

And before Grandmother caught her at it, too. She still looked mad about the conductor refusing to delay his train on Rogan's account. Which meant she'd be extra mad about Rogan not showing up and ruining her plans.

She strode across the platform with another round of loud, indignant clomping.

"Let's go, Callie Mae," she said sharply. "We'll leave without your father and have a wonderful time, just the two of us."

She snatched the satchel and stormed toward the train. In her fury, she didn't take Callie Mae's hand, as she always did, and before her grandmother could notice, Callie Mae took a breath, bolted from the bench and ran in the opposite direction.

Dodge City, Three Days Later

Rogan had the sick feeling something was wrong.

He sat in the Long Branch Saloon and stared broodingly into his glass of whiskey. His plans didn't include sitting at this table, in a dark corner, alone. Durant should be with him, fine-tuning the details that would close the deal against Carina.

He wasn't. In fact, Durant wasn't anywhere in this stinking cow town. Rogan had scoured every hotel, every boardinghouse, every brothel, looking for him. He walked the streets, up and down, and hadn't found a sign. He searched the liveries and the saloons and even the local jail.

Nothing.

Rogan lifted the glass, frowned, thought of how he'd escaped Salina in the dead of night, before his mother had an inkling he was gone. He'd endured the long ride to Dodge City solely on the anticipation of meeting up with Durant again to finish the last phase of their scheme. They'd agreed upon the day, the time, the place.

Durant wouldn't have forgotten.

Where was he?

Did Mother have something to do with his absence? Her wrath could be formidable, her vengeance nothing less. Had she been so furious from realizing Rogan had no intention of going to Europe that she tried to ruin his plans in revenge?

It'd be just like her, the conniving shrew.

But then, she'd have to know he'd retaliate, too. Incriminate her by telling of her part in their blackmail plan first chance he got. Why would she risk it?

Rogan swirled the amber liquid, shifted his thinking toward possible motives for the gunslinger's disappearance. Was Durant out on the trail, following Carina, making sure she stayed cooperative? Had something happened to her or the herd to throw them off the trail and off schedule? Or had Durant changed his mind about the blackmail?

As soon as the last thought formed, Rogan discarded it. Durant wouldn't walk away from all that beautiful money. Not a chance.

No, he had to be in trouble. How or where or by whom, Rogan didn't know yet, but if it wasn't Mother, the idea Penn McClure might have something to do with it turned his skin clammy from a cold sweat.

He threw back the last of the whiskey. The burn in his throat cleared his mind, filled him with a rush of comfort.

There was no way Penn McClure could connect him with Durant.

Was there?

Rogan vowed to be more careful than ever, just in case. He had to think through every angle, expect the unexpected. He was so close to getting Carina's money. So close…

Hell, maybe Durant was just fine and had tried to contact him about his whereabouts. A possibility Rogan hadn't thought of until now. The gunslinger could've sent a wire while Rogan was in Salina, and the message might be waiting for him at this very moment.

Rogan set his glass down, pulled the brim of his hat lower over his eyes and hustled out of the Long Branch. It didn't take long to reach the telegraph station. Took even less time to read the paper the operator gave him.

Rogan's blood chilled at the words.

Durant's dead.

The message was signed by Penn McClure.

Chapter Sixteen

Outside of Dodge City

Carina sat on the lush Kansas grass, tilted her head back and stared up into the night sky. Stars sparkled down at her; crisp evening air filled her lungs. A short distance away, her beloved herd rested, their long-horned, blackened shapes visible as far as she could see.

She'd lost track of the hour, knew only that Sourdough would've cleaned up supper by now, and the outfit would be sprawled around the chuck wagon, bellies full from his infamous son-of-a-bitch stew, bodies tired from this, their last day on the trail.

She should've been exhausted, too. Relieved the drive had finally come to an end. Filled with cautious hope and anticipation of finally getting her daughter back soon.

She was all those things, yes. Yet she battled a strange melancholy that left her with the need to spend some time alone to sort through it.

McClure had been gone for five days, and she missed him more than she'd ever thought she could miss a man.

At some point, Carina gave up fighting it. Which would've been about the time she accepted the fact she'd fallen in love with him.

It shouldn't have happened. She'd broken her own rule about getting involved with one of her hired men, but this feeling, this obsession, was unlike anything she'd felt since she fancied herself in love with Rogan Webb back in her wild, foolish days.

And look where *that* got her.

She had plenty to think about now that they had finally reached Dodge City. Like how she'd have to toughen up instead of feeling all mushy inside whenever she got to ruminating about Penn McClure. Which was just about every spare minute. Or when she looked for him to ride up from over a bluff, or around a curve in the trail. Which was the whole day through.

Sighing, she removed her hat and set it on the ground beside her. Ironic he hadn't been the one to drive her cattle to Dodge City, after all, but saw to it that Jesse and Stinky Dale did in his place. He'd taken Durant's body into Ashland for the local mortician to care for, said he had some business to attend to once he got there.

Secret Service business. What else could it be? Her pride kept her from asking for sure or even when he'd be back, but she couldn't help being struck by how Durant's death had changed the cards on her. Put them in

McClure's favor. Helped bring him one step closer in satisfying his revenge against Rogan.

Carina didn't care about revenge, McClure's or anyone else's. She just wanted Callie Mae home again.

Troubled, she loosened the strip of rawhide tied at her nape, allowed her hair to fall in a heavy mass over her shoulders, her back. Unbound and free.

If only she could be free, too, of this awful heartache, this terrible fear of being alone. Of being without her little girl.

Or not having a man in her life.

McClure, at her side.

Why did she have to go all weak and let him mean something to her? The days had been long, too long, since he left. He was always on her mind, some way or another. Why had she allowed him to be?

She shouldn't have. It just happened, out of her control. When she least expected it.

Maybe he wasn't coming back. He could have figured his debt to her had been paid in full now that her herd arrived in Dodge City, thanks to Jesse and Stinky Dale. He could think there was nothing to keep him in the C Bar C outfit anymore.

Nothing to keep him with her.

She covered her face with her hands and despaired over how it would all end. How she would survive if she lost everything. Her daughter, her ranch, the man she'd grown to love.

"Carina."

The low voice penetrated her thoughts and brought her straight up with a jerk. She twisted to find him walking toward her from the direction of the chuck wagon. McClure, in the flesh. Masculine, tall, lean in the dark night.

She bolted to her feet, her pulse racing. He'd come back when she'd all but convinced herself he wouldn't. He strode toward her, a vision of power and agile grace, and in that moment, she wanted to be less boss and more woman. She wanted to throw herself in his arms so he could kiss her senseless.

"You shouldn't be out here alone," he said. "It's getting late."

"I needed to think."

He halted in front of her, so close she could smell the saddle leather on him. The day's ride and the night's tobacco, too.

He reached out his hand, as if he intended to touch her. But drew back, as if he decided against it. "You've got a lot on your mind."

God, but she wanted him to hold her. "More than you know."

"Don't be so sure." He regarded her, long moments between them. She sensed he had plenty on his mind, as well. "It's almost over, Carina."

She crossed her arms, shivered from all she stood to lose. "We've got a ways to go yet."

"Tomorrow, everything will change."

So little time left. Only minutes and hours. Yet it seemed like forever.

"What's going to happen, McClure?" she asked quietly. The shadows hid the planes and angles of his face, but his strength soaked into her. "Will Rogan give me my daughter like he said he would?"

McClure hesitated. "There's a chance he won't. At least, not right away. And maybe not even then. You have to be prepared for it."

She swallowed, hated the truth in his words. "How can any mother prepare herself?"

"All of us, we'll do what we can to find her, bring her home. You know that."

Her men. The loyal C Bar C outfit. Their moods had been somber around the campfire tonight. Their silence grim while they ate their stew.

"They didn't want to go into town tonight," she said, staring into the sky. Their devotion moved her then, as it did now. "They don't feel like celebrating the end of the drive."

"They don't want you to give your herd over to him."

"They know I don't have a choice."

"Carina."

At the roughness in his voice, her gaze snapped to him. "We've been through this before, McClure. It doesn't matter you disagree with me. It has to happen."

"Rogan is wanted by the United States government. He has serious crimes to pay for. You can't make it easy for him to commit another one by blackmailing you."

"The hell I can't!" Her voice rose in frustration. Did he think it was something she *wanted* to do?

"I have a plan, Carina." Suddenly, he stilled, slashed his dark gaze toward the low rise of the bluffs behind her. "Someone's coming."

She turned, spied a horse and rider emerging from the shadows. Moonlight glinted on the barrel of a revolver.

McClure kept his eyes on the man who rode boldly

toward them from the opposite direction of their camp and nowhere near the herd. By the cut of his clothing, the style of his hat, his daring to approach with a drawn weapon, Carina knew he wasn't any cowboy of her acquaintance.

McClure tensed, breathed a terse oath. "Let me handle this."

He pulled the brim of his Stetson lower over his forehead and stepped back from her, shaking his head as if he was disgusted about something.

"He's about as lazy as a hound dog in the sun, Miss Lockett," he said in a loud, exaggerated drawl Carina had never heard before. "I'll tell him to pack up his gear and hit the road, then, like you said." He ignored her confusion, glanced up and smiled amiably at the rider. "Evenin'. You lookin' for the C Bar C boss?"

"I am." The rider reined in.

"Well, you just found her. I'll let you two have at it, but don't be too late, y'hear, Miss Lockett? Ain't safe for you out here by yourself. I'll keep an eye out for you, just in case."

He touched a finger to his brim, turned and sauntered away, leaving her to play along and keep his identity safe. A match struck flint, and the flame illuminated Rogan Webb's face.

"Hello, Carina. You made it to Dodge City, I see," he purred.

"Where's Callie Mae?" she demanded.

"They told me at the stockyard office your herd had arrived." The match flame licked at the end of his cigar. "And right on schedule, too."

"I won't give you a single cent until you tell me where she is."

He puffed once, twice. The air filled with the scent of the tobacco. "Do you think you're in control here, Carina? Because you're not. Not at all."

He might be right in that regard, but she had the advantage over him, in ways he had yet to realize. She aimed for a new angle of attack.

"Where's Durant?" she taunted.

"He's gone."

Her brow arched in mock surprise. "Is he? Where?"

"So the money from your herd is all mine."

"Did the law catch up with him, Rogan?"

"It's none of your damn business where he is!" Rogan snapped.

Ruthless, she pressed on. "Just like the law will catch up with you. Then you'll find out your blackmail scheme wasn't as perfect as you thought."

"I'll be long gone by then. And rich enough to stay that way." He puffed furiously. "They've left, Carina. Headed toward Europe."

Her mind scrambled to keep up with his. "Callie Mae and Mavis?" Pain sliced through her. "How do you know? Have you seen them?"

"Of course I have. Before they boarded the train headed East. She was right here in Kansas, Carina, dear. And you didn't even know it."

Carina began to bleed, deep inside. Oh, God. Close. So damned close. "Where is she now?"

"On the ship, I suspect."

"Which one?"

"I have the itinerary with all that information. Locked safely away, of course. When you give me the cattle money, I'll tell you how to find the itinerary." He lowered the cigar and smiled.

Furious impatience roared through her to give him what he wanted and see the scheme done.

"What do I have to do?" she grated.

"Tomorrow, a cattle buyer by the name of Edward Lonner will approach you with an offer to buy the herd. Don't take it."

"Why not?"

"He's the man my mother chose to handle the arrangements. I'm going to change them."

"To what?" she asked, taken aback.

"George Satterfield has bought C Bar C herds for years, hasn't he?"

Rogan had been thorough in his investigation. Woollie preferred working with Satterfield over the scores of other cattle buyers who swarmed into cow towns and stockyards to bargain for beef.

"Yes," she admitted.

"Deal only with him," Rogan ordered. "Business as usual, understand? Have him pay you in my name and leave the bank draft at the Wright House on Front Street. Return in twenty-four hours, and the itinerary will be waiting for you."

"Twenty-four hours!" How could she wait that long?

"It's as simple as that, my dear Carina." His smile came again, cold and calculated.

"Go to hell."

"I have places far more pleasurable in mind." He

nudged his horse into a slow turn, kept the revolver trained on her. "Until tomorrow, then. And let me remind you, any attempts to put a bullet in my back in the next few minutes will keep you from finding Callie Mae for a long, long time."

Had she ever hated a man more? Fuming, frustrated, all but frantic, Carina had no choice but to stand there and watch him disappear into the black night.

It was all Penn could do to let him go.

He crouched behind some brush and strained to hear what he could of the conversation. He gleaned enough to know Rogan had set down some ground rules to carry out his plan; Penn could see from the rigid stance of Carina's body the control she struggled to keep while he did.

But to ride after him now would only jeopardize Callie Mae's return, and Penn couldn't risk it. Once Rogan recognized him, he'd bolt to avoid arrest. Or shoot. Or worse. Penn had come too far to chance losing him to the criminal underworld and be forced to hunt him down all over again. Better to play the game until the odds were better for Carina, and Rogan fell complacent, assured he was in control.

For now, Carina concerned him more. She looked so damned alone, watching Rogan ride off. The sight of her tore at Penn's insides.

He rose and left the brush. He halted next to her and had to fight hard to keep from taking her into his arms.

"I'll do everything I can," he said simply.

She turned toward him. "Yes." Her voice sounded hushed, resigned, in the night. "I know you will."

"It won't be much longer." The words sounded trite, but they were the truth.

Her shoulders lifted as she drew in a breath, then exhaled it all in a rush. The anguish she struggled to contain. "What if she doesn't want to come back?"

This time, he couldn't help it. He hooked his arm around her neck, over that thick mass of brunette hair, and pulled her against him. "Carina, she will. You're her mother. The C Bar C is her home."

"Oh, McClure." She sank into his chest with a moan. "What if Mavis has been filling her head with lies? What if Callie Mae's having so much fun that she'll never want to live on the ranch again?"

He'd never seen Carina this unsure. This afraid. He slid his palm along her spine in long, slow strokes, searched his brain to find words of comfort and truth. And failed.

There weren't any.

Instead, he fisted his hand into the silken weight of her hair and gently tugged her back to look at him.

"No more what-if's," he growled.

The time had passed for useless assurances, for going through the motions of commiseration, no matter how genuine. Her fears ran too deep. They were too real. Too much like his own, besides, and he sought to reassure her in the only way he knew how.

He lowered his head to take her mouth to his. A small, hungry sound slipped from her throat, and she curled her arms around his back, pressed her body against him. She opened her mouth, and he angled his head, changed the purpose of the kiss to something far more selfish. He plunged his tongue into the warm, wet recesses of her mouth.

She met him with an eagerness he didn't expect. Her acceptance of his consolation fused into a bold invitation, a blatant *need,* that pushed him toward the edges of constraint. A side of Carina Lockett she'd let no man see, no man experience.

Except now.

Except him,

The heat in his blood flared into a burning desire to discover more. To tear apart the cool authority she always wore and lay open the warm femininity she always tried to hide.

And yet from the first moment he met her, he knew Carina Lockett was more woman than even Abigail had been. An intriguing blend of power and vulnerability that left him wanting. And fascinated.

He was fascinated still. Now. More than ever.

His hand slid from her back in a journey toward her breast. His palm anticipated the feel of those globes of supple flesh meant to be enjoyed by a man, by him, but suddenly, she curled her fingers around his wrist and stopped him before he got there.

Her breathing ragged, she broke off the kiss. Her dark gaze opened onto his. "Tell me one thing, and make it the truth."

His brain strained to exchange lust for coherent thought. "What?"

"Do you think of her when you kiss me?"

He stared stupidly down at her. "Who?"

"Abigail, McClure," she said. "Abigail."

"Hell, no," he said, without hesitation. He wanted her to believe him. It was important that she did. "She doesn't exist for me anymore, except as a bad mistake that should never have happened."

It'd been a long time in coming, he knew. His love for Abigail dying. Her betrayal had been a festering wound on his heart, but being with Carina these past weeks, trailing her cattle, fitting into her world, had been the balm he needed to heal.

Carina angled her face away. She would've stepped back if he let her.

"How can you not think of her? She was your betrothed. You loved her," she said.

There was that pride and vulnerability again. Both always managed to get under his skin, into his blood. He cupped her chin, forced her to look at him.

"Not anymore. I hold you in my arms, and you consume me," he said, his voice low, husky, his need to convince her running strong. "The things you make me feel—damn it, the thoughts in my head are of you alone, Carina." He pulled her hips to his, let the thickening of his manhood show he meant what he said, in a way where his words couldn't. "If I lied to you about that, then I'd be no better than she was."

Her gaze lingered on him, her mind working.

"Yes," she whispered.

He sensed the crumbling of her doubts. Felt it in the way her body softened against him.

"I told you I wanted you, remember?" He thought of the time, the place. The two of them together like this. His fingers lifted to the top button of her blouse, flipped it open. Did the same with the one below. "I didn't lie about that, either." She filled him with a craving to know how her hands would feel moving against his skin, her breasts snuggled warm against his chest. How many times had he hungered for it? "And I've always made it a practice to get what I want."

With the decisiveness so much a part of her, Carina eased away and plucked his Stetson from his head. "Well, then." She gave the hat a careless toss to the side, where it landed next to hers on the ground. "I appreciate a man who wants what I want." She removed her holster and guns; they landed with a soft thud. "So let's get to it."

His breath hitched. He replayed the words in his head to make sure she said what he thought she'd said.

And from the way her fingers parted his shirt and pulled it off his shoulders, he'd understood just fine. She dropped the garment next to their hats. His bandanna followed. The gun belt, too. When she set to unfastening his Levi's, Penn was all but panting from the anticipation.

He was going to be one hell of a lucky man soon.

But there were a few details which concerned him.

"It's chilly out here," he said, the words at odds with his fingers, fast unbuttoning her blouse. "That going to be a problem for you?"

"Not if we do this right." She pulled the blouse free of her riding skirt and off her body, leaving the ribbons of her pink camisole for his untying.

Which he did. In record time.

"Someone from the outfit might see. Could be embarrassing for you." A breach of the privacy that meant so much to her. "Lift your arms."

"He'll know to stay back and keep his mouth shut." Her arms lifted. "Or he's fired."

The camisole joined her blouse. Made her naked from the waist up. Penn stood stock-still and stared at her full, rounded breasts, shaded by moonlight and tipped with dark nipples, already pebbled from the cool air. Erect and ripe for suckling.

Fire roared through his veins.

"Carina." He strove to keep the fiery heat from raging out of control. "You're a damned beautiful woman, y'know that?"

She trembled in response, and they both went for the button holding her skirt closed, fumbling with the thing until it came open. The skirt rustled past her hips and legs and landed in a heap at her ankles.

Penn left her to the pantaloons. He saw to his Levi's. They both took care of their boots, and finally, *finally,* they stood together, naked and breathing rough from the desires raging through them.

Penn hovered on the brink of seeing them satisfied. Warred with the need to take her fast and hard—or to prolong the pleasure of the coming minutes, the ecstasy of sating his lust and hers.

He wouldn't have another chance like this. Not after tomorrow, when he saw his revenge against Rogan done. Carina would hate him for what he had to do. The plans he'd already made. She wouldn't understand. Not with Callie Mae first and foremost in her mind.

Penn only had now, this moment, and suddenly, a

raw urgency coursed through him. A need to take this time with her and lock it away, deep inside his chest. Make it precious and pure.

His very own, forever.

"Penn," she whispered.

His thoughts fled at the hushed intimacy in that lone word. His name, rarely spoken. He took her into his arms, held her in a tight, possessive embrace that had him reveling in the intoxicating feel of skin against skin. Breasts to chest. His blade quivered against the warmth of her belly. Her slim thighs pressed to his broader ones. His head lowered, and he took her lips to his. Their mouths clung with tongues twisted and curled.

This need for her…he hadn't known it could be this strong. This consuming. She stole his strength, filled his heart to bursting with an emotion he had no time to name. So full it hurt.

He eased her down with him to the ground, their clothes a blanket against the prickly grass. He rasped her name again and again, dragged his kisses from her mouth, to her cheek, down the satiny curve of her neck. He filled each palm with a delectable breast, flexed his fingers. And savored.

The ache built in him, fierce and intense. Demanded to be quenched. His senses filled with her musk, her heat. His mouth opened over one pert nipple, and he drew the swollen nub in with his tongue, swirled and teased and suckled until she speared her fingers into his hair with a moan. Holding him to her for more.

He repeated his pleasure on the other, gently nipped

the sensitive tip with his teeth, prolonging her arousal. Prolonging his own. His hands traveled lower, past her ribs, her waist....

Carina, pure female. Pure perfection. Penn had to know all of her. Every silken inch, and his fingers slid along the smooth skin to the nest of curls at the juncture of her thighs. Her feminine folds held the sweetness of her dew, invited him to taste her sensuality, her blatant need for him.

And his own raged higher still.

Her hips began to move. Her thighs loosened, parted beneath his touch. Her breathing quickened into little rasps.

"Come into me," she whispered, the sound aching. Her dark hair haloed her head, a pillow of brunette satin. "Now, Penn. Come."

She reached for him, and he obliged, rising above her with muscles trembling. He entered her silken depths with a single, slick thrust, found her tight, gloriously tight. He reveled at the feel of her heat sheathing him like this.

"Carina," he groaned, on the brink of falling into heaven. "Carina, Carina."

Her back arched, her hips moved, her urgency built. High, as high as his. Taking him with her to create a fierce rhythm, a rocking dance that sent them soaring, catapulting, up to the stars in a blindingly sweet explosion of release.

There was something primitive and carnal in their union, Carina mused, pleasant aftershocks still lingering in her body. Natural and untamed. Symbolic, too, maybe, lying here in McClure's arms with her cattle not far in the distance.

Two of the things that had become most important in her life.

Tomorrow, she would lose them both.

She could hardly bear to think of it. She chose to think instead of how he made her feel complete by filling the emptiness inside her. Woman and man, together as one.

If only for a little while.

"Cold?" His low voice sounded muffled against her hair.

"No." Far from it, not with the way she lay next to him, their arms and legs tangled.

He burrowed her closer anyway. Her fingers splayed against the taut muscles of his back; her palm flattened and glided over his heated skin with slow, lazy strokes.

When before would she have taken the liberty to touch him so freely?

When would she again?

"You're going back to the Secret Service, aren't you, McClure? When this is all over." Carina had to hear it. Maybe, then, it would be easier to accept.

"You called me 'Penn' when you were lovin' me up a few minutes ago."

Her mouth softened. "Did I?"

"I prefer it." He kissed the top of her head.

"You're avoiding my question."

A moment passed. "I find the job satisfying, Carina."

Her heart squeezed with sadness. "Because of Rogan's counterfeiting ring, I suppose."

She sounded petulant, and she chastised herself for it. She had no right to interfere in his life and want more than he was ready to give. Something hopeless like being with her on the C Bar C to live a life herding cattle. Far different than one the government would require.

"Bringing Rogan to justice is at the top of my list at the moment," he said. "I figure the agency will appreciate it well enough and won't much care how I got the job done."

"But—"

She felt a sudden flare of impatience in him.

"Enough, Carina."

He shifted his body over her, and she welcomed his weight, the delicious distraction of his warmth and strength. His blade stirred against the inside of her thigh. Pulsed with his growing desire.

"Rogan's not worth wasting what little time we have left together," he murmured.

His head lowered, his lips hovering a feather's breadth above hers. He filled her with the sweet anticipation of what he wanted. Of what she would soon have again. His mouth curved with a decidedly wicked, devastatingly male, grin.

"I, on the other hand, am."

Chapter Seventeen

The Next Morning

George Satterfield sat behind the desk in the tiny stockyard office and signed his name with a flourish. The bank draft bore the amount of payment in full for Carina's herd. At top market price. Nearly the entire worth of the C Bar C Ranch.

Callie Mae's legacy. Right there on that piece of paper.

Carina tore her gaze away. She should've been prepared—she'd had three long weeks on the trail to brace herself for today, this moment, the ugly knowledge that she would have to give it all away.

But she wasn't. Not even close. The numbers scrawled in black ink were too real. They only made the nightmare worse. The fortune she would lose.

Reaching over from the chair beside her, McClure, looking grim, took her hand into his. Despising her weakness, that she needed him to be here with her, she grasped his fingers tight.

Only one more line remained to be filled in. Satterfield's pen hovered above it.

He appeared as grim as McClure. "You sure about this, Carina? You want me to put Rogan Webb's name on this check?"

"It's nothing I want, George, believe me. It has to be done, that's all."

Beneath his gray moustache, his lips thinned but he said nothing more. The sound of the pen scratching the paper, laying down the ink, would be forever imprinted into her memory.

Finally, he set the writing instrument down and handed her the check. "I'm sorry, Carina. I wish it were easier for you."

"Easier?" Her brow arched at the odd comment. "To be blackmailed? Or pay ransom for one's child?"

He exchanged a glance with McClure. "Take your pick, I suppose."

"I'd rather not, I assure you." Carina released McClure's hand, folded the check and put it in her pocket. She stood up.

"I'd be happy to buy you a drink, if it'd help," Satterfield said, rising with her.

She managed a wan smile. "I might not know when to stop."

"If there's anything more I can do, just ask."

"There isn't, but thank you."

They made their goodbyes, and with his hand at her waist, McClure guided her out of the office. They paused on the boardwalk, and Carina contemplated the stockyards beyond. Huge pens filled with cattle, for as far as she could see. Great masses of beef on the hoof that would be loaded onto railcars for hungry markets back East. Soon, the C Bar C herd would join them.

The sharp feeling of loss, the terror of not being able to survive, of starting over again from nothing nearly crumpled her to her knees. What if she failed? What if she was never able to regain the Lockett legacy?

"You don't have to go to the Wright House alone," McClure said.

She strove for strength. The need to go on. Forced herself to look up, into eyes a troubled shade of brown. McClure had argued about her decision this morning. He'd argue again now if she allowed him.

"It's broad daylight. Rogan will recognize you if he's anywhere around," she said.

"I'm not going to hide under a rock just because the sun's shining."

"I can't risk it."

She strode toward her Appaloosa, hitched at the post next to his gelding. Nothing could go wrong. Nothing.

Untying the reins, she climbed into the saddle. He set his hands on his hips, watching her. His silence unnerved her.

"Don't do anything, McClure. Promise me."

He scowled. "He deserves to be behind bars."

"Yes." Or rot in hell, she didn't care which. "You can arrest him after I bring Callie Mae home. I have no doubt you will, besides." She deplored another argument where anyone could overhear. And Rogan would be waiting for her. She thought of the long hours stretching ahead before they heard from him again. "Why don't you go somewhere and have a drink or two? Think of me while you do."

"I don't need a saloon to think of you, Carina."

The growl set her nerve endings alive with the memory of their heated lovemaking only hours ago. The feel of his hands hungry over her body.

The smolder in his dark gaze revealed he thought of it, too. She gripped the reins to keep from vaulting out of the saddle and into his arms, to have him hold her one last time before she had to give away her precious world.

But she didn't, of course. She wouldn't get back on her horse.

"I'll see you back at camp," she said.

Carina turned the Appaloosa toward town, changed her focus to what she had to do, banking her trust on Rogan that he'll keep his end of their deal and Callie Mae would be hers again.

Penn swore at her stubbornness. That damnable pride. Wasn't right she had to be alone when she walked into the Wright House, gave away her money and walked out again, empty-handed.

He sighed. But the she-boss was tough. She'd manage it with that stubbornness and pride. And her leaving gave him the time alone he needed to fine-tune a few details.

The plan she didn't know about. And wouldn't, until he saw it through.

He mounted up. Out of habit, he skimmed his surroundings with a slow perusal of who might be around, watching. Nothing seemed out of the ordinary. This time of year, every season, cowmen from surrounding states filled the stockyards and mingled throughout the pens doing business one way or another.

He shifted his study toward the rail yards, too. Long ribbons of track laced the prairie; railcars waited to be loaded with livestock. Some already were, needing only the steam engine at the front of the line to stoke up its boilers and pull out.

And yet…his gaze snagged on something red. Plaid. A child walking beside one of the cattle cars. A little girl alone.

Penn shook his head in disapproval. Some cattleman's daughter, left to entertain herself while he conducted his financial affairs, most likely. She had no place being out there by herself. Too bad she was. He hoped her father found her soon enough and gave her a good scolding for wandering off. She had it coming, for sure.

Penn dismissed her from his mind. He turned the gelding, rode the short trip into town and headed toward the Long Branch Saloon. Horses lined the hitching posts along the front, but he found room for his on the end. Dodge City was booming, no doubt about it. A steady deluge of cowboys came at the end of their drives with their payroll in their pockets. Establishments like this one helped them spend it.

He walked in. Past the faro table, past the mahogany bar, past the curious glances from poker-playing wranglers, none of whom he recognized. He strode straight into the back room and closed the door.

Woollie glanced up from his beer. Penn grinned. Damned good to see his friend again.

"You got my message," he said.

"And you got mine." Woollie stood up, shook Penn's hand, his smile broad through his curly beard. "How's she doing?"

"As well as can be expected, I guess. She's determined to give him the money."

"The hell of it is, you can't blame her, but we can't let her do it."

When he'd arrived in Ashland with Durant's body, Penn was pleased to find the telegram from Woollie waiting for him. Carina's foreman had had his fill of convalescing back on the trail and made up his mind to go to Dodge City on his own to meet up with the outfit there. Penn set up the rendezvous and left instructions for him to come here, to the Long Branch.

"Looks like you healed up all right." He noted the absence of a sling, necessary for the injuries Woollie incurred after the stampede. Now, he appeared strong, relaxed, in good health all around.

"Well enough to ride and shoot, I reckon," Woollie said.

"Glad you're here." Penn meant it.

His scrutiny shifted to the other men in the room—Jesse and Stinky Dale, Ronnie and Billy, Orlin Fahey. Carina's men, gathered under a veil of secrecy to fight for her.

"She have any idea you're here?" he demanded.

Jesse shook his head. "After she paid our wages this

mornin', she told us to quit lookin' as sad as blood-hounds and get out of camp to celebrate the end of the drive." He shrugged. "We left. We just didn't mention we was meetin' you here."

Penn nodded his approval. "Good."

Finally, his glance settled on the last man. Harvey Whalen, all the way from Washington. The Treasury Department, and one of the best Secret Service agents Penn had the pleasure to meet.

"Mornin', Harv," he said.

"Penn."

Dressed in a gray suit and tie, he appeared out of place amongst the C Bar C cowboys, but Penn couldn't have had a better man on his side. He was meticulous with details, shrewd in his thinking, and his help so far had been invaluable.

"I trust all went well with the cattle buyer," Harv said.

"Smooth as silk. She didn't suspect a thing."

"Of course not." He smiled.

Penn smiled back, his relief that the first step of their plan had been executed without a hitch.

His smile faded. But from here on out, things would get more complicated. One miscalculated move on Rogan's part would tear their scheme apart. They had to be prepared for anything.

"She's at the Wright House now." He swept a glance over them. "So listen up, boys. This is what we're going to do."

During cattle season, the Wright House had more business than they could handle. In addition to providing sleeping rooms for the drovers and cowboys coming off the Western Trail, the hotel also offered a restaurant and general store.

People crowded the place. Male voices filled the air. Boot soles scuffed the wooden floor; spurs clinked. The smell of tobacco warred with the aroma of brewing coffee and the day's dinner menu being prepared in the hotel's kitchen.

The female part of Dodge City's citizenry came, as well, to buy their necessities in the mercantile, and Carina found a discreet place among them. She'd be far less conspicuous with her own gender than she would in the hotel with all those men.

And here, she could watch for Rogan. Bolts of fabric and piles of blankets, stacks of hats and tall pairs of leather boots, kept her all but hidden while she maintained a clear view of the hotel clerk's counter.

She didn't have long to wait for Rogan to appear. With his coat swept back to one side to reveal the gleam of his revolver, he slid a prudent glance around him, but didn't see her, of course. Not with the brim of her hat low on her forehead and business booming as it was. He said something to the slick-haired clerk, who turned to the rows of mail slots behind him and retrieved the envelope Carina had left only a short time ago. After checking its contents, Rogan smiled, tucked the envelope into his white shirt pocket and left.

As easy as that.

Her stomach tightened. God, she hated him.

She did her part by giving him the money. Now, he

had to do his by telling her where Mavis had taken Callie Mae.

Except Carina intended to change the rules a bit. To hell with tomorrow, the twenty-four hours he'd instructed her to wait. He would tell her today.

Now.

Her feet moved. Out of the mercantile. Out of the Wright House. She raked her gaze through the throng of men, women and horses to find him, refused to give in to the fear that he'd head straight out of town with her money, without giving her the itinerary as he'd promised.

He had little to gain by keeping his end of the scheme, she knew. She'd be foolish to think he would.

Nor would he trust her to sit back and do nothing to retaliate. He'd want to escape her. In a hurry.

She had to stop him before he did. If he didn't tell her where her daughter was, she'd grab him by the throat and choke the information out of him.

Carina spied him mounted and trotting away from the hitching posts at the far end of the hotel. She rushed off the boardwalk and vaulted onto the Appaloosa to follow.

The narrow corridor of space separating Hoover's Cigar Store and Zimmermann's Dry Goods kept Penn hidden in their shadows. He stood far enough back from the boardwalk to prevent folks from noticing he was there, keeping a close eye on the Dodge City Bank right across the street.

Rogan could show any minute. He would've snatched

Carina's check by now, but Penn was convinced he wouldn't keep the draft with him. The evidence of his blackmail. He'd want to get her money deposited in an account fast, keep it locked away safe and ready to withdraw after he escaped.

He wouldn't get far, Penn vowed. And then sweet revenge would be his.

Plenty of horses and rigs lumbered noisily up and down Front Street. Penn studied them all, just in case one of them held Rogan. Folks went about their business back and forth on the boardwalk—men, women, children—and he studied them, too.

Made the time pass in a hurry. Kept him from thinking of Carina. How she'd be feeling pretty low about now. Sick at heart from what she had to do, with no guarantees giving up her herd would free her daughter from Mavis Webb's clutches. Penn wished—

A young girl wearing a plaid dress passed by the narrow opening, and his thoughts stumbled to a halt. *Red* plaid. All by herself, as she'd been in the rail yards.

His lips thinned. Where the hell were her parents? She should be with someone. Anyone. Why wasn't she?

He stepped out between the two stores, his gaze clinging to her as she continued down the boardwalk. She could get hurt in a cow town like this. Get caught up in some of the wildness that tended to break out with no warning. She'd be all but helpless against it. An innocent victim, and who would know? Who would care?

He set his hands on his hips, threw a glance across the street. The Dodge City Bank appeared quiet, with no one going in. No one coming out. It'd take only a minute or two to talk to her….

He turned back to the girl, walking away at a steady pace. His feet moved of their own accord, his need to make sure she was all right compelling him to go after her. His stride outpaced hers, and he caught up with her in front of the City Drugstore.

"Hey there, young lady," he said.

She started at the sound of his voice. Her step quickened.

"Name's Penn McClure," he said, fitting his stride to hers. "Mind if I ask what yours is?"

She threw a wary glance up at him. Walked faster.

"I'm not going to hurt you, honey. I promise. You're all by yourself, though, and you shouldn't be. Someone could try to hurt you. Are you lost?"

He kept a close watch on her. From the way she inched closer to the edge of the walk, he was pretty sure she planned to bolt into the street.

"Go away, mister," she said.

"Where are your parents?"

Quick as a sprite, she swerved away from him, but expecting it, Penn swung in front of her and blocked her path.

Fear flickered in the depths of her eyes. Eyes as blue as a summer sky.

"It's none of your business, so just leave me alone, will you?" She stood with her feet braced, fists clenched, glaring up at him, defying that fear.

Penn admired her for it. The girl had spunk, for sure.

"I'll help you find them or get someone who will," he said. "Will you tell me your name so I can?"

"No."

He had little experience in dealing with children, but he had to persist. He couldn't let her go now that she'd raised the concern in him.

He bent, clasped his thighs, brought himself down to her level. She locked her gaze on him, those eyes, filled with fatigue and wariness, but vivid and direct.

A resemblance tugged at his memory. He clawed through his brain to decipher it, to remember, to figure out why he had the distinct impression of something familiar....

"Where're you headed then?" he asked. "Maybe I can help you get there."

"I said I don't need your help, mister."

"Well, if you don't let me help you, I'll just have to take you to the sheriff's office. It's his job to take care of lost girls anyway. Not mine." He straightened. "C'mon. Let's go."

She didn't move. Acutely aware of the time ticking away, the distance separating him from the Dodge City Bank, too, Penn waited.

"The Wright House," she said finally.

The hostelry, located a couple of blocks over, catered mostly to cattle buyers and Texas cowmen. Penn took in her expensive-looking red plaid silk dress, all but covered with dirt and wrinkles. The scuffed and dusty bow-topped patent leather shoes.

"Does your daddy buy cattle?" he asked with a frown.

Her chin lifted. "No."

"Did he trail a herd up here?"

"No." She bit her lip. A moment passed. "My mother did. Leastways, I think she did."

Penn went still. "Your mother."

His gaze sharpened over her tousled reddish-brown curls, streaked by the sun and in sorry need of combing. Again that sense of familiarity came. He struggled to define it, an elusive something he should know.

Her hair is the perfect shade of cinnamon.

An image dropped into his brain.

Her eyes as blue as the sky.

Clear and concise and as real as if he held the thing in the palm of his hand.

Hell.

The picture Carina kept tucked inside the pink camisole. Against her breast and next to her heart.

"You're Callie Mae, aren't you?" he breathed, stunned.

Her dirt-streaked face lit up with surprise. With a rush of raw hope. "How did you know that? Do you know my mother?"

"Yeah, I know her." And wasn't that an understatement. A knowing so deep he'd never forget her. "I'm her trail boss."

Suddenly, a rush of anger changed Callie Mae's hopeful expression. She smacked him on his chest with both her fists. "You're lying! You're not her trail boss. Woollie is!"

"Whoa, honey." Appalled at his poor choice of wording, Penn held up a hand. He didn't dare tell her how the man had gotten hurt, the reason why Penn had taken his place. "You're right. He's her trail boss. Has been for a long time. I just helped him with the job for a spell, that's all."

"You did? You trailed the C Bar C herd up from Texas?" she asked, but her mouth flipped into a suspicious pout. "So how come I've never seen you before?"

"Because I was hired out on your ma's roundup, and you'd already left home with your grandmother by the time she hired me to help drive the cattle."

"You know about my grandmother, too?" she asked.

"I do." And more, besides. "Where is she?"

A guarded look stole into her expression. "I don't know. I haven't seen her since we were in Salina. Is Mama here? Is Woollie?"

"Yes, to both your questions." Had Callie Mae traveled to Dodge City *alone?* How had she managed it? And what happened to Mavis Webb?

Callie Mae sucked in an excited breath. "Where? Are they at the Wright House?"

Questions circled inside his head, answers that needed to be found. Again, Penn's gaze slid toward the Dodge City Bank. Locked over a man reining in at the hitching rail. A dandy dressed in a dark suit and a fashionable bowler hat, different than the Stetson hats every one else in town wore, and he knew, then, that Rogan Webb had arrived.

His pulse kicked in to a fast beat. Whatever transpired in the coming minutes, Callie Mae didn't need to see it. Her father was a chiseler of the lowest caliber. Something she probably already knew, but she was just a kid, and Penn didn't want her to witness what he had to do.

He declined to answer her questions. Took her hand instead. Tugged her off the boardwalk and into the dirt street. He figured they were far enough away from the bank that she wouldn't notice Rogan down the block, but Penn couldn't risk it. He had to keep her occupied for a while. Get her out of harm's way.

"Are you hungry, Callie Mae?" He fished with his free hand into a hip pocket, pulled out a few coins. Kept her walking across the street toward an eatery with yellow gingham curtains in the window. "Why don't you buy yourself something to eat while I—"

"I want to find my mother." Callie Mae tugged at his grip. He held her fast. "Why won't you tell me where she is?"

"I will, honey. Soon. I promise. It's just that she's busy right now. And so am I. Going to take some doing to track her down, and there's something I have to do first, so let's just go in here and you can buy yourself some dinner, okay?"

He slid another glance down the boardwalk. Rogan had the bank's door open, had just stepped through it….

"Here." He handed her the coins. Callie Mae eyed them with clear indecision. "Buy yourself whatever you want. But stay right here, and I'll come for you in just a bit, y'hear?"

At last, she took the money. "I guess."

"Don't go anywhere, Callie Mae. Stay right here. You're going to see your mother real soon. I'm going to help you do that, I swear it. *But just stay here.*"

She peered up at him through a thick veil of lashes.

Penn wondered what she was thinking. She had more courage, more perception than any ten-year-old should.

"Okay," she muttered finally.

He ushered her in the doors, pulled them closed behind her before she could think of another protest. He took the time to mutter a prayer to the Almighty to keep her there and save him from Carina's wrath for doing what he was doing. Leaving Callie Mae behind.

But the lure of revenge was powerful. Too powerful to ignore. He could taste it on his tongue, feel it buzzing in his veins, and drawing his revolver, he broke into a full run toward the Dodge City Bank.

Chapter Eighteen

If there was one stroke of good luck Carina could claim for the morning, it had to be that Rogan didn't go far. Only to Front Street. The Dodge City Bank, to be exact. Did he intend to wire the money to some prearranged account? Bury it so deep the law might never find it?

He disappeared inside, but before Carina could dismount and go in after him, movement caught her eye.

A man carrying a gun, sprinting down the boardwalk from the opposite side of the block, toward the bank.

The hair stood up on her arms.

McClure. And he intended to wreak the revenge that was more important to him than anything, even Callie Mae, but especially *her,* and oh, God, what would happen when Rogan recognized him?

Callie Mae stuck her head outside the eatery's door and watched Penn McClure run as quick as a lobo. She just plain didn't know what to think about him claiming to know Mama.

Maybe she shouldn't believe him.

But then again, maybe she should.

He'd guessed her name. And he knew about Grandmother. Woollie, too. He seemed genuinely worried about her, mostly, wanting to make sure she got something to eat and all. Callie Mae guessed if he'd wanted to hurt her, he would've gone about it different.

She clutched the coins he'd given her tighter, inched farther out of the restaurant and more onto the boardwalk to see him better.

Strange about him being in such a hurry. Made her wonder if he was coming back, and she'd be blasted mad if he didn't. He said he'd take her to her mother, and she'd been so hoping he would.

Dodge City was plenty big, and Callie Mae didn't know all the right ways to look for her, even though she'd come this far by herself. Had even checked at the stockyard office to see if the C Bar C herd was penned outside of town. The nice man at the desk told her the cattle were, so she had a pretty good idea her mother— or someone in her outfit, at least—might be around town.

Her eyes narrowed over Penn McClure. He'd stopped running but now he was going into the Dodge City Bank. Was he after someone in there? Why?

Shoot. She didn't know what to make of it, but it wasn't much her business what he was up to. Her empty belly demanded her attention more, and she turned to go back into the eatery.

Except a woman across the street from the bank distracted her. A woman on an Appaloosa. Callie Mae lifted a hand, shaded her eyes against the sun. And squinted hard.

The woman dismounted and hurried across the street. She strode straight and tall, and she wore a riding skirt and a holster and a wide-brimmed hat, and suddenly, pure joy soared through Callie Mae.

Mama!

Penn reined in the adrenaline surging through him. Forced himself to keep his pace even, to push open the door and enter the bank lobby like any other customer.

Once inside, he paused, skimmed a glance around the place. He took note of who was where—the man in a gray suit, seated on a burgundy, tufted chair reading a newspaper; a cowboy standing near the plate glass window, emblazoned with Dodge City Bank in bold letters. Near a tall, potted fern, a couple of cowboys talked quietly while they enjoyed a smoke.

A normal business day, it seemed. Nothing out of the ordinary.

He resumed walking across the lobby, toward the row of teller windows. Three of them, side by side. Two were occupied by cowboys, intent on their financial affairs with the cashiers who assisted them. Rogan stood at the far right one, his back to Penn as he withdrew an envelope from his coat pocket.

Carina's money. Penn halted behind him. Rogan wouldn't know he had a gun pointed at him while he conducted his thievery. Not until it was too late.

The smooth-shaven cashier—Henry Fringer, Penn had learned—smiled at Rogan in greeting. "Good morning, sir."

"Indeed it is. Deposit this for me, will you?" Rogan passed George Satterfield's bank draft under the barred window. "Here's the number of the account." A slip of paper followed.

Fringer studied the penciled markings on that little slip. "I believe this account belongs to our correspondent, Donnell, Lawson & Simpson, in New York."

"That's right."

"You want the money to be available there?"

Rogan nodded crisply. "I do."

The efficient-looking cashier glanced down at the bank draft next. His scrutiny lingering, his smile stayed on his face. "A good sum, Mr. Webb. Let me guess. For your cattle?"

"None of your damn business what the money's for," he snapped. "Just do what I told you."

"Certainly, sir. I'll be but a moment."

But instead of retrieving the bank's ledger, Fringer opened a drawer, removed a magnifying glass, and held it over the check. His brows knitted in concentration; he slid the lens from one side to the other, then back again.

Rogan stiffened. Tension shimmered off him, like desert heat off sand. He leaned closer.

"Is there a problem?" he hissed in a low voice.

The man straightened. Ignored him. Angled his head toward an open office beyond the teller windows. He lifted his arm and waggled his fingers at someone only he could see.

George M. Hoover stepped out. One of the leading merchants in Dodge City, owner of the cigar store a short way down Front Street, he helped establish the Dodge City Bank and now proudly served as its president.

"Come look at this, Mr. Hoover," Fringer said. "Tell me what you think."

Handsome, with a stocky build, Hoover took the magnifying glass into his thick fingers and pored over the check draft, just as his cashier had.

"What?" Rogan grated, his narrowed gaze bouncing between them.

Finally, Hoover straightened. Set down the glass with a firm thunk. He leveled Rogan with a stern expression.

"We cannot accept this check for deposit, Mr. Webb," he said firmly.

"What do you mean you 'can't accept it'?" Rogan snarled.

The bank president drew himself up, imperious in his disdain. "The note is forged."

Rogan stared.

"Would you like to use the magnifying glass to see for yourself?"

"You're lying."

"I assure you, I am not. The draft isn't worth the ink wasted on it."

Rogan stood stock-still while his brain clearly put two and two together. And came up with trouble.

"Damn her." He swore. Violently. *"Damn* her!"

"If I were you, Mr. Webb, I would damn no one but yourself. Because, you see, you've been set up."

Rogan jerked, as if slapped. "What?"

Penn moved, then. Right on cue. Wedged himself in between Rogan and the cowboy on his left. He pulled the hammer back on his Peacemaker.

"How does it feel to be cheated of thousands of dollars of someone's hard-earned money?" he murmured.

Rogan spun toward him. The blood drained from his cheeks. "McClure!"

"We meet again." Penn's lips curved in a cold smile.

The bank's door opened, and the sound of a wagon rumbling down Front Street drifted into the lobby. The door closed again and silenced the sound.

"You're about to be arrested by the United States government for all your counterfeiting crimes," Penn went on, refusing to let himself be distracted by anything but the bulge beneath Rogan's jacket. "So why don't you just slide your hogleg under the teller window before someone gets hurt. Slow and easy. Mr. Hoover will know what to do with it when you do."

Rogan didn't move. But his gaze darted from Penn, to Fringer, to Hoover. As if weighing his odds against all of them.

Jesse moved out from behind Penn and pulled out his gun. "Reckon you're taking a long time to obey Mr. McClure's order, Webb."

"Best do it now, while you're still able." Stinky Dale showed himself from the farthest window, and his weapon made three aimed at Rogan's chest.

Beads of sweat appeared beneath the bowler's brim. Penn figured Rogan knew he was close enough to hell to smell smoke if he didn't comply.

Gritting an oath, Rogan laid his shooting iron on the counter. Hoover snatched the weapon and hustled toward his office for cover, taking his cashiers with him.

"Agent Harvey Whelan traveled across this fine country for the pleasure of throwing you in the cooler, Rogan. Compliments of the Treasury Department and the Secret Service," Penn said. The contempt which chilled the blue of Rogan's eyes kept his senses fine-tuned. The man had nothing to lose right now, and that made him plenty dangerous. "Come on over here, Harv, and I'll let you arrest him."

But it wasn't the sound of the agent rising from the burgundy chair and striding forward in the firm, even tread of shoe leather that reached Penn's ears, but the sharp jangle of spurs from the direction of the bank's front door.

"Not yet, McClure," Carina said. Her slender fingers gripped the pearl handles of each Colt, the firepower she needed to get what she wanted. "Not until he tells me where my daughter is."

His heart slammed against his chest. His brain spun with all he needed to explain to her. All she didn't yet know. "She's here, Carina. I'll take you to her when—"

"He's lying," Rogan said. "She's not."

Confusion darkened the violet depths. "What are you talking about?"

Rogan's lip curled. "Just like you lied about the money, Carina."

"From the herd?" Her gaze jumped to Penn, dragged back to Rogan. "I never lied, damn you."

Impatience snapped inside Penn. Her confusion was

a distraction he couldn't afford. There'd be time for explanations later—after Rogan was in jail.

"Woollie!" Penn barked. He made a fierce gesture with the nose of his Peacemaker. "Get her out of here!"

Woollie, looking grim, stepped away from the plate glass window. Carina whirled toward him with a shocked gasp.

Suddenly, Rogan leaped toward her with more speed, more agility, more *cunning* than any of them could have expected. His body rammed against hers, and thrown off balance, she cried out. He whipped the Colts from her holster, flung his arm around her neck and pressed the nose of one to her temple. Holding the other in a white-knuckled grip, he kept her body tight against his chest.

One after the other, C Bar C hammers cocked.

Barrels leveled.

Fingers stroked triggers….

"Don't shoot!" Penn roared. "Don't shoot!"

Sweet Mother. If any of them missed, if any of them shot Carina…

The horror rolled through him in waves. His perfect plan for revenge had been knocked to its knees. Carina being here, at the worst possible moment, had given Rogan the bait he needed to save himself.

"I'm so glad you've come, Carina, dear," he said against her ear, his voice as smooth as oil. "Call off your wolves for me, will you?"

"Let me handle this, Carina," Penn grated.

Her bosom heaved; her eyes, cold, a little wild, turned on him. "Callie Mae is more important to me than your revenge could ever be to you, McClure. You're not going to make an arrest until I have what I need out of him."

"And maybe not even then," Rogan cooed.

"Tell us what you want us to do, Mr. McClure." Ronnie moved away from the potted fern, Billy beside him, both their weapons aimed and steadied. "Just tell us."

"Easy, boys," Woollie said, tense, his hand up. "Back off."

"Carina, listen to me," Penn said. He had to convince her. He had to make her understand. "She's here, in Dodge City. I swear it. Just trust me to—"

Something red streaked in his vision. His head whipped toward it. Specks of color through the plate glass window. There one moment, gone the next, and then the door burst open. Callie Mae, out of breath, excited, jubilant, barreled into the bank lobby at a full run.

"Mama, Mama!"

Even with the Colt against her temple, Carina jerked her head around, a scream tearing from her throat. "Callie Mae!" She strained against Rogan's grip, her arms reaching for her daughter. "Oh, Callie Mae!"

Callie Mae skidded to a halt. Her eyes rounded like moons, and her dirty face scrunched. She shrieked in fury.

"Let her go, Rogan! Let her go!" she screamed.

Like a cornered she-cat, she flung herself at Carina and grasped her hands, pulling, pulling to break her free.

"Take her away!" Rogan shouted, sidestepping to

evade her, dragging Carina with him. "You hear me? Take her away from here!"

"Sweetheart, sweetheart." Tortured tears streamed down Carina's face, her anguish from her daughter seeing her like this. Captive. Helpless. "I'll be all right."

"Come here, Tea Cup!" Woollie rushed forward, scooped her into his arms. Callie Mae screamed. Her fists flailed, her feet kicked, her back arched in protest. "You can't be in here right now, honey."

He had his hands full with her, but he managed to get her out the door, spare her from the harshness of her father's sins. Jesse and Stinky Dale, Ronnie and Billy, each stood immobile, stricken from the grief of their she-boss, the little girl they loved as their own, their uncertainty about what to do next written on their sun-brown faces.

Rogan held Carina in a tighter grip to her neck, hard enough to turn her breathing ragged.

"Make them drop their guns, Carina," he commanded. "Or I'll shoot. You got the girl, don't you? But I don't have anything. You hear me? I don't have anything. So you're going to write me another check. A real, genuine bank draft this time. Every dime that your precious herd is worth. Else you'll die right here. I'll kill you. I'll *kill* you!"

She clutched his arm with both hands, her body rigid. Her gaze lifted to Penn, her violet eyes deep pools of torment, of raw dignity. She all but tore his heart out of his chest.

"You heard him, McClure," she said.

Beautiful Carina, too strong to beg for her own life.

To order her men to defend her when she needed it most.

Her pride, her courage... Penn had never loved her more.

He lowered the Peacemaker. Tossed it somewhere off to the side, out of reach. The gun clattered against the floor. Soon, four more shooting irons followed. The C Bar C outfit, completely unarmed.

"Penn." Harv's throat bobbed above his white shirt collar. "Are you sure?"

"Drop yours, too." Penn's voice snapped the order.

The agent's gun joined the rest with a hard thunk, a fitting punctuation to the vow pounding in Penn's head.

Unheeled, he'd find a way to save her. He'd get back at Rogan for what he'd done. Show no mercy...

"Let's go, Carina." Rogan inched toward the door, pulling her backward with him. "You know I'll shoot you, don't you? So don't do anything stupid, like try to get away or anything. Nothing stupid, no, sirree. I'll kill you."

He was almost there, through the door. Onto the boardwalk, his horse tethered right outside.

"What do you think your mother would say if she saw you now, Rogan?" Penn asked. He kept his tone easy, as if he spoke about the weather. "Might be she'd cut you out of the family fortune if she knew about all your crimes. You suppose she'd do that, Rogan?"

Rogan flinched. "Leave her out of this!"

"She'll need to be notified of all you've done, you know. No matter what happens." Penn persisted, homed in on a weak spot a man like Rogan had. "'Course, she's guilty of a little blackmail herself, isn't she? She may even have to testify against you in front of a judge and jury. Think about it. The respected Webb name, dragged through the dirt. She won't want to do that, will she?"

"Shut up!"

"You're the only family she has, except Callie Mae. Guess your daughter will get all the Webb money some day. Because you're going to be in jail the rest of your life, Rogan. Or dead. You decide which."

"Just shut the hell up, McClure! You hear me?"

"Might be the Treasury Department will cut you a deal." Penn took a step closer to the door. To Carina. "Tell everything you know about the counterfeiting underworld, and well, things might get better for you."

A drop of sweat trickled down Rogan's cheek.

"You're not going to get away with stealing C Bar C money, Rogan." Ruthless, Penn persisted. "Not a chance. The Secret Service, the police, they'll be crawling all over the country looking for you. No place big enough for you to hide, so you may as well give up now, while you're still alive."

He detected the faintest weakening in the man's grip on Carina. She seemed to breathe easier from it, at least. Penn moved a careful step closer.

"Word's going to spread fast around here about you, Rogan. No cattle buyer is going to do to Carina what you want him to do. He won't write her a check when he knows she has to give it to you. No one will pay her blackmail. No one."

Rogan's breathing quickened into agitated pants that revealed him hovering on the breaking point. The truth he was fighting.

"What's it going to be?" Penn halted. Only a few yards kept him from Carina. "Make up your mind, and make it fast."

Rogan's teeth bared. "Damn you, McClure!"

Suddenly, roaring in fury, he yanked his arm from around Carina's neck and shoved her away, the unexpectedness of it sending her hurtling toward Penn before she could right herself. Instinctively, his arms opened, and he took her staggering against him.

Rogan stood outside, on the boardwalk, one of Carina's Colt pistols aimed at Penn, the other at her, his expression black with vengeance. But before he could pull the triggers, the deafening bark of a bullet from somewhere outside reverberated throughout the bank lobby. Rogan's body arched from the force. His eyes, once blue as the summer sky, darkened and rolled back in his head. He dropped into a heap and didn't move.

For a moment, no one acted. No one understood.

Orlin appeared, then. In the doorway. A revolver hung loose in his hand. The acrid scent of gunpowder clung to him.

Carina twisted to see the man who had saved her life and Penn's.

"He weren't no better than them Injuns that killed my family, Miss Lockett," he said quietly. "I did it for them."

The nightmare was over.

Carina sagged against McClure. She needed a few

moments to recover, to allow the aftershocks of the violence to quiet throughout her body.

She needed his strength, too. Hers was all but gone, and she'd yet to brace herself for what would come next.

McClure leaving.

Her eyes closed, hating it.

"You could have told me, you know," she said against his shoulder. "About the forged check."

"You would've refused to go along with the ruse. You would've been afraid for Callie Mae in case anything went wrong." His mouth moved against her hair as he spoke, his voice hushed, somber.

His recklessness unnerved her, that untamed part of him which gave him the cunning to lay the trap for Rogan. She shivered.

His embrace tightened, warming her. Giving her comfort.

"Tell me I figured you right," he murmured.

She soaked him in. "You did. I never would've agreed to it."

"It was the only way to capture him, Carina. Beat him at his own game."

"He could've shot you. Or me. Where would that have left Callie Mae?"

"I knew it could happen. I laid awake at night worrying that it would. But I had to try."

She suspected his plan took shape after he left the Western Trail to tend to Durant's body. He'd been gone for days, she recalled. The time he'd taken to set Rogan up.

He did it for himself, she knew. For the case he'd been determined to close. The revenge he needed to satisfy.

But he did it for Callie Mae, too. And her.

Especially her.

Carina's eyes opened. Gathering up her will, all the strength she possessed, she drew back.

His hand lifted to her cheek in a gentle caress. His expression turned grave, oddly vulnerable. "Carina."

The words he needed to say, the life he needed to live, hung in the air between them. Unspoken. But as blatant as if he'd shouted them out.

Penn McClure was destined for great things, a prize for the government that meant so much to him. Driven to enact justice against those who chose to take the wrong side of the law.

Her destiny included things far simpler. A ranch. A herd of cattle. And being a mother.

God, she loved him.

The Secret Service agent, Harvey Whalen, cleared his throat. "Excuse me, Penn. Sheriff Sughrue would like to talk to you."

She had no more time left. Her heart all but tearing in two, Carina stepped out of his arms. "Go on, McClure. You've got a job to do."

He didn't move. "I'm not finished with you yet, Carina."

"There's no reason for you to stay. Your debt to me is paid in full." She managed to smile. "The saloon damages, remember?" She steeled herself against the fierceness in his gaze. "You're free to do all the office work you want. You can—" Her throat worked. She refused to cry. To let him see her pain from letting him go. He didn't need her to tell him what he could do, besides. He'd decide well enough on his own. "You were a hell of a cowboy, you know," she said instead.

"Rogan being dead hasn't changed that."

"No, I guess not."

"It'll always be in my blood, playing cowboy for you."

"Will it?"

The admission stirred up the ache in her heart, made her wish he'd be with her, for always. A permanent and loyal part of her outfit. Her life.

"I'm going back to the C Bar C with you, Carina."

She didn't move, but the sound of his voice spun in wild circles around her brain, leaving her confused and certain she hadn't heard what she thought he said. "You're going where?"

"These past few weeks have showed me there's more satisfaction in working hard under the sun with the woman I love than there is in an office fighting crimes I hate."

She blinked. *With the woman I love…*

"A hell of a lot more," he amended with a growl.

Hope warred with the confusion. "But your case against Rogan and counterfeiting—"

"Stopped being my case the day I walked away from the Secret Service and headed to Texas."

"But—" she said again.

"The case is Harv's. Has been since I left. I just took care of the revenge end of it."

She swiveled toward the gray-suited agent, who seemed to understand her bewilderment.

"That's right, Miss Lockett," he said, smiling. "But don't let him tell you he didn't have a big part in helping me close it. He did, and the Treasury Department owes him plenty for it. We're going to miss him, that's for sure." He turned toward McClure. "I'll let the sheriff know you'll be out shortly."

"Thanks." The door closed. "I love you, Carina."

She swung back toward him. Her heart grabbed onto the words and held on tight, the fear running through her that he might not mean them. Or say them again. She lifted shaking fingers to her lips. "You'll change your mind. You'll be bored tending cattle. You'll want to work in an office again and catch criminals and—"

"I don't want anything but you in my life." At some point, he'd moved closer. So close their bodies nearly touched. "I couldn't walk away from you if I tried. Which I'm not going to. Not ever."

Carina forgot to breathe, her hopes, her yearning for him soaring.

"I want to build the Lockett legacy with you," he murmured. "Make it stronger for Callie Mae. For all our children. Starting today. Now."

Her eyes brimmed. Her fears began to dissipate, like cool mist beneath the hot sun. "Oh, McClure." She slid her arms around his neck. Easily, as if he'd done so a hundred times before, he fitted her into his embrace. "I love you. More than I ever thought I could love a man before."

Their mouths met, hungry and wet. Again and again.

And after long moments of hungry kisses, his dark head lifted.

"Carina," he said in mild exasperation. "Wives don't call their husbands by their last name. You're going to have to start calling me 'Penn.' Every day. For the rest of our lives."

Incredibly happy, she laughed. She was about to embark on a new beginning, having him in her life. He'd be the center of her world, and she'd devote herself to him for always.

But as for his name, she made no promises.

Some habits were harder to break than others.

Epilogue

Late Summer

Carina dipped the knife into a bowl of water and carefully smoothed the powdered sugar frosting with the wet blade, a trick Sourdough taught her to make icing a cake easier.

Lord knew she needed all the help she could get.

Baking and cooking never ceased to be a challenge. Sometimes a disappointing one, at best, but she was getting better at both.

Callie Mae's finger guided her reading of the recipe.

"'Frost each layer and sprinkle with grated coconut.'" She glanced up with a grin, showing the gap from the tooth she'd lost just yesterday. "Is that why they call it a 'Snow Flake Cake'? 'Cuz the coconut is supposed to look like snow?"

Carina set down the knife and eyed the results of her handiwork. "Guess so."

"Can I sprinkle the coconut on?"

"Sure." Carina handed her the bowl heaped with the shredded fruit meat. "Make it pretty."

Callie Mae carefully scattered the flakes until the top

and sides were covered. Carina marveled at the end result. The cake really did look as if it had snow on top.

"Can I have a piece?" Her daughter eyed the dessert as if she'd never tasted one before.

"Absolutely not." She slid the plate toward the center of the table so the icing could dry. "You can have one after supper. How about that?"

"Can I go out with Grandpa then? He's waiting for me."

"When there's dishes to do?" Carina asked, her brows arched, her tone half teasing, half chiding.

Callie Mae sighed dramatically. "I'd rather play checkers with him."

"I'm sure you would." She gave her a playful swat with a towel. "Go ahead. But you'll do dishes later, for sure."

"I will. I promise. Thanks, Mama!" Grinning again, she reached up for a kiss. Carina gladly obliged. "I love you. Bye!"

She took off at a full run out the back door, the hems of her flowered cotton dress trailing behind her. Carina peered through the kitchen window and watched her go, her gaze clinging as her daughter happily loped across the yard. A beautiful bundle of energy. Of spirit and innocence. Grandpa sat beneath the ash tree with his checkerboard already laid out, and he greeted her with a hug.

Carina's heart swelled with love for both of them. At the thought of how different being a family was these days.

Being a wife, too.

And mother.

Again.

The tiny life growing inside her had made itself known a couple of weeks ago. She hadn't shared the news with anyone but her handsome husband yet, but the swelling of her belly would make it a necessity before long. Callie Mae and Grandpa would be as excited as a couple of jaybirds when they found out. Carina decided then and there she'd break the news while they were all having a piece of Snow Flake Cake tonight after supper.

The heat of the afternoon beckoned her from the kitchen to the porch to rest a spell. She filled a cup with steaming coffee, added a good portion of canned Borden's milk and stirred it in, then strode through the front room and out the door, her concentration locked on the coffee sloshing to the cup's rim and the threat of burning her thumb. She didn't see the woman standing at the top of the step until she almost ran into her.

Carina leaped back with a startled squeak. Hot brew spilled over the back of her hand, and she yelped at the sting of pain. The cup dropped, and the coffee pooled into a murky puddle at her feet.

Mavis Webb, dressed in black henrietta and crape— mourning clothes, for the son she'd lost—pressed a thin, blue-veined hand to her bosom in alarm.

"Did you burn yourself?" she asked.

Carina stiffened. "Yes. You nearly gave me heart failure standing there. And the coffee was fresh-made."

Mavis didn't move, though her careful glance drifted over the reddened knuckle. "I'm sorry. I didn't mean to startle you."

Whatever pain remained from the burn was lost in the apology Mavis Webb humbled herself to offer. Had Carina ever heard one from her before?

Except for her driver waiting in the yard, it appeared she'd arrived alone in her fancy rig. Carina's mind stirred with suspicion.

"Why are you here?" she demanded.

"I—I couldn't stay away any longer." A faint quaver replaced the hoity-toity inflection normally present in her voice. "Some things are meant to be said in person, and oh, Carina, there are so many things I must say to you."

Carina figured there wasn't much of anything Mavis Webb could say that would make Carina want to listen, but she strained to be civil. "Like what?"

She drew in a breath. "I put Callie Mae through a terrible ordeal, taking her away from you like I did. I've been thinking of her constantly."

"Have you?"

"Yes, and—and how is she? Does she hate me overmuch?"

"She's a strong child." Carina laid the truth out. "But she doesn't stray far from me. I think her sense of adventure has been satisfied for a while. She's learned the hard way what's important and what's not."

"She's happy, then?"

"Very."

"What Rogan and I did—"

"Was unforgivable and something neither of us will ever forget. We don't talk about him much. I hope the day comes when we never will again."

Mavis flinched, her pride broken. "I'm most grateful you declined to press charges against me. You should have, I suppose, to the fullest extent of the law."

"I wanted to."

"So why didn't you? I deserved it."

"Because you're Callie Mae's grandmother, and Callie Mae loves you. Still." So many times, Carina had questioned the wisdom of her decision, the reluctance to throw the old witch in jail where she belonged. "She's lost her father. I didn't want her to lose her grandmother, too."

"Thank you." Mavis bit her lip. "She's all I have, you know."

"Yes."

But Carina thought of all Callie Mae had gained. Penn, at the top of the list, who embraced honor and ideals and who'd grown to love her as a father should, something Rogan had never been able to do.

Mavis angled her head toward the ash tree in the backyard. Her gaze held on the old man and young girl seated around the checkerboard, both oblivious to her presence. For long moments, she appeared at a loss for words.

Carina swallowed hard. Dug in deep to find the forgiveness that most days proved elusive. And found a shred to cling to.

"Would you like to come in, Mavis?" It took a valiant effort to extend the offer, but once it was made, Carina had no regrets. "I've just baked a cake, and—"

"No, but thank you." Seemingly with great effort, she turned back to Carina. "I only wanted to stop for a moment." Her eyes filled with watery hope. "But maybe—maybe next year, I could come for a visit, a short one, of course, to—to see Callie Mae."

"Yes," Carina said quietly and vowed to find a way to endure it, for her daughter's sake. "I think she'd like that."

"Thank you. Oh, thank you, Carina."

As if she feared she'd lose what little remained of her composure, she pivoted toward the steps. In the next moment, however, she pivoted back.

"You're wearing a dress," she murmured. "I've never seen you in one."

"Yes, well." Of course, Mavis would notice. "It's just percale. Nothing fancy."

"It suits you, you know. You're a beautiful woman."

Her smile with the rare compliment, though hesitant, was genuine. She turned, and with a rustle of black henrietta, hurried down the steps. Carina's thoughtful gaze lingered on the departing rig until it disappeared from sight.

But she didn't go into the house. Instead, her glance shifted toward the horse corral. Lifting a hand to shade her eyes from the sun, she found Penn with TJ Grier, both of them inside the rails, working together to tame a feisty yearling.

Watching them, love and pride rushed through her. The C Bar C was a better place with her husband beside her at the helm. Strong and enduring.

Peace settled around Carina.

The Lockett legacy would continue, for many years to come.

* * * * *

Every Life Has More
Than One Chapter

Award-winning author Stevi Mittman delivers another hysterical mystery, featuring Teddi Bayer,
an irrepressible heroine, and her to-die-for hero,
Detective Drew Scoones. After all, life on Long
Island can be murder!

*Turn the page for a sneak peek at
the warm and funny fourth book,
WHOSE NUMBER IS UP, ANYWAY?
in the Teddi Bayer series,
by STEVI MITTMAN.
On sale August 7*

Before redecorating a room, I always advise my clients to empty it of everything but one chair. Then I suggest they move that chair from place to place, sitting in it, until the placement feels right. Trust your instincts when deciding on furniture placement. Your room should "feel right."

—TipsFromTeddi.com

Gut feelings. You know, that gnawing in the pit of your stomach that warns you that you are about to do the absolute stupidest thing you could do? Something that will ruin life as you know it?

I've got one now, standing at the butcher counter in King Kullen, the grocery store in the same strip mall as L.I. Lanes, the bowling alley cum billiard parlor I'm in the process of redecorating for its "Grand Opening."

I realize being in the wrong supermarket probably doesn't sound exactly dire to you, but you aren't the one buying your father a brisket at a store your mother will somehow know isn't Waldbaum's.

And then, June Bayer isn't your mother.

The woman behind the counter has agreed to go into the freezer to find a brisket for me, since there aren't any in the case. There are packages of pork tenderloin, piles of spare ribs and rolls of sausage, but no briskets.

Warning Number Two, right? I should be so out of here.

But no, I'm still in the same spot when she comes back out, brisketless, her face ashen. She opens her mouth as if she is going to scream, but only a gurgle comes out.

And then she pinballs out from behind the counter, knocking bottles of Peter Luger Steak Sauce to the floor on her way, now hitting the tower of cans at the end of the prepared foods aisle and sending them sprawling, now making her way down the aisle, careening from side to side as she goes.

Finally, from a distance, I hear her shout, "He's deeeeeeaaaad! Joey's deeeeeaaaad."

My first thought is *You should always trust your gut.*

My second thought is that now, somehow, my mother will know I was in King Kullen. For weeks I will have to hear "What did you expect?" as though whenever you go to King Kullen someone turns up dead. And if the detective investigating the case turns out to be Detective Drew Scoones...well, I'll never hear the end of that from her, either.

She still suspects I murdered the guy who was found dead on my doorstep last Halloween just to get Drew back into my life.

Several people head for the butcher's freezer and I position myself to block them. If there's one thing I've learned from finding people dead—and the guy on my doorstep wasn't the first one—it's that the police get very testy when you mess with their murder scenes.

"You can't go in there until the police get here," I say, stationing myself at the end of the butcher's counter and in front of the Employees Only door, acting as if I'm some sort of authority. "You'll contaminate the evidence if it turns out to be murder."

Shouts and chaos. You'd think I'd know better than to throw the word *murder* around. Cell phones are flipping open and tongues are wagging.

I amend my statement quickly. "Which, of course, it probably isn't. Murder, I mean. People die all the time, and it's not always in hospitals or their own beds, or…" I babble when I'm nervous, and the idea of someone dead on the other side of the freezer door makes me very nervous.

So does the idea of seeing Drew Scoones again. Drew and I have this on-again, off-again sort of thing…that I kind of turned off.

Who knew he'd take it so personally when he tried to get serious and I responded by saying we could talk about *us* tomorrow—and then caught a plane to my parents' condo in Boca the next day? In July. In the middle of a job.

For some crazy reason, he took that to mean that I was avoiding him and the subject of *us*.

That was three months ago. I haven't seen him since.

The manager, who identifies himself and points to

his nameplate in case I don't believe him, says he has to go into *his cooler*. "Maybe Joey's not dead," he says. "Maybe he can be saved, and you're letting him die in there. Did you ever think of that?"

In fact, I hadn't. But I had thought that the murderer might try to go back in to make sure his tracks were covered, so I say that I will go in and check.

Which means that the manager and I couple up and go in together while everyone pushes against the doorway to peer in, erasing any chance of finding clean prints on that Employee Only door.

I expect to find carcasses of dead animals hanging from hooks, and maybe Joey hanging from one, too. I think it's going to be very creepy and I steel myself, only to find a rather benign series of shelves with large slabs of meat laid out carefully on them, along with boxes and boxes marked simply Chicken.

Nothing scary here, unless you count the body of a middle-aged man with graying hair sprawled faceup on the floor. His eyes are wide open and unblinking. His shirt is stiff. His pants are stiff. His body is stiff. And his expression, you should forgive the pun—is frozen. Bill-the-manager crosses himself and stands mute while I pronounce the guy dead in a sort of *happy now?* tone.

"We should not be in here," I say, and he nods his head emphatically and helps me push people out of the doorway just in time to hear the police sirens and see the cop cars pull up outside the big store windows.

Bobbie Lyons, my partner in Teddi Bayer Interior Designs (and also my neighbor, my best friend and my private fashion police), and Mark, our carpenter (and my dogsitter, confidant, and ego booster), rush in from next door. They beat the cops by a half step and shout out my name. People point in my direction.

After all the publicity that followed the unfortunate incident during which I shot my ex-husband, Rio Gallo, and then the subsequent murder of my first client—which I solved, I might add—it seems like the whole world, or at least all of Long Island, knows who I am.

Mark asks if I'm all right. (Did I remember to mention that the man is drop-dead-gorgeous-but-a-decade-too-young-for-me-yet-too-old-for-my-daughter-thank-god?) I don't get a chance to answer him because the police are quickly closing in on the store manager and me.

"The woman—" I begin telling the police. Then I have to pause for the manager to fill in her name, which he does: *Fran.*

I continue. "Right. Fran. Fran went into the freezer to get a brisket. A moment later she came out and screamed that Joey was dead. So I'd say she was the one who discovered the body."

"And you are…?" the cop asks me. It comes out a bit like who do I *think* I am, rather than who am I really?

"An innocent bystander," Bobbie, hair perfect, makeup just right, says, carefully placing her body between the cop and me.

"And she was just leaving," Mark adds. They each take one of my arms.

Fran comes into the inner circle surrounding the cops. In case it isn't obvious from the hairnet and bloodstained white apron with Fran embroidered on it, I explain that she was the butcher who was going for the brisket. Mark and Bobbie take that as a signal that I've done my job and they can now get me out of there. They twist around, with me in the middle, as if we're a Rockettes line, until we are facing away from the butcher counter. They've managed to propel me a few steps toward the exit when disaster—in the form of a Mazda RX7 pulling up at the loading curb—strikes.

Mark's grip on my arm tightens like a vise. "Too late," he says.

Bobbie's expletive is unprintable. "Maybe there's a back door," she suggests, but Mark is right. It's too late.

I've laid my eyes on Detective Scoones. And while my gut is trying to warn me that my heart shouldn't go there, regions farther south are melting at just the sight of him.

"Walk," Bobbie orders me.

And I try to. Really.

Walk, I tell my feet. *Just put one foot in front of the other.*

I can do this because I know, in my heart of hearts, that if Drew Scoones was still interested in me, he'd have gotten in touch with me after I returned from Boca. And he didn't.

Since he's a detective, Drew doesn't have to wear one of those dark blue Nassau County Police uniforms. Instead, he's got on jeans, a tight-fitting T-shirt and a tweedy sports jacket. If you think that sounds good, you should see him. Chiseled features, cleft chin, brown hair that's naturally a little sandy in the front, a smile that…well, that doesn't matter. He isn't smiling now.

He walks up to me, tucks his sunglasses into his breast pocket and looks me over from head to toe.

"Well, if it isn't Miss Cut and Run," he says. "Aren't you supposed to be somewhere in Florida or something?" He looks at Mark accusingly, as if he was covering for me when he told Drew I was gone.

"Detective Scoones?" one of the uniforms says. "The stiff's in the cooler and the woman who found him is over there." He jerks his head in Fran's direction.

Drew continues to stare at me.

You know how when you were young, your mother always told you to wear clean underwear in case you were in an accident? And how, a little farther on, she told you not to go out in hair rollers because you never knew who you might see—or who might see you? And how now your best friend says she wouldn't be caught dead without makeup and suggests you shouldn't either?

Okay, today, *finally*, in my overalls and Converse sneakers, I get it.

I brush my hair out of my eyes. "Well, I'm back," I say. As if he hasn't known my exact whereabouts. The man is a detective, for heaven's sake. "Been back a while."

Bobbie has watched the exchange and apparently decided she's given Drew all the time he deserves. "And we've got work to do, so…" she says, grabbing my arm and giving Drew a little two-fingered wave goodbye.

As I back up a foot or two, the store manager sees his chance and places himself in front of Drew, trying to get his attention. Maybe what makes Drew such a good detective is his ability to focus.

Only what he's focusing on is me.

"Phone broken? Carrier pigeon died?" he asks me, taking in Fran, the manager, the meat counter and that Employees Only door, all without taking his eyes off me.

Mark tries to break the spell. "We've got work to do there, you've got work to do here, Scoones," Mark says to him, gesturing toward next door. "So it's back to the alley for us."

Drew's lip twitches. "You working the alley now?" he says.

"If you'd like to follow me," Bill-the-manager, clearly exasperated, says to Drew—who doesn't respond. It's as if waiting for my answer is all he has to do.

So, fine. "You knew I was back," I say.

The man has known my whereabouts every hour of the day for as long as I've known him. And my mother's not the only one who won't buy that he "just happened" to answer this particular call. In fact, I'm willing to bet my children's lunch money that he's taken every call within ten miles of my home since the day I got back.

And now he's gotten lucky.

"*You* could have called *me*," I say.

"You're the one who said *tomorrow* for our talk and then flew the coop, chickie," he says. "I figured the ball was in your court."

"Detective?" the uniform says. "There's something you ought to see in here."

Drew gives me a look that amounts to *in or out?*

He could be talking about the investigation, or about our relationship.

Bobbie tries to steer me away. Mark's fists are balled. Drew waits me out, knowing I won't be able to resist what might be a murder investigation.

Finally he turns and heads for the cooler.

And, like a puppy dog, I follow.

Bobbie grabs the back of my shirt and pulls me to a halt.

"I'm just going to show him something," I say, yanking away.

"Yeah," Bobbie says, pointedly looking at the buttons on my blouse. The two at breast level have popped. "That's what I'm afraid of."

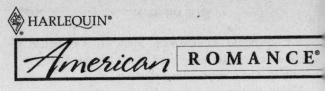

HARLEQUIN®

American ROMANCE®

TEXAS LEGACIES: ᴛʜᴇ CARRIGANS

Get to the Heart of a Texas Family

WITH

THE RANCHER NEXT DOOR

by

Cathy Gillen Thacker

She'll Run The Ranch—And Her Life—Her Way!

On her alpaca ranch in Texas, Rebecca encounters
constant interference from Trevor McCabe, the
bossy rancher next door. Rebecca becomes very
friendly with Vince Owen, her other neighbor and
Trevor's archrival from college. Trevor's problem
is convincing Rebecca that he is on her side, and
aware of Vince's ulterior motives. But Trevor has
fallen for her in the process....

On sale July 2007

www.eHarlequin.com

HAR7517

REQUEST YOUR FREE BOOKS!

Harlequin® Historical
Historical Romantic Adventure!

2 FREE NOVELS PLUS 2 **FREE GIFTS!**

YES! Please send me 2 FREE Harlequin® Historical novels and my 2 FREE gifts. After receiving them, if I don't wish to receive any more books, I can return the shipping statement marked "cancel." If I don't cancel, I will receive 6 brand-new novels every month and be billed just $4.69 per book in the U.S., or $5.24 per book in Canada, plus 25¢ shipping and handling per book and applicable taxes, if any. That's a savings of close to 15% off the cover price! I understand that accepting the 2 free books and gifts places me under no obligation to buy anything. I can always return a shipment and cancel at any time. Even if I never buy another book from Harlequin, the two free books and gifts are mine to keep forever.

246 HDN EEWW   349 HDN EEW

Name	(PLEASE PRINT)	
Address		Apt. #
City	State/Prov.	Zip/Postal Code

Signature (if under 18, a parent or guardian must sign)

Mail to the **Harlequin Reader Service®**:
IN U.S.A.: P.O. Box 1867, Buffalo, NY 14240-1867
IN CANADA: P.O. Box 609, Fort Erie, Ontario L2A 5X3

Not valid to current Harlequin Historical subscribers.

Want to try two free books from another line?
Call 1-800-873-8635 or visit www.morefreebooks.com.

* Terms and prices subject to change without notice. NY residents add applicable sales tax. Canadian residents will be charged applicable provincial taxes and GST. This offer is limited to one order per household. All orders subject to approval. Credit or debit balances in a customer account(s) may be offset by any other outstanding balance owed by or to the customer. Please allow 4 to 6 weeks for delivery.

Your Privacy: Harlequin is committed to protecting your privacy. Our Privacy Policy is available online at www.eHarlequin.com or upon request from the Reader Service. From time to time we make our lists of customers available to reputable firms who may have a product or service of interest to you. If you would prefer we not share your name and address, please check here.

Mediterranean NIGHTS™

*Glamour, elegance, mystery and revenge
aboard the high seas...*

Coming in August 2007...

THE TYCOON'S SON

*by
award-winning author*

Cindy Kirk

Businessman Theo Catomeris's long-estranged
father is determined to reconnect with his son, so
he hires Trish Melrose to persuade Theo to renew
his contract with Liberty Line. Sailing aboard the
luxurious *Alexandra's Dream* is a rare opportunity for
the single mom to mix business and pleasure. But
an undeniable attraction between Trish and Theo is
distracting her from the task at hand....

COMING NEXT MONTH FROM

HARLEQUIN®
HISTORICAL

- **WHIRLWIND BABY**
  by **Debra Cowan**
  (Western)
  When rancher Jake Ross finds a baby on his doorstep, he has to
  hire a nanny—and fast! All he needs is someone to take care of
  the child, so why can't he get Emma York out of his mind?

- **DISHONOR AND DESIRE**
  by **Juliet Landon**
  (Regency)
  Caterina Chester has kept her passionate nature tightly confined
  After she is forced into marriage, it seems that her most improp
  husband may be the only man who can free her!

- **A NOTORIOUS WOMAN**
  by **Amanda McCabe**
  (European)
  Venice is a city filled with passion, mystery and danger. Especi
  for a beautiful perfumer suspected of murder, when the only ma
  who can save her has been ordered to kill her.

- **AN UNLADYLIKE OFFER**
  by **Christine Merrill**
  (Regency)
  St. John is intent on mending his rakish ways. He won't seduce
  an innocent virgin. But Esme is determined and beautiful, and h
  offer is very, very tempting....